Angel
and the
Enemy

by Marnie L. Pehrson

Enjoy!
Marnie L Pehrson

To my friend, Cathy…
for inspiring me to write
this story and her constant
encouragement along the way.

Acknowledgments

I would like to thank my friend and editor, Julie Coulter Bellon, for her tireless patience in tutoring me in the skills of good writing and for helping me work and rework this manuscript to a polished state. Julie's unique talent for helping me see my stories through new eyes has been invaluable in adding a richness that never would have been there without her assistance.

Also, a special thanks to Cathy Nattress, Betty Morton and Rachael Crook for their encouragement and assistance in proofreading the manuscript.

Chapter 1

August 1864

Angelina stomped her weathered work boot down on the shovel. It jarred her entire body, but her efforts did little to break through the unyielding earth. She was discouraged by the insignificant amount of dirt that resulted from her efforts, but tossed it into the pile forming under a large hickory tree. She and her brother had been working for some time, but the hole still wasn't deep enough for a decent grave.

With each shallow scoop of earth Angelina removed, the thunder cracks grew louder and the lightning flashes brighter. Again her foot pounded on the shovel, and then as if choreographed to match her footwork, rain broke through the heavy gray blanket overhead. Within seconds, Angelina's blouse and skirt soaked up the moisture.

The rain softened the ground somewhat; making it a little easier to break the soil, but Angelina knew from experience that Georgia clay only becomes heavier when wet. She quickened her pace as ragged lightning attacked a helpless dogwood on the other side of the pasture. Angelina's eyes moved from the tree to the thick clouds above her. She glanced at her lanky younger brother, Cal, who motioned for her to give him the shovel so he could take a turn again. He took it, pushed up his shirtsleeves on his tanned arms and started digging.

"This may have to do. No point 'n gettin' ourselves killed too," Angelina looked from the shallow grave to the corpse. Without shifting her eyes away from the body, she extended the shovel to her brother.

I'm sorry, boy, so, so sorry! Angelina shook her head as she stared at the dog's white fur. Her mind darted back to the previous afternoon when Sam had trotted alongside her, wagging his tail happily as he accompanied her to the barn. He'd been such an enjoyable companion, sitting with her as she milked old Gerty every morning and night. *Such a good listener!* A wistful smile flickered across her face as she remembered pouring out her troubles to the dog. Her mouth hardened into a quivering line, and she blinked back the threatening tears, for the eighteen-year-old couldn't shake the feeling that it was her fault.

The rain fell in buckets now, and Angelina's blouse and skirt clung to her feminine form. She brushed her hand across her forehead, but water continued to drizzle down her face. Her long brown eyelashes batted in a vain attempt to stop the river of liquid from pouring into her vibrant green eyes.

"This 's gonna have to do, Cal," she reached toward the dog. Cal took one set of legs while Angelina took the other, and they dragged the stiff, seventy-pound animal into the shallow grave. Having only one shovel between them, Cal scooped dirt from the pile onto the dog while Angelina shoved her gloved hands into the mound and threw clods of earth over it. The dirt was even heavier than expected because the clods clung together, connected by mangled strands of grass and buckwheat.

As Angelina's gaze shifted from the corpse to the mound of dirt, she wasn't convinced this was enough soil to keep the carcass from stinking later on in the sweltering August sun. It would have to be enough, though. They must finish the job now. She certainly didn't want to come back later to complete the task. It broke her heart to see Sam already turning yellow around his mouth and eyes. It was bad enough to face his death once, but the thought of returning when the body would be rotting, wet and stinking was more than Angelina could take.

A loud crack of lightning rumbled, sending a shiver up Angelina's spine. Her wide eyes met her brother's. The pair threw clods of dirt and grass upon the animal as fast as they could until the carcass was covered with a layer of earth. Satisfied they'd done all they could in the little time they had, the teenagers took off running.

They stopped at the gate, opened it, and Angelina ran toward the house, leaving Cal to latch the gate behind them so the horses wouldn't get out of the corral. "Toss 'at shovel down," Angelina called back over her shoulder. "Metal just draws the lightnin'!"

Sixteen-year-old Cal dropped the shovel by the gate and soon his lanky legs caught up with and surpassed his sister. As they ran up the hill toward home, Angelina swiped at the torrents of water cascading down her face and obstructing her vision.

Panting from their quick ascent up the hill, the siblings stopped on the front porch to catch their breath. Angelina tried to wring the water from her blouse and skirt, letting it splash on the wooden porch while Cal stripped off his wet shirt and tossed it on a rocking chair, then reached to remove his muddy boots.

A little girl's fingers opened the door a crack, her chubby face peeking out to observe her older siblings and the torrential storm.

"Did ya bury 'im?" eight-year-old Eleanor flinched at the deafening thunder crack that rumbled on for several seconds. A second chubby face joined her at the door. The little girl clasped his hand protectively, her fist tightening around six-year-old Joseph's fingers until his appendages looked more like little red sausages than fingers. His big blue eyes grew even wider as his head darted toward another flash of light.

"Yep, done the best we could," Cal answered in a relaxed even tone, unruffled by the lightning and thunder so typical of a Georgia summer rain. Even though her brother was two years her junior, Angelina always felt safe knowing he was nearby. She remembered the day their father rode off for war and how Cal gave her hand an assuring squeeze then pulled her into a comforting embrace, letting her soft cries melt onto his shoulder. Cal had wanted to join with their father to fight for the Confederacy, but of course, he was far too young at the time. Everett made his son promise that no matter how long the war lasted, he'd stay with the family and look after them while he was gone. Cal obeyed with reluctant agreement, but once the promise was made, Angelina felt safe because she knew her brother was always true to his word.

Cal's muddy hand shoved the door wider as he tromped inside in his sock feet. Angelina twisted a few more cupfuls of water from her hair, then gave up and tried to wring out her clothing. Finally, giving up on the hopeless endeavor, she stepped inside with the objective of finding a secluded spot to remove the heavy garments. Her mother, Lelia, hurried to the door carrying a towel in each hand and extended them to her children.

~*~

As Angelina's now dry body lay on her cot in the loft, she looked up at the log planks that her father had placed himself when he'd built the house after he and Lelia first married. The piece of Georgia property just South of Chattanooga, Tennessee had been their home for almost twenty years. They'd been happy there until the day Everett left to join the Confederate forces about two years earlier. The family had received periodic letters from him, but they'd heard nothing in nearly six months – ever since word came that he'd been incarcerated in a Union prison.

Whether he lived or not was anyone's guess. A tear trickled down Angelina's cheek, and she rolled over on her side, brushing the moisture away. Sam's death only served to increase her fear that her father was gone along with his favorite dog. She berated herself for not burying the scraps from the previous night's supper further away from the house. Sam had managed to unearth one of the chicken bones and choked on it that morning around daybreak.

"What a waste! What a complete and utter waste!" Lelia had lamented as she stood over the dog's stiff body with tears welling in her eyes.

Life seemed suddenly so precarious, so fragile and fleeting. One moment a body was alive and hopping about and the next it was snuffed out of existence. None of them verbalized it, but Cal, Lelia and Angelina all harbored in their hearts the secret dread that the dog's passing meant that Everett too was gone.

Angelina looked across the room to Eleanor who lay curled in a ball napping on her own cot. The poor child had cried herself to sleep in sadness over the loss of their family pet. Cal and Joseph were equally heartbroken, and it felt to Angelina as if a thick, muggy blanket of gloom draped itself over the household - smothering, relentless and sticky like the humid Georgia afternoon.

At the sound of horse hooves approaching, Angelina rolled over and slid out of her bed, kneeling by the loft window. Two Union soldiers dismounted their horses and tied them to a tree. With firearms drawn, they approached the house with determination in their footsteps. Angelina leaned over the loft and looked down at her mother and Cal who stood on either side of the front door.

"Yankees!" Angelina's anxious whisper hissed over the loft railing.

Lelia gestured affirmatively and waved her hand, motioning for Angelina to stay hidden in the loft. "Keep the children out of sight!"

Cal stood on the other side of the door, his rifle raised, his arms flexed and ready to defend his family.

The two soldiers stepped onto the front porch and approached the door. The stocky one adjusted his navy cap on his head, smashing down his greasy mouse-colored hair. He raised his muddy boot in preparation to kick down the front door, but his companion outstretched an arm to stop him. He tightened his bearded jaw with a negative nod, and shot an irritated glance down at the shorter soldier.

"No need in that," he said and lifted his knuckles to the door and knocked.

Angelina could sense her mother's fear, but watched with pride as she pushed it down and put a resolute hand to Cal's chest and then opened the door. Cal stood beside his mother, his rifle raised.

Lelia eased open the door a crack and peered out, "Yes, how may we help you, gentlemen?"

"I'm Lieutenant Elijah Willoughby and this is Captain Jacobsen," the dark-headed soldier removed his hat, ran his hand through his thick black hair and pointed to his companion. "We . . . " he hesitated. His pensive blue eyes softened and he tilted his head as if he were groping for some polite way to say what needed to be said. "We were wonderin' . . ."

Impatient with Lieutenant Willoughby's delay, the gruff one called Jacobsen pushed his way forward and barged into the house. He spit a wad of tobacco juice on the floor, "We'll be commandeering your home as a base of operations."

Lelia's eyes followed the stream of spittle as it splattered on her fresh swept floor. Her eyes closed and she drew in a deep breath.

Willoughby grimaced and his apologetic eyes swept from Cal to Lelia. His thumb and forefinger unconsciously twirled a silver rope-design ring on his right hand as he seemed to be silently assessing the situation.

"What if we don't want you in our home?" Cal pointed his rifle at Jacobsen, but Lelia raised her hand gesturing for Cal to move the weapon to a less threatening position.

"It's all right, Cal," she muttered. Angelina's anxiety increased, her pulse throbbing in her ears as she peered down from the loft. She knew her mother's first concern was always for the safety and peace of her family. Being alone without her husband, she would attempt to comply with the enemy. She wound't confront them and risk harm to her family.

Angelina watched the Captain closely as he ordered Cal to relinquish his rifle. Cal hesitated but their mother nodded for him to cooperate. Jacobsen took Cal's rifle and holstered his own pistol.

Willoughby looked up toward the loft, his gaze traveling from one fair countenance to the other until his eyes met Angelina's. The fear searing through her veins ever since she'd observed the Yankees' approach subsided and the expression of apology in the soldier's penetrating blue eyes sent a warming calm throughout her body.

His eyes broke from hers with an abrupt shift and trained on her mother. "We could set up our headquarters in the barn, Ma'am, so's not to be in your way," Elijah Willoughby offered. His companion looked at him as if he'd lost his senses.

"I don't think so!" Jacobsen retorted. "If the house is good 'nough for rebs, it's good 'nough for us!" Jacobsen's stomping stride resounded through the house. He inspected every corner as if he owned the place.

Angelina's anxious eyes watched the ruthless officer shove open the door to her parents' bedroom.

"This room will do nicely," Captain Jacobsen barked and stepped into the room.

Cal lurched forward, "That's my Mama's room. No Yank'll be sleepin' in my Mama's room!"

Jacobsen turned his expression of disdain to Cal, and then raked his lascivious countenance over Lelia from head to toe. "I don't know, boy. Your Mama might be needin' a real man in her room."

"Lay a finger on a single member of my family and you'll find a bullet through your head," Cal threatened, his eyes meeting the Captain's with an icy glare. Angelina's heart hammered as she witnessed her brother stepping

12

closer to the man, staring down the barrel of his own rifle, which the Captain now pointed at him.

"That's enough!" Willoughby stepped between the two men. "There's no call to treat these folks like this."

"Just let me gather a few o' my things, and I'll join my children upstairs," Lelia countered with the charm of a Southern lady simply making room for invited guests.

Willoughby stood in front of Jacobsen letting Lelia pass into the room. The pair waited while she gathered her belongings and handed them to Cal. The young man stood on the second rung of the loft ladder lifting the items to Angelina while his protective eyes remained on his mother.

"We expect supper within the hour, so get that brood of yours to work," Jacobsen barked at Lelia and pointed toward the loft.

Willoughby's face turned red and his eyes clenched shut for a brief instant. His broad chest rose and fell with controlled indignation. Jacobsen pulled Elijah's arm, tugging him into Lelia's room and shut the door.

"Damn Yankees!" Cal spat, "Come in 'ere, barkin' orders like they own the place!" His furious gaze remained on the bedroom door. "I've half a mind to show 'em what a reb's really made of."

"Shhh, they'll hear you," Lelia whispered.

Angelina climbed down the loft ladder and approached her mother. "Cal's right, Mama. You're too accomodatin'. This is our home and they're intruders," she whispered.

"Better to be accommodatin' than dead!" Lelia said.

"I wish Daddy were here. He'd a sent 'em packin'!" Cal retorted.

"I wish your Daddy were here too," Lelia muttered as she reached for an iron skillet and set it atop the stove.

Chapter 2

Angelina sat at the large rectangular wooden table in the dining area, peeling potatoes into a pot. Her head lifted as Captain Jacobsen opened the bedroom door, tromped into the kitchen and thrust his fists to his sides, surveying the family as if he were now master of the house. Angelina's gaze dropped to her task while his eyes traveled to the wood-burning stove where Lelia worked.

Lelia, who had her back to him, dabbed the perspiration from her brow with her handkerchief and glanced over her shoulder. Turning to face the soldier, she motioned to Eleanor and Joseph, indicating they should get to the loft. The children obeyed her unspoken command the instant it was given. They rose from their seats at the dining room table, and scurried up the ladder.

Jacobsen's gaze traveled along the rows of oak cupboards, past Angelina and toward the living area to his right. An unlit fireplace stood along the center of the wall. His attention shifted back to Angelina. She could feel his gaze trailing slowly over her, starting at her face and down the length of her as he slowly licked his lips. Angelina lowered her head, focusing on the potato and knife she held in her hands.

"That's enough potatoes," he gestured toward the pot beside Angelina. "You come with us and show us around the property."

Angelina put her palm to her chest and looked side-to-side. Was he talking to her?

"You," he pointed straight at her now. "We need to see the lay of the land before we send for our troops tomorrow."

The vision of hundreds of soldiers like Jacobsen came to Angelina's mind, and a rattling wave of anxious nausea coursed throughout her body. They'd soon be overrun like boll weevil on cotton.

Lelia stepped beside her daughter, sliding her protective arm around Angelina's narrow shoulders. "Cal can show you the property when he gets in from roundin' up the horse that got out of the corral."

"We don't have time to waste," Jacobsen gestured for Angelina to stand and come along with him. But she sat motionless, her eyes shifting toward Willoughby, whose masculine form filled the bedroom doorway. He took three long steps and came to stand beside his vile companion. Jacobsen may have been superior in rank, but he definitely wasn't Willoughby's superior in manner, character or physique. Her heart leapt a little, hoping this man would temper his companion's unreasonable commands.

"I'll show you the farm," Lelia untied her apron and set it on the table in front of Angelina. "You finish supper, Angelina."

Jacobsen swiped the apron from the table and threw it back at Lelia, hitting her in the chest. She caught it and set it back on the table.

"Now look here," Lelia's jaws clenched, and her eyes narrowed. Angelina recognized that glare. It was the

15

expression her mama wore when she'd hit her limit. "I've let you come in here and take over our home. We're cookin' you supper, but my daughter's not goin' anywhere with you two."

Angelina felt her stomach churning as trouble brewed. Lelia looked as if her eyes were shooting daggers across the room at Jacobsen. Every muscle in the man's body tightened in response, and he returned her defiant glare. It was like watching two bulls square off, ready to gore each other to death.

"Either she shows us the property, or we'll torch the place and move on to the next farm. It's your choice. You make it." Jacobsen folded his arms across his chest, issuing the ultimatum as if he were forcing a child to either eat her vegetables or go to bed without supper.

"Look, Captain," Elijah moved toward Jacobsen. "We don't need . . ."

"Stay out of it, Willoughby," Jacobsen's curt reply sliced off the end of Elijah's peacemaking attempt.

"You're not serious?" came Lelia's incredulous retort. Her stance matched Jacobsen's, her tightened fists mounted to her hips.

"I am," Jacobsen countered coolly, his hateful black eyes glaring back at her.

"You'd burn down our cabin over somethin' as insignificant as who shows you around the farm?"

"I would, and think nothin' of it," he retorted, reaching for the oil lamp burning at the center of the kitchen table.

Willoughby stepped forward putting a staying hand on Jacobsen's outstretched arm. "There's no need for threats. I'm sure the woman is just concerned for her daughter's well being." Elijah's kind blue eyes met Lelia's, "Ma'am I'll take personal responsibility for your daughter's safety. She will not be harmed." Angelina noted the honest dignity in his voice and the valiant expression in the firm set of his bearded jaw. Would her mother trust him? He was a Yankee after all. But Lelia had very little choice. A Captain outranked a Lieutenant, and Angelina knew Willoughby could only go so far in contradicting Jacobsen's orders. Yet, she sensed he would not allow her to come to harm.

Lelia made no indication she would relinquish her position. Angelina rose to her feet in an abrupt motion, her wooden chair scraping noisily across the floorboards.

"I'll go, Mama. The children need you." If someone were to face danger, it would be better that it were her, Angelina reasoned to herself. A mother of small children should be kept from harm's way.

"Angelina," Lelia put a hand on her daughter's shoulder.

"It'll be all right, Mama," Angelina turned her green eyes to meet her mother's gaze and hoped they conveyed confidence even though her insides quivered like jelly on a plate.

Angelina moved toward Willoughby's side.

"If anythin' happens to her, I'll shoot a bullet through you myself," Lelia warned as Jacobsen exited the house. He ignored her threat and kept on walking. Elijah hesitated in the doorway, letting some distance develop between himself and Jacobsen. Then he motioned for Angelina to step outside. As he started out the door, he looked back at Lelia, his eyes holding hers with confident assurance, "I promise you, Ma'am, she will not be harmed."

Elijah and Angelina caught up to Jacobsen who had now turned around and was staring at Willoughby with an impatient scowl.

17

"What would you like to see first?" Angelina directed her question to Willoughby because she couldn't stand to look at Jacobsen's sinister dark eyes. Men like him sensed fear like a wild animal, and Angelina wasn't going to give him the satisfaction of knowing he frightened her.

"Just show us the perimeter of the property for now," Jacobsen barked.

"We need a good spot for the men to camp," Willoughby explained further, his apologetic smile directed toward Angelina. "Do you have a spring or creek nearby? It would be best to camp near water."

"We do," she replied and turned east.

The soldiers walked on either side of her. Willoughby bent down and picked up a twig, his large hands breaking it into small pieces as he strode along. Every once in a while, he would toss one toward a tree trunk and watch it bounce off into the grass. His relaxed manner would have set her at ease, but she could sense Jacobsen's eyes on her. She turned slightly and through her peripheral vision observed him gawking at her hair, her face, her figure. At one point, he even slowed his pace, lagging behind her to inspect her from behind.

Angelina tried not to show her immense discomfort, but her nervous fingers twisted the drawstrings of her skirt. Willoughby glared at Jacobsen then engaged Angelina in conversation. "I guess this 's the springhouse over here?"

"Yes," she answered.

"It looks fairly new," Elijah noted, looking back toward the barn and the smoke house, comparing the structures to the whitewashed springhouse.

"Our old one got hit by a tornado a couple years back so Daddy built this new one right before he left."

"So your father's with the Confederacy?"

Angelina's eyes shifted to Elijah's navy uniform. She squared her narrow shoulders, "He sure is," she answered proudly, lifting her chin.

Elijah cocked his head with a sympathetic gesture, "Must be difficult havin' your pa away like that."

"We miss 'im," she replied as her wary eyes followed Jacobsen. The Captain had walked several yards away from them and started to go inside the springhouse.

"Where's he goin'?" Elijah muttered under his breath, his head leaning to one side and his shoulders slumped. Just as he started to follow Jacobsen, Angelina extended her hand and without thinking about what she was doing, tugged his sleeve.

Elijah turned back toward her expectantly, noting her slender fingers clinging to his navy jacket. His gaze lifted to her anxious eyes.

Aware of having touched him, she drew back her hand. "Are you really gonna bring troops here?" she whispered. She didn't think she could stand more men like Jacobsen swarming around their property.

"Uh . . ." Elijah glanced back toward the springhouse. Jacobsen had disappeared inside. "It's only about fifty men. I'll try to keep 'em out o' your way."

"When will they be here?"

"We'll go back for 'em in the mornin'."

"Will there be any fightin'?"

"Probably not, hope not," he glanced back over his shoulder, but Jacobsen still hadn't exited the whitewashed building.

"You don't like 'im," Angelina observed.

"I don't have to like 'im," Elijah's voice lowered as he slipped his silver ring up to his knuckle and back into place. "Problem is I don't trust 'im." Just as he faced the springhouse and took a step in its direction, Jacobsen emerged with a chunk of cheese in one hand and an apple in the other. He burnished the fruit on his coat and took a bite. The juice ran down the corner of his mouth, and he dried it on his sleeve.

"They're makin' supper," Willoughby scolded.

Jacobsen said nothing but swaggered away from them alongside the spring in the direction of the field.

"Did you want an apple too?" Angelina offered.

"No thank you," he followed Jacobsen at a slower pace, keeping some distance between them and the Captain.

"How did you get saddled with the likes o' him?" Angelina wondered aloud.

"I'm good with maps and directions. The Captain gets lost easy. So he brought me along to scout out the area."

Angelina wished Jacobsen would get lost right now. At least he wasn't leering at her at the moment.

"What's this?" Jacobsen called out, pointing to a mound of dirt on the edge of the field.

"We just buried our dog there," Angelina replied.

"What? What did she say?" Jacobsen hollered.

"She says they buried a dog there," Elijah yelled back at Jacobsen, then lowered his voice, directing his next comment to Angelina. "Looks like a fresh grave."

"Very fresh. We buried 'im earlier today." She could feel her chest tightening and the moisture gathering in her eyes just thinking about Sam.

"I'm sorry," Elijah's attention stayed on the grave as they approached it.

"Me too. He was a good dog. He'd been with us for years." Her hands gripped the folds of her skirt.

"That's too bad. What happened to him?"

Angelina paused and stood over the grave, bowing her head as a wave of deep remorse threatened to engulf her. She swallowed the lump forming in her throat and blinked back the excess dampness in her eyes in an effort to maintain the appearance of control.

"He got hold of a chicken bone and choked," Angelina's voice quivered a little. She cleared her throat as she turned her back to Willoughby and stared off toward the forest that ran alongside the pasture.

"That's a shame," came his soft, sympathetic reply.

"Uh hmm," she blinked back the tears. "It was my fault," she confided and then wondered why she would admit such a thing to a stranger.

"How's that?"

She cleared her voice once more, hoping she could speak without her voice cracking. "I should've buried the scraps farther away from the house so he couldn't find 'em."

"That's not your fault. Dogs 'll be dogs. They've got a keen sense o' smell. Not much you can do 'bout it short o' tossin' the bones in a creek or somethin'. Can't hardly bury 'em deep enough."

"Yes, well . . ." she wasn't certain she agreed with him, but she appreciated his willingness to make excuses for her negligence.

"I've got a dog waitin' back home for me. She's a collie. Good dog, helps with the sheep and goats. A good companion too." They continued their stroll, side by side.

"I guess she keeps your wife comp'ny while you're away," Angelina replied, instantly scolding herself internally for her outright attempt to determine the

21

Lieutenant's marital status. But her guilt only flickered for a moment; she was too relieved by his answer.

"Not married. Happy's with my sister."

"Happy?" Angelina's full lips curled into a smile.

Elijah shrugged. "She's the happiest dog I've ever seen. Always waggin' her tale and runnin' out to meet me when I come home from workin' in the fields."

"Sounds like Sam," Angelina replied. "I miss 'im already." She brushed the back of her hand to her eyes. "He followed me everywhere. He was my Daddy's dog. He and I were always taggin' along after Daddy. So when he left, Sam became my shadow."

"It's hard losin' someone ya love," Elijah observed in a somber voice. She sensed he wasn't talking about dogs anymore, but she didn't want to pry.

"Willoughby!" Jacobsen's voice broke their conversation.

"Yes, sir."

"Get over here!"

Elijah jogged toward Jacobsen's position in the middle of the field.

"Let's make camp over yonder along the creek," Jacobsen began gesturing and explaining where he wanted the men positioned and where he wanted the artillery to go.

Angelina didn't pay much attention to their conversation. She couldn't hear most of it, anyway, because she'd remained several yards from them. She raised her head to watch Lieutenant Willoughby as he spoke with the Captain. If she'd been asked to identify the higher ranking officer between the two, she would've selected Willoughby with his confident carriage and impressive build.

Engrossed in their planning, they didn't seem to notice her standing there anymore. It gave Angelina the opportunity to observe Willoughby from a distance. She believed he was just about the handsomest man she ever did see. He pulled his cap down lower on his dark hair, shielding his eyes from the afternoon sun. His prominent cheekbones rose even higher as he squinted.

She wondered whether his black mustache and beard made him hot. Counting her blessings that women didn't have aggravatin' facial hair, she fanned herself with her hand. It was bad enough that she had to wear all these petticoats beneath her skirt. She'd hate to have all that hair to deal with too.

As Angelina continued to examine him, she could tell Lieutenant Willoughby took a certain amount of pride in his appearance. Not to say she thought him vain, but he did wear his beard in the popular style of the day. She supposed keeping it as neatly trimmed as he did cut down on the heat. His uniform also appeared to be in better shape than the Captain's. He smelled much better too. The Captain, in contrast, did not seem to take such pains with his personal hygiene. Just as her mind turned to little Joseph and his aversion to bathing, the men started in her direction.

"We can head back to the house now," Lieutenant Willoughby motioned for her to join them. She hesitated and then eased forward, not eager to get too close to Jacobsen. He reeked of tobacco and sour perspiration. But she forced herself to join the two men, staying closer to Willoughby.

Jacobsen could evidently see that she tried to position herself next to Willoughby. He grabbed her by the arm and held her fast against his side. "Come along," he said in her ear, his voice raspy and grating.

Angelina almost gagged from the stench of his breath, his missing teeth whistling slightly when he spoke. "Get your hands off me!" she hissed, trying to quell the fear. She pulled at his fingers to pry them off of her tender flesh, but he only laughed at her efforts and gripped her harder.

"I like 'em feisty," he breathed. "We could have some fun together, you and me," he leaned in, his mouth coming dangerously close to hers.

She jerked her arm in an attempt at freedom and was about to kick him in the shins, when in an instant Willoughby wedged himself between Angelina and the Captain. He used his strength to clamp his hand on Jacobsen's wrist, prying the man from her. With both hands, he shoved Jacobsen backwards. The Captain staggered a step or two and then regained his stance.

"Leave 'er be!" Willoughby ordered.

"You better watch your step, Lieutenant, or you'll be finding yourself court-martialed. I'm still the commanding officer here, and you do what I say!"

"Court-martial me if you must, pull rank on me, whatever you want, but you're disgracin' the uniform of the Union army, and I'll be hanged by my toes in the pits o' Hades before I see you touch this young woman again."

"You are no judge of my actions, Willoughby. Attention!" he shouted.

Willoughby gave Angelina an apologetic look that belied his exasperation, but he dropped her arm and stood erect, looking forward.

Jacobsen stared up into Elijah's face. "Lieutenant Willoughby, who is your commanding officer?"

"You are, sir," Willoughby shouted.

"Are you in any position to question your commanding officer?"

"No sir," Willoughby shouted.

Jacobsen smiled. "You just remember your place, boy," he said. He turned on his heel after a leering glance at Angelina. "Come along girl. Now that you've seen a real man in charge, I want you and your ma to serve me my supper."

Willoughby relaxed his stance, and lagged behind Jacobsen with Angelina. "Are you all right?" he asked, his voice low.

"I'm fine," she muttered, rubbing her arms where she was sure the bruises in the shape of Jacobsen's fingers would be forever branded on her skin.

"Hurry up!" Jacobsen shouted. "Don't make me come back for you."

Angelina and Willoughby quickened their pace. "Don't go anywhere alone with him," Willoughby whispered, his voice anxious. "He's a loaded gun, and there's no tellin' what he could do."

Angelina was afraid because his tone was so serious, but she nodded her head in agreement. "Don't worry, I can take care o' myself," she said, her voice shaking a little.

"You're a strong woman," Willoughby agreed as he gave her a small smile, "but once Jacobsen gets something in his head, I'm afraid no one can stop him." His words were ominous and as they walked back to the house, there was an eerie silence as if all of nature agreed with Willoughby's words.

Chapter 3

Elijah stepped into the house and looked around the room. Lelia was cooking. Cal sat with the children playing a game, but Jacobsen was nowhere in sight.

"Where's the Captain?"

"He stomped off to the bedroom and slammed the door," Cal replied.

"Oh," Elijah turned to look beside him and noticed Angelina was no longer with him. He spun around searching for her. "Where did she go?" he muttered to himself.

Lelia pointed her paring knife toward the window, "She stopped to check on the goats."

Willoughby looked in the direction Lelia had indicated and saw Angelina squatted down, petting a small kid. He smiled and retraced his steps outside.

"Need some help?" he called out as he drew near the small goat pen.

"Oh, Wilma's just got herself all tangled up here." Angelina pulled at the long green vines twisted in a mass around the kid's hooves and legs.

"Here," he knelt on the ground beside her and pulled a jackknife from his pocket. With careful strokes, he cut away the vines and then patted the animal on the back.

He reached inside his jacket and pulled out a small apple, cut a wedge from it and fed it to the kid. Angelina wondered how a man like this could be a soldier. He seemed too kind-hearted to kill anyone. He patted the animal's back, running his fingers through the soft fuzzy fur.

"She's a cute little thing," he smiled.

"I think it's the cinnamon color of her coat that makes her so pretty," Angelina observed.

"That and her face." Elijah put a hand on either side of the goat's small snout and turned it toward Angelina. "Now that's a cute face for a goat."

Angelina smiled in agreement. Elijah and Angelina sat there on the ground for several minutes taking turns feeding apple wedges to the goat until they heard Eleanor ringing the bell for supper.

As they ate, Lelia treated the Union soldiers as if they were honored guests, giving them the largest portions and seeing they were made comfortable. Cal eyed them with contempt, making no effort to hide his emotions. Lelia instructed Eleanor and Joseph to eat their meal upstairs. She said it was so there would be room at the table for the officers, but Angelina knew it was because her mother wanted her little ones kept safe. At first, she'd suggested Cal and Angelina stay upstairs as well, but Lieutenant Willoughby insisted that the family keep to their normal routine.

As Angelina sat across the table from Elijah Willoughby, she tried not to meet his unusual eyes directly, but she kept finding herself drawn to them. She wondered how someone with such dark hair and complexion could have such crystal blue eyes. Elijah Willoughby was a dichotomy in more ways than just his appearance. He seemed so gentle yet powerful, softhearted yet willing to fight for a cause. But who could really trust a Yankee? He could be pretending to be kind only to steal everything they owned or ransack their house and leave them dead.

She'd heard horrific tales of the destruction the Yankees left in their wake and of the foul atrocities performed upon women. The remembrance of those stories caused an evil chill to climb her spine. Out of the corner of her eye, she caught Jacobsen leering at her again. If anyone was capable of violence, Jacobsen was. She shuddered involuntarily and closed her eyes. She inhaled and exhaled deeply, trying to calm her nerves.

When Angelina opened her eyes again, Lieutenant Willoughby was staring at her. Their eyes locked, thunder rumbled in the distance and a flash of lightning brightened the dimly lit room. Everyone else's attention shifted toward the window, watching the sheet of rain dropping from the sky and slapping on the porch and roof. But Elijah did not break his gaze from Angelina's.

A smile twinkled in his eyes, tugged at his lips and the dimple in his bearded cheek deepened. Angelina fought the emotions inside her. Under other circumstances she would have found him incredibly attractive, felt drawn to his gentle nature and the endearing light in his eyes, but . . . *What was she thinking?* Her nervous gaze fell to her plate, and her slender fingers twirled the fork through her potatoes.

"Can I pour you some milk, Captain Jacobsen?" Lelia asked.

Captain Jacobsen snickered. "I don't drink *milk*," he informed her. He pulled a flask from his pocket. "I'll take care of my own drink." He took a long swig, wiped his mouth on his sleeve and put it defiantly on the table.

Angelina watched her mother's faint expression of disgust, then pushed her chair back and stood, "I think I'll see if Joseph and Eleanor need anything else to eat."

"I'm sure they'd like some more rolls," Lelia lifted the basket, and Angelina snatched two.

Elijah rose to his feet and his head moved in courteous acknowledgement of her. She stepped around the table, trying not to meet his gaze. Jacobsen did not rise to his feet, but leaned back in his chair, rubbing his stomach satisfactorily, his lewd eyes following her movements as he picked at his teeth.

Elijah's brows narrowed with his frown as he stepped in front of Jacobsen, blocking his view of the young woman. "We should get some sleep so we can leave at first light."

"In a little while," Jacobsen muttered and let the front legs of his chair pound to the floor, then reached out to grab another roll.

A few minutes later, Angelina returned with the children's cups. While she poured the milk from the pitcher, she tried to avoid meeting either man's gaze directly. Jacobsen made her blood run chill, but the warm shiver that her attraction for Elijah produced was no less unnerving. She wished they'd both take Elijah's suggestion and retire early.

Anxious to get her milk, Eleanor scurried down the ladder to join Angelina, but Jacobsen intercepted her, grabbing her and plopping the little girl on his knee. Running his hands through her blonde curls, his sinister voice deepened lower than usual, "You're a pretty little thing." Eleanor squealed in fright and tried to wiggle free, but Jacobsen tightened his arm around her.

"Eleanor!" Lelia cried out and shoved her chair back from the table, scraping it loudly across the floor. Rising, she scrambled to rescue her wide-eyed child.

Angelina jumped at her mother's outcry, tipping the cup and spilling milk across the table. Elijah bolted toward Jacobsen, but Cal beat him there. He snatched the child from Jacobsen's arms and pulled her to his chest. "Keep your hands off her, you blasted Yank! Touch my sisters and I'll kill you!"

Lelia rushed toward them and gathered the child into her arms. "Eleanor, honey, are you all right?" Lelia transported her daughter to a far corner of the room, consoling the child against her bosom. She stroked the child's downy hair as the girl choked back tears against her mother's shoulder.

Angelina scrambled to clean up the mess she'd made while Jacobsen rose to his feet, slamming his chair backwards, crashing it to the floor. Swearing a stream of expletives he bellowed, "Can't a man comment on a pretty girl without everyone carrying on like he's committed a crime?"

Elijah strode toward the Captain and put a hand on his shoulder, "Perhaps we should just retire for the evening and let her put her children to bed. We have an early mornin'."

Jacobsen lurched away from Elijah's touch and stomped off into the bedroom, his entire body stiffened, almost trembling as he tried to contain his rage. "Get in here, Lieutenant," he growled through his gritted teeth. "We need to talk."

"I'm sorry, Ma'am," Elijah gave Lelia and then Angelina an apologetic shrug. Angelina returned to wiping up the spilt milk when Elijah followed Jacobsen and drew the door shut.

Angelina quickened her pace in cleaning up the milk when she heard angry voices murmuring from inside the room. What sounded like furniture crashing startled the whole family, and Lelia's anxious eyes met Cal's and then Angelina's.

"Let's get the little ones upstairs and stay with 'em. We can clean up this mess in the mornin'," Lelia instructed.

Cal lifted Eleanor, carrying her up into the loft. His mother and Angelina followed on his heels. Lelia gathered her children about her on a straw bed, putting little Joseph on her lap. Cal held Eleanor in a protective embrace. Angelina joined the rest of the family on the bed as they listened to the soldier's angry voices.

"We need to say a prayer," Lelia grabbed Cal's and Angelina's hands, and they took one another's. Lelia bowed her head and began praying for the safety of her family and the speedy return of her husband. Then, she thanked God for Lieutenant Willoughby's kindness and commended his protection to the Lord.

When Lelia prayed for Captain Jacobsen's lost soul and that the Lord would soften his heart, Angelina opened one eye and met Cal's cocked eyebrow. Angelina knew Cal doubted the likelihood of that ever happening as much as she did, but a smile still crept over her lips thinking about her mother's kind heart and her willingness to pray for their enemies.

Chapter 4

Angelina couldn't sleep. Normally the sound of the pattering rain on the roof would have helped her relax, but not tonight. She kept seeing his face, the way he ran his hand through his dark wavy hair and his nervous habit of fidgeting with his ring. Finally, she managed to doze off.

She could feel Lieutenant Willoughby's strong arms about her, holding her, his piercing blue eyes staring deep into her soul. His hand slid to her cheek, an exhilarating shiver enveloping her with his caress. She felt her lungs tighten in anticipation as his mouth drew within inches of her own. At that moment, she awakened and bolted upright in her bed, every cell of her body alive with electricity, her mouth parched and dry for want of liquid, or was it for want of his kiss?

Angelina shook her head and ran her fingers through her blonde locks in frustration. *He's a Yankee, for heaven's sake!* she scolded herself. She had no business thinkin' on Lieutenant Willoughby or feelin' anything for 'im. He was the enemy, invadin' their home, ready to perform who-knew-what kind of villainy upon them.

She lay there for several minutes in the darkness of midnight, reining in her thoughts after such a dream. Then, slowly, Angelina crept from her cot and descended the ladder in search of water. She found the pitcher and poured herself a cup. As she drained it, her eyes lingered on her parents' closed bedroom door. She could hear soft snores coming from behind it and wondered if it was Willoughby. Willoughby - she wished he would come out, that she could spend a few minutes alone with him, without Jacobsen's leering presence. What would it be like to be alone with him? Her dream still fresh in her memory, she allowed herself to linger on it for a moment, and then scolded herself for her wayward thoughts. Dreaming was one thing, but to dwell upon it was improper.

She stared at the closed door, realizing she did not wish it to open for Jacobsen also slept behind it. Willoughby's warning about Jacobsen being unstoppable once he got something in his head echoed through her mind. He'd warned her never to be alone, yet here she was downstairs alone in the kitchen at night. Her anxious gaze flickered toward the front door. She really needed to make a trip to the outhouse. Perhaps she should waken Cal to go with her. But she could hear the snores and deep breathing of a houseful of sleeping people. Surely, she could slip outside and return without notice. She'd be all right.

Angelina tiptoed toward the front door, lifted the latch, turned the knob and opened it a crack. She widened it a little further, giving herself only enough room to slip out. The hinges creaked and she froze, her pulse quickening. Her eyes darted back to the closed bedroom door. She held her breath, waiting and listening. The sounds of sleep continued uninterrupted and she slipped out, easing the door closed behind her.

The sky was cloudy, offering no light to find her way, but she knew the path like the back of her hand. The darkness would hide her like a trusted friend. Quickening her step, she opened the door to the outhouse, the familiar hinges squeaking as she did so. As she sat in the darkness, she thought she heard the door to the house creak closed. Her thoughts turned to Willoughby, wondering if he'd heard her come out.

Easing the outhouse door open, she peered into the darkness. "Who's there? Is that you, Lieutenant Willoughby?"

When no one answered, Angelina stepped onto the path and felt a cloth go round her head, catch between her lips and tug until she bit down on what felt like a handkerchief.

"I knew you fancied that stupid Lieutenant," the man behind her rasped. "But it's not him you'll be with tonight." The familiar voice made Angelina's heart almost stop. Jacobsen! She tried to scream, but no sound came out.

Her stomach twisted in knots as the adrenaline charged through her veins. She elbowed Jacobsen and heard a groan. She tried to run, but before she got far, he grabbed her again and pressed her close against him.

"I like 'em feisty," he hissed in her ear, repeating his words from earlier in the day.

The tears poured down Angelina's cheeks, and he cruelly twisted her arms behind her back and propelled her toward the barn. The closer they got to the doors, the heavier his breathing became and Angelina tried to dig her heels in, knowing what was coming.

He dragged her through the barn door, and threw her into the hay where she landed on her backside. Scrambling to her knees she tried to get to the stall where the pitchforks were hanging, but Jacobsen caught her and slapped her hard across the face. Her cheek stung as she fell backward and hit her head on the dirt floor. Before she could react, he was there again, gripping her arms and forcing them over her head.

The vise grip he held on her wrists cut off the circulation to her hands, and her legs ached from his knees pressing them to the floor. Again, she screamed, but only a muffled sound could be heard. The cow above her gave a low moo, something Angelina would have found comforting in the past, but instead she thought of the glowing eyes of the cow being an unwilling witness to what was happening to her.

Before she could finish the thought, he jerked her head to the side and slobbered kisses across her cheek. Angelina shook her head violently, fighting with every ounce of strength she had left, thinking that if she concentrated and fought hard enough, she could hurl his body from hers. But the harder she struggled to free her hands, which he held above her head, the harder he pressed his full weight on her.

For a moment he released his weight as he fumbled with his belt. She tried again to slide herself away from him, but he grabbed her nightgown with both hands and ripped it down the front. She pushed against him, but he was too strong and pressed down upon her, suffocating her, making Angelina wish she could just disappear into the floor.

She knew that no one inside the house would hear her muffled screams, but she did not relent for they drowned out his moans and heavy breathing. Her stomach wrenched with nausea, not only from the terror of the situation, but also from the rank odor of his breath in her face. Tears streamed from her eyes, and her nose filled with moisture. She couldn't breathe. She had to stop crying or she'd smother to death. Then again, better to smother to death than to face what was happening.

No! No! No! The words repeated through her mind. *Please No! Please No! Help me, Lord!* Her thoughts cried out and transformed into an anguished prayer as the excruciating pain enveloped her body and soul. Surely this couldn't be happening! *"Help me! Help me!"* her internal chant pleaded for what seemed like an eternity of torment. And then, just as she was about to sink into utter hopelessness, as if in answer to her prayers she heard a loud wooden crack, felt a sudden jolt hit the man, and sensed his body separate from hers with a thud and crackling rustle of hay.

When she felt hands on her shoulders, she kicked, her arms flailed, and she screamed through the cloth. The hands released her, and then she heard the striking of flints. A small flickering flame hovered in the air, floated and caught hold of the wick in the lantern hanging on the barn wall.

"Miss, are you all right?" Elijah Willoughby's voice held deep concern.

Angelina clutched at her shredded gown, gathered it the best she could to her neck, and tucked her legs back under her nightgown. His eyes narrowed, then all color drained from his face as his mouth dropped open for a moment. His eyes scanned the room, searching for something and then rested upon Jacobsen.

She tugged the gag from around her mouth, over her head, and flung it across the barn. She licked her lip and tasted the metallic saltiness of warm blood. Her eyes shifted from Willoughby to Captain Jacobsen's lifeless body that lay in the hay, blood oozing from his temple, and a two-by-four lying beside him.

"Is he? Is he – dead?" Angelina whispered, afraid yet hoping it to be true.

Elijah pulled one suspender strap over his bare torso and squatted down, putting his hand to Jacobsen's throat.

He shook his head, "No, his pulse is weak, but he's alive."

Angelina scooted farther away from the men until her back hit the barn wall.

"I'm so sorry, Miss," Elijah eased toward her.

"Stay away from me!" she tried to scream, but to her surprise found her voice hoarse and unable to rise above a scratchy whisper. "Just stay away from me!"

"I'm not gonna hurt you, Miss. I promise," Elijah lifted his hands, his palms in the air as a gesture of innocence.

"Stay away," she shook her head. Her arms encircled her legs, which she had tucked under her, and the tears started to flow again. She looked at Willoughby and thought how her dreams of a romantic hero had been shattered and replaced by the vile man lying on the dirt floor. Her eyes fell to the monster, whose stinking foul breath would be forever seared in her memory, incinerating any hope for sweet romantic love.

"Let's take you inside to your mother," Elijah approached her as if he were attempting to befriend a frightened doe.

"No!" she raised her hand in a halting motion. "Stay away from me!" She struggled to her feet, still clutching the shredded rag of a nightgown to her throat. Willoughby's eyes cast about, scanning the barn. Angelina wanted to retreat but felt the horrid nausea swell in her stomach. A thick tunnel of darkness closed in on her. Before she hit the ground, just as her legs gave way beneath her, Elijah was there, gently lifting her in his arms and carrying her bruised body back to the house.

The loud burst from Elijah kicking open the door and carrying Angelina into the house awakened Lelia and Cal. They scrambled to the edge of the loft and peered down into the kitchen watching the soldier tromp across the wooden planks, carrying Angelina into her mother's bedroom. He set her gingerly upon the bed.

"What's happened?" Lelia cried and scurried down the loft ladder.

Cal went for his gun that he kept under his straw mattress. In a flash, he descended from the loft, joining his mother. Lelia hovered over the bed where Willoughby sat next to Angelina, covering her with a blanket. Cal raised his weapon toward the Union officer, but halted with his finger on the trigger.

"What's happened? You tell me what's happened to my daughter this instant!" Lelia demanded, shaking Willoughby by his bare shoulders. Cal stomped across the room and pressed his pistol to the center of Elijah's back.

"Jacobsen attacked her in the barn," Elijah answered, raising his arms in an indication of surrender. "I came upon them, hit 'im over the head and brought her in here."

"I'll kill ya, ya worthless Yank! I should've shot ya the minute ya stepped foot on our porch!" Cal growled and shoved the pistol deeper into Elijah's back.

"I tell you it was Jacobsen. Go out in the barn and see for yourself, before he comes to and escapes," Elijah answered in his own defense.

Cal looked to his mother who gestured for him to do as Willoughby suggested.

Cal stomped out of the room, across the kitchen and out the front door. Lelia sat on the edge of the bed by her daughter, and Elijah went for a washcloth and dipped it in a washbasin. Just as he handed it to Lelia, a shot cracked the humid midnight air.

Lelia glanced toward the front door as her hand flung to her bosom. Elijah's apprehensive eyes met Lelia's. He reached for his pistol, hurried out of the bedroom and into the kitchen just as Cal stepped inside the house, his weapon still smoking. Lelia was on Elijah's heels and ran to her son in the kitchen, taking his shoulders in her trembling hands. "Cal, what have you done?"

"I did what should've been done the moment he stepped foot on our property."

With the hard-steeled expression of contempt on his face, her son looked as if he'd aged ten years in the last ten minutes. He raised his gun, pointing it at Elijah Willoughby, and cocked the trigger.

Instead of pointing his pistol at Cal in retaliation, Elijah lowered his weapon to the kitchen table and raised his hands in the air, "I mean your family no harm, Cal. I promise you; I had no part in this other than to stop it."

"Don't matter; you're one of 'em and you've gotta die."

"No Cal, it's not right. You can't do this," Lelia put her hands on her son's arm, attempting to calm his fury.

Just as Cal was about to fire, Angelina hobbled from the bed. She clung to the blanket around her shoulders and

39

leaned heavily against the doorframe. Her movement jarred the door, and the three of them turned to look at her. She panted, her bruised and bloody lip quivering, "No Cal, ya can't do it. He saved my life."

At the sight of his sister on her feet, Cal lowered his weapon. "Ya've got one minute to gather your belongin's and get the blazes out o' here."

Lelia approached Angelina and helped her back to bed while Elijah followed them into the bedroom to gather his things. He put on his shirt and hat and approached the bed.

"I'm awfully sorry, Miss Angelina," he said, a pained expression in his sad blue eyes as he bent over her and pressed something into her hand. Angelina could only offer him a numb stare as he tipped his hat, walked into the kitchen, and out the front door. When her eyes fell to her open palm, she found Willoughby's silver ring. Her mind flashed back to when they had walked through the field, and he reached for the ring whenever he appeared nervous. It meant something to him, yet he'd given it to her. She closed her fist around it and shut her eyelids, letting a single tear spill onto her cheek.

Why hadn't she listened to Willoughby's warning never to be alone? Why hadn't she taken Cal with her to the outhouse? Why did the soldiers even have to come here?

~*~

While Lelia tended to her daughter's cuts and bruises, Cal stood in the doorway watching Elijah drape

Jacobsen's body over a horse. Elijah then mounted his own and rode away.

"I should kill 'im too. What if he comes back with troops?" Cal murmured under his breath.

He heard his sister's sobs, and his resolve to kill the other soldier strengthened. He picked up his gun, but when his mother's voice begged him to prepare a bath for Angelina, he stopped. Putting down the gun, he turned back to the window, just in time to see Willoughby staring at the house, his horse stomping with impatience, before he turned and rode slowly away. "Hurry, Cal," his mother shouted.

"What's wrong?" he asked as he went to the doorway of the bedroom. Angelina was crying uncontrollably on the bed, yet when she looked at him, it was as if she looked past him, her eyes vacant and staring.

"I've got to bathe," Angelina said, murmuring it over and over. "He's on my skin. I need a bath. I've got to take a bath."

Lelia's worried eyes met Cal's. "I'd send you for the doctor, but it's not safe. Let's get her bathed and warm."

Cal nodded, his shoulders slumping. Watching his sister suffer was difficult, but knowing it was his fault for not protecting her was unbearable. He should've followed his instincts about them Yanks. How would he ever face his sister again? And what of his father? Cal took a deep breath. This war was destroying the country, but he wouldn't let it destroy his family. Squaring his shoulders, he turned to his task. The days for courtesy were over. Cal had proved tonight that he was capable of doing anything to protect his family. Anything.

Chapter 5

February 1865

Lieutenant Elijah Willoughby's heart pounded beneath his uniform as he strode purposefully toward the two soldiers who lifted a covered corpse onto a stretcher. Catching up with them, he drew back the scratchy wool blanket to reveal the dead man's face. A wave of relief swept over him as he studied the casualty and realized it was not Old Stone.

He nodded at the medics, and they hefted the body to the far side of the Rock Island prison facility. Elijah straightened and looked toward the building in front of him. He took a deep breath, knowing it would be the last breath of fresh air he would enjoy for the next ten hours. Raking his hand through his thick black hair, he steeled himself to face the degrading conditions inside the barracks. It sickened him to see the appalling treatment of Americans against Americans day in and day out. As he entered the compound, he headed toward his usual post guarding Confederate prisoners, and a faint smile turned up his lips. The one bright spot for Elijah in this wretched war was the southern gentleman whom the other prisoners referred to as Old Stone.

Just before he reached the bunk area, Captain Allen stopped him, spitting his tobacco juice near Elijah's boot. "You just comin' on?" he asked.

Elijah drew his coat closer about him, feeling the items he had stashed there and not wanting Captain Allen to discover them. "Yeah, I'm on tonight."

"You just be sure to keep an eye on 'em. We want the prisoners quiet and orderly, ya hear?" He leaned closer and Elijah could smell his foul breath. "I know you have a soft spot for 'em, though I don't know why. They're rebels and good for nuthin'." He rocked back and gave Elijah an evil smile. Nodding, he waited for Elijah to salute him, then turned on his heel. Elijah sighed deeply, having witnessed firsthand how Captain Allen meted out his judgment against the "rebels," and he was glad Allen wouldn't be around tonight.

The repulsive stench of human filth, sweetened with hay, filled Elijah's nostrils. Even though the odor was familiar, its pungency startled him. A wave of nausea lurched in the pit of his stomach, and he fought the uncontrollable urge to gag. He quickly covered his nose and mouth with his hand.

As he approached Old Stone's bunk he noticed with some alarm that several more prisoners were missing since he'd been there three nights earlier. Stone's bunk stood empty. Evidently, the illnesses and deaths had escalated in Elijah's absence. Had it taken his friend?

His heart raced and his chest tightened as his frantic eyes peered around the darkened barracks searching for his friend. In the corner, a prisoner knelt by a bed and hovered over a man sprawled out on the straw mattress.

Elijah approached the pair, "You two need some help here?"

"Willoughby?" Old Stone squinted into the darkness. "Is that you?" The coarse raspy voice held a strain of hope.

Elijah raised his low-burning lantern to illuminate the prisoner's face. "It's me," the smile on Elijah's face fled when he saw the condition of his friend. The lines on his face were deeper and the usual flicker in his eyes absent. They were so hollow and sunken that Elijah was surprised at the change that had taken place in the few days he'd been on leave.

His gaze shifted to the man lying on the straw cot, and recognized him as one of the newer arrivals. He looked as if he'd just received a beating. Overall, he appeared much healthier than Stone, but his face was battered and his left eye swollen almost shut.

"What happened?" Elijah asked.

"Capt'n Allen's out o' sorts this evenin'. Decided to take it out on Harry," Stone related.

Elijah squatted down, "Here, let me take a look."

Stone moved aside and watched as Elijah withdrew a clean handkerchief from his pocket, poured some water from his canteen onto it and dabbed at the man's face. Harry winced.

"What set 'im off this time?" Elijah asked.

"I didn't move fast 'nough to suit him," Harry gritted through clenched teeth as his right hand gripped the blanket upon which he lay and his left went protectively to his thigh.

"Harry's leg's still achin' him," Stone's quivering hand patted the young man's head and straightened his tousled hair.

44

"Maybe we should take you to the infirmary?" Elijah suggested. "This eye looks pretty bad."

"No, no . . . don't send me there. No one comes back from the pest houses."

"All right . . . settle down, son," Old Stone soothed.

"Nobody's gonna make ya go anywhere. It was just a suggestion," Elijah cleaned closer to the man's swollen eye, and Harry winced, releasing a low groan.

"Are ya about done with that?" Harry snapped through clenched teeth.

"Just 'bout," Elijah completed the task and asked if there was anything more he could do for him.

"Just let me rest. I just want to sleep," Harry muttered, closing his swollen eyes as he shifted his back to them and cursed the war.

"All right, sleep well," Old Stone patted Harry's shoulder, rose to his feet and went back to his bunk. He sat down on his straw stuffed cot and leaned his back against the cold drafty wall.

"Did ya enjoy your leave?" Stone asked.

"I did, and I brought ya somethin'," Elijah whispered as he crouched by Stone's bedside. He looked left and right, assuring that no one observed him and that the men around him were still sleeping. He eased his hand inside his uniform and pulled out a small bundle.

The prisoner took the gift. His trembling hands unfolded the handkerchief to find a bundle of dandelion greens bound together with twine and two large strips of beef jerky. The man's eyes lit up and glistened with moisture. An expression of amazement caused his bearded jaw to drop at what he saw next. An orange!

"Where did you get this?" Stone whispered in wondering awe, holding the piece of fruit as if it were a diamond. "I couldn't take somethin' like this." He extended the orange back to Elijah.

"I want you to have it. You need it," Elijah insisted, placing his warm hand over Stone's icy one.

"But, where did ya get it?" Stone whispered.

"Never mind where I got it. Enjoy it," he replied. "Just be careful no one sees it . . . or . . ." he looked around the barracks, "smells it."

Old Stone bowed his head with understanding. He put some greens in his mouth and began working on the orange. Elijah watched as Old Stone picked at the orange peel with his dirty brittle fingernails, trying to pull away just a small section to reveal a wedge. He worked for some time to extricate two sections. Then he wrapped up the remainder in the handkerchief and shoved it into the straw of his mattress.

Stone extended a piece in Elijah's direction.

Elijah removed his cap and shook his head side to side, "No, you need it more than I do."

As if he were sampling a piece of heavenly ambrosia, Old Stone put the glistening orange slice between his parched lips and bit off the tip. Elijah felt his own eyes mist at the pitiful sight of a grown man showing such gratitude and reverence over a tiny morsel of fruit.

"You're an angel from heaven, ya are. My guardian angel," Stone's coarse whisper was only audible to Elijah's ears. The howling wind kept anyone else from being awakened by their conversation.

A single dimple on Elijah's left cheek deepened and the lantern light twinkled in his blue eyes as he rose to his feet, took his guard position and watched his friend turn two orange sections into a feast. Upon finishing his small snack, Old Stone sat up a little in his bed, propping his head against the wall.

He cleared his voice, "Have I told ya about my eldest daughter?"

Elijah's lips turned up in amusement. He'd heard about Old Stone's daughter several times. He enjoyed listening to him speak of his family, but most especially his daughter.

"Oh, she's a fair one, my daughter. Will make a man a fine wife," he smiled and sighed before continuing, "that is if I ever dare to part with her. She brings a smile to my face every time I look at her. Perty as a picture. My wife always tried to find a gold ribbon to match her hair. I said it should've been green to match her eyes. But she's the kind o' girl who can't stand to have anythin' about her tied down. My fondest memory is of her hair flowin' wild and free behind her."

"Is that so," Elijah pretended not to have heard this description before.

"It is, but mind ya, she's a stubborn one. Got 'er pride she does, but she's got spirit."

"Spirit's a good thing," Elijah noted and thought that the daughter must get her spunk from her father.

"It is! That it is. And she's got it – that and perseverance." Stone sniffed the air around him. "You had chicken for supper, didn't ya?"

Elijah lifted the lapel of his coat to his nose, "Yeah, I did. Sorry," he gave Stone an apologetic look, marveling at the man's keen sense of smell.

"It's all right," he waved his hand, "Puts me in the mind of a story though."

Elijah smiled. Everything put Stone in mind of a story.

"I remember the first time my wife sent our daughter out to kill a chicken for dinner. She was about twelve, I reckon. She chased that fowl around the barnyard for nearly an hour before wrestlin' it to the ground. And when I say wrestle, I mean wrestle!"

Elijah thought Stone was choking when he heard the raspy rattle coming from the man's chest. He lifted his lantern and his anxious eyes studied Stone. Upon closer examination, he realized the man was laughing.

Brushing the tears of mirth from his eyes, Stone continued, his voice getting louder as he went along. "She was covered in mud and chicken mess . . . nearly head to toe! It was smudged all over 'er cheeks and covered 'er flowered dress! What a stink she brought with 'er when she stomped proudly into the kitchen carryin' that dead chicken by its wilted neck! She stretched the bird out toward 'er Mama as if she'd won first prize at the county fair!"

"'That's good, now go clean it' her mama says. See, my wife had 'er back to 'er whilst she was cookin' at the stove. So she only saw the bird danglin' there. If she'd seen our daughter, she'd 've been fit to be tied! I was sittin' there at the kitchen table hidin' behind my newspaper, tryin' to keep from bustin' out laughin'! You should've seen the girl's eyes fall. She'd thought her work was done. Then she discovers she has to drag her filthy self outside and starts ta pluckin' feathers!" Stone laughed again, that raspy almost choking giggle.

He rubbed his dirty sleeve against his eyes and continued, "Of course, I went out and helped 'er gut it, but left 'er to deal with the feathers. Next time she come in,

48

that layer of dirt was like the glue that held on a coat o' feathers! White feathers – big ones and downy ones stuck everywhere on her body, in 'er hair, and clingin' to 'er face! She looked like she'd had a run in with a chicken coop full o' mad layin' hens and come out as a great big bird herself!"

Elijah laughed, picturing the beautiful young girl Stone usually described in such a pathetic condition. He imagined her now as a girl of fourteen or fifteen, driving the young boys to distraction with her antics.

"This time when she handed over the bird, my wife still didn't see 'er. She had 'er nose in the oven checkin' on some biscuits. So she just motioned for 'er to put the bird on the table. I thought I'd bust a button to keep from laughin'. I says, 'Better wash up for supper now, Sugar.' The next time my wife saw 'er, she'd been to the pond and cleaned herself up. She was so determined not to let 'er Mama learn of the mess she'd made of herself, she even scrubbed down 'er dress and hung it out to dry on the line. To this day, my wife doesn't know about what happened, but it sure keeps me amused on lonely nights rememberin' my perty daughter turned into a chicken!"

Stone sighed long and hard, a happy, remembering-days-gone-by sort of sigh. And Elijah noticed that Stone's face didn't seem to have so many lines anymore. His eyes didn't seem as hollow either.

Stone continued on with one story after another. He told of his courtship, his marriage, the life he and his wife had built together. Other prisoners had awakened and now leaned closer in their cots to hear, but Elijah didn't mind. The other guards were always nearby, but didn't get as close as Elijah did. Elijah did notice that Old Stone never mentioned his family members' names. He assumed Stone guarded those like jewels lest the stray ear of a malicious Union soldier were to seek out his dear ones to inflict harm.

"What about you, then?" Stone prodded. "Tell me about your family. You don't have a wife, you said."

Elijah looked around, his audience of prisoners watching him with interest. It reminded him of all the times he and his school friends had gathered in his barn for late night storytelling. Only now, he was surrounded by men who were dirty, beaten, and sick, but hadn't entirely lost hope. That was one thing Elijah knew, that the human spirit was strong. He looked pointedly at Old Stone. "No," Elijah shook his head. "No wife."

"But you've got a baby sister."

"Nancy," Elijah replied with a nod.

"That's right, Nancy. Tell me 'bout Nancy," Old Stone prodded.

"Well," Elijah leaned his broad shoulders against the wall as he stood beside Stone's bed. His eyes rolled back in his head as he tried to think of a good story to tell. Settling upon one, his twinkling eyes met Stone's. "To appreciate this story you have to know a little bit about my sister."

Stone nodded, smiling in anticipation.

"She's the kind o' girl that's got to have everythin' just so. She always made good marks in school, never got in trouble in class, always followed the rules."

"Nothin' like her brother," Stone gave the bundle Elijah snuck into the barracks a discreet pat.

Elijah snickered, "No, I suppose not."

"So Nancy's a good girl."

"Very good. Does everythin' the way it ought 'o be done and would be plum mortified to find out she'd done anythin' less than perfect or made a fool of herself in the slightest way. Anyway, Nancy took piano lessons from Mrs. Cravitt in town every Thursday afternoon. Mama made me walk into town with her and wait outside on Mrs. Cravitt's front porch while Nancy took her lessons. Sometimes I'd go climb a tree or sneak off to Marty Jules' house for a while, but I'd always come back to walk Nancy home."

"A good big brother," Stone noted.

"Well, you might not agree after I tell ya the rest," Elijah winked. "Anyway, I got this idea to tease Nancy," his eyes brightened with the memory of it. "I made sure I stood outside the window as she was finishin' up her lesson so she'd see me when she turned 'round and started to leave. When she came out the front door, I took her piano book all gentlemanly like, and we walked a few steps down the road. Then I took Nancy's arm all consolin' like and I says, 'Nancy, I'm sorry 'bout what happened back there.'"

"'What's that?' she says."

"I said, 'It was plum awful the way Mrs. Cravitt smacked your hand with the ruler when ya messed up on your lesson. You weren't doin' that bad.'"

"Nancy whips 'round and stares up at me and cries, 'She didn't smack my hand with no ruler!'"

"'Oh, yes she did. I saw it, and it wasn't very nice o' her either. I should probably tell Mama how mean she was.'"

"Nancy got all upset and says, 'You're makin' that up! Mrs. Cravitt has never once smacked my hand with a ruler! I always study my lessons.'"

"I knew I had her goin' good so I just went on with it, 'Now Nancy, I won't be tellin' Mama and Papa about it cause I know Mama might make you stop takin' lessons from Mrs. Cravitt, but she did smack your hand. Now admit it.'"

51

"She got her feathers all ruffled, clenched her fists at her sides, just all torn up over it," Elijah laughed remembering his sister's indignation, the way her cheeks turned almost as red as her hair and her eyes grew fiery mad.

"So Mrs. Cravitt didn't smack 'er with the ruler, then?" Stone deduced.

"Oh no! She never touched Nancy. But, boy, Nancy sure did get her bloomers in a wad over me actin' as if she had! I suppose she thought if I'd make it up to tease her, that I might go home and tell Mama that Nancy hadn't studied her piano lessons proper and that Mrs. Cravitt's had ta give 'er a swat!"

"Why that was plum mean!" Stone affected disappointment, but then his stifled smirk gave way to a belly laugh.

"I told ya I wasn't such a good big brother."

~*~

It was the last evening of Elijah's guard duty, the night before he would be transferred back to the battlefront, that Old Stone leaned on his elbow in his straw bed and tugged at Elijah's coat. Elijah crouched down beside Stone and looked into the man's bearded face and hollow eyes. Stone's tongue moistened his cracked, bleeding lips, "Friend, when this plague is over, when we've turned our swords into pruning hooks once more, ya must come to Georgia and let me repay your kindness."

Elijah could only smile at the gentleman. War or no war, he couldn't imagine the hostilities between the North and South would ever die down enough for him to set foot back on Georgia soil. Granted, he had a Southern accent of his own, being from Northeast Tennessee. Blending into Georgia culture wouldn't be too difficult. He certainly wouldn't wear a Union uniform if he did return; but Elijah knew if he ever did make it home, he'd have no desire to leave again.

Old Stone's insistent gaze met Elijah's own. Whispering quieter still, he gave Elijah directions to his farm and made him promise to visit.

Elijah simply inclined his head in agreement, took Old Stone's cold withered hand in his and eased his other over the top, hoping to transfer some of his body heat to the poor man before leaving him forever. Emotions thick and painful formed as a lump in Elijah's throat when he realized he most likely would never see his friend again.

"God be with you," Elijah whispered as he released Stone's hand and left the barracks for the last time. Shielding his eyes from the stark brightness of the morning sun, Elijah breathed in the fresh air, then his eyes widened in understanding.

"Of course! I should've known!" he whispered to himself and turned around to face the door to the barracks, ready to run back inside to his friend. He took two steps in that direction then came to an abrupt halt. Anxiety spread over him.

No, he could never tell Stone he had met his family months earlier, that he'd sat at their supper table and seen the loveliness of his wife and children, and especially the beauty of his green-eyed daughter. The daughter Stone always described seemed like a child, not the beautiful young woman Elijah had met.

Waves of guilt engulfed him as he thought of her, guilt that had haunted him since that terrible night. The war had changed him, he'd seen and done things he'd never in his wildest dreams imagined he'd be forced to do. But knowing what had happened at Stone's farm, knowing it was his fault, he knew he could never face Old Stone again.

Chapter 6

Lelia sat on her front porch with Pastor Jackson's wife, Delilah. The only sound breaking the silence was the rhythmic squeak of their rockers and the occasional call of a songbird.

"How long's she been like this?" Delilah asked. Her deep-set brown eyes still fixed on Angelina, who sat on a rock in the distance with her blank stare cast upon the fields.

"Been nearly six months since it happened, and she hasn't been the same since."

"Does she speak at all?" Delilah asked, leaning forward as if they were discussing something that shouldn't be talked about.

"Just the bare minimum. Yes, ma'am's, No ma'ams and the like, but that's about it," Lelia answered, her voice low.

"What 'bout the other youngins? Does she speak to them?" Delilah continued rocking, but her gaze didn't leave Angelina's form.

"Nary a word." Lelia stopped rocking. "I just don't know how to help her."

"Such a shame, such a pretty girl, and once so lively," Delilah's head moved side to side in a gesture of disappointment and pity. "So the soldier, what he done to her . . ." Delilah hesitated as if she were unwilling to speak of the foul deed.

"Unspeakable, just unspeakable things," Lelia brushed a tear from her eye.

"So she told you of it?"

"No, no, she won't speak of it, but from the condition of her afterwards, I know it was bad," Lelia replied.

"Does she sit like that all the time?" Delilah gestured over to where Angelina sat.

"No, she still works as hard as ever, but when she finishes with her chores, she goes off by herself and stares so forlornly, it just breaks my heart."

"At least the war is over now, and Everett will be returning. Maybe he'll help her heal," Delilah offered.

Lelia only moved her head in agreement, pretending she believed it could happen, but inside she feared her husband was dead. There had been no word of Everett in a year. Odds were he had died in prison or on some unknown battlefield. After what happened to her sweet Angelina, Lelia had given up hope on happy endings. But she didn't voice her concerns aloud. She dared not dash her children's hopes or give force to her fears by speaking them into the air. As her mama always said, "The devil has ears and he feeds on our fears."

Lelia looked toward the door when she heard Cal step outside with Eleanor holding one hand and Joseph the other.

"We're gonna go see if Angelina wants to take a walk with us today," a cheery smile graced Eleanor's face.

The two women watched as Cal led the children toward the slab of limestone upon which Angelina sat.

"Will she join them?" Delilah asked.

"Some days she will. She has her good days and her bad like the rest of us, I suppose."

"Today must be a good day," a smile twinkled in Delilah's eyes as Angelina rose to her feet and stepped into stride with her siblings.

"It is unseasonably warm for early spring. Perhaps that's why she's decided to be sociable," Lelia replied.

~*~

As the children reached the peak of the grassy knoll and descended the other side, Cal caught sight of a ragged figure approaching. The bearded man paused long enough to rake a hand through his scraggly brown hair and to adjust the lapel on his threadbare gray uniform. Then he resumed his belabored pace, limping along with the aid of a stick for a cane.

It wasn't unusual to see war-torn individuals making their way South, returning home to their families and what remained of their property. Most found their homes ransacked or burned to the ground. Defeated and depressed they sat among the ashes and somehow mustered the courage to continue and rebuild with their limited resources.

Here before them was another such man. Cal would greet him as he did the others and invite him for a meal. They treated each soldier who passed as if he were their father, hoping and praying heaven might repay their act of kindness to their own loved one.

The children halted while Cal descended the hill and

approached the ragged man. "How do, sir? You on your way home?" Cal queried as he drew closer to the veteran, an odd tingle drizzling throughout his body.

The man's posture straightened a little and his hollow brown eyes glistened. The veteran swallowed hard, giving an affirmative nod. Cal looked into the man's face for several moments, trying to place the familiarity in the eyes. They were the only things that appeared human behind the mane of shoulder length hair and full scruffy beard. Suddenly, recognition flickered within Cal, then joy and relief filled his heart. He stepped closer and draped his slender arms around the figure, holding him tight. "Papa, papa," he whispered into the man's shoulder.

After several moments in his father's embrace, Cal's mind turned to Angelina. Perhaps there would be hope for her now. As he came out of his father's embrace, Cal looked over his shoulder at his sister who stood between Joseph and Eleanor at the top of the knoll. With tears running down his cheeks, Cal's eyes met his sister's with a nod. Angelina released Eleanor's hand and covered her mouth in astonishment. She started running and Eleanor followed at her heels. Soon, the girls united in the familial embrace.

"We missed you so much, Daddy!" Eleanor cried. Joseph, who had been so young when his father left for war, stood apart from the rest of the family, eyeing the strange scruffy soldier.

"You don't remember me do you, Joseph?" Everett knelt before the child, cocking his head to one side and smiling at his small son. Everett extended one hand and stroked his beard with the other, "Maybe you'll recognize me better once I've shaved this mess."

Joseph took the man's hand and shook it, squinted,

and studied Everett's eyes. A gradual smile crept across the child's face, and he thrust his arms around his father, resting his head on Everett's shoulder.

When Everett turned his attention to Angelina, she melted into his embrace, tears spilling in an uncontrollable rain.

Everett's careworn face drew up with concern as he took her shoulders in his hands and searched her eyes, "Sugar, all is well now, your Daddy's home."

But his compassionate words only served to bring more tears. As Cal watched his sister, he could see the dam of pent up pain, sadness and loss break through in a deluge of emotions.

Everett's helpless eyes questioned him, and Cal could barely control his anger as his mind went back to the night of Angelina's attack. His mouth hardened into a grim line, his muscles tightened, and his fists clenched at his sides. This should have been a happy reunion, but because Cal had failed in his care of the family, Angelina was damaged, never to be the happy girl their father once knew. Cal's guilty eyes met his father's, but there was no condemnation there, only love and concern. Just the expression on his father's face helped to ease Cal's burden.

He put an arm about his sister and another around his father's shoulder, "Here, let's get back to the house. Mama will be upset if she finds out you were here this long, and we didn't take you to her."

As they grew closer to the house, Cal watched recognition dawn on his mother's face. She rose from her rocker, lifted her skirt and leapt off the porch. Running toward them, she clasped her hands to Everett's bushy bearded cheeks and searched his hollow smiling eyes. He put a dusty hand to her cheek, staring at her with the same loving expression Cal had witnessed the day his father left for war. With tears in her eyes, she threw herself into his arms and gripped him tight.

~*~

After accompanying Everett and the children back to the house, Lelia's first instinct was to feed her emaciated husband. Her heart ached for the pain he had experienced, and her stomach wrenched at the thought of the days and nights he must have endured without a decent meal.

She'd already started a stew a few hours earlier, so she enlisted Delilah's help in setting the table while the children gathered around their father.

Before the incident, Lelia would have asked Angelina to help, but she knew that more than anything else, Angelina craved her father's attention. She'd always been a daddy's girl. He'd been the one she ran to with bee stings, skinned knees and nightmares. As a little child, Angelina would sit on his lap listening to him play his harmonica until she drifted off to sleep. Lelia could see in Angelina that same blonde-haired child, long deprived of her father's presence. The young woman's eyes now sparkled with the first glimpse of hope Lelia had seen there in months. No, she would not deprive her daughter of time in Everett's healing presence.

It wasn't until after the children settled into their beds and Everett and Lelia climbed into their own that Lelia related Angelina's frightening experience.

She knew Everett felt a horrible mixture of pain, anger, and helplessness. The wrinkles on his face and the lines around his eyes seemed to convey every emotion he felt within. She saw guilt there as well, and Lelia knew he berated himself for not being able to defend his family, especially his sweet Angelina. Like father, like son she thought. Tears trickled from the corners of his eyes at Lelia's retelling.

Lelia thought how she couldn't remember a time when she'd seen her husband cry. In all the twenty years they'd been married, even at the loss of their third child, even upon the death of his own parents, she'd never seen more than a glistening in the man's eyes. But now, tears trailed down his cheeks as he buried his forehead in his palms. She could do no more than to drape her arm about his shoulder. War had changed him. She'd expected war would harden a man, but a year in the wretched, filthy prison had softened the husband she'd known. He'd become acquainted with grief and suffering on an intimate level, and it left him acutely compassionate.

Finally, Lelia decided to stop analyzing and snuggled into his arms, willing herself just to enjoy his homecoming. She'd have plenty of time for these thoughts later.

~*~

Over the next weeks and months, Lelia watched as Everett made special efforts to spend time with his oldest daughter. They went for long walks in the woods, worked in the fields together, and over time Angelina came out of her shell and began to speak more. She still wasn't the cheery youth she'd once been, but she did begin to initiate conversations and become a little more like her old self.

One evening, Lelia and Everett lay beside each other on their feather bed talking and listening to the crickets and cicadas. Lelia shifted to her side and draped an arm across her husband's chest as he lay on his back, looking up at the rafters.

"Everett," she whispered.

"Yes, dear."

"Has Angelina ever spoken to you about . . . about that night?" Lelia hoped Angelina had been able to open up to her father, for she still hadn't confided in her.

"Not really," he replied.

"I worry about her holdin' all that in. I don't know the full extent of . . . of . . ." Lelia's words trailed off, unable to voice her fears about what had happened to her daughter.

"I can understand why she doesn't want to talk about it. Some things are best left unsaid."

Lelia wasn't so certain of that. She knew Everett understood better than anyone else why Angelina did not want to speak of the event. He'd been no more willing to speak of his own season in hell.

"I wonder if a mind can heal when it's holdin' all that inside. Seems like keepin' it all bottled up would be like not lancin' a festerin' wound," she observed.

"What a perty picture that paints across the mind," Everett quipped with a sarcastic tease.

"Well, just seems dangerous to hold it in like that," Lelia defended her rather graphic analogy. She hoped her husband realized she was admonishing him as much as she was discussing Angelina.

He must have understood because after several moments of silence his deep measured voice selected his words, "When you endure somethin' unmentionable, somethin' so traumatic, you just want to forget. You're afraid to face it again by speakin' of it."

Lelia said nothing, but let her hand move with assurance and comfort against his chest, trying to show him she understood.

Nothing but the crickets chirping cut through the darkness until Everett finally spoke again in a quiet deep voice, "It was filthy."

When he paused, her mind searched to regain its bearings with his sudden change of topic.

"Dank. Cold – so bone chillin' cold." She could feel him shudder beneath her palm. "Rats were everywhere. Some men ate them as if they were rabbit or squirrel. The smell was . . . I thought I'd never wash it off o' me. My first day out, I couldn't find a stream fast enough. Didn't matter that the water was ice cold, I had to wash it off. I would o' given anythin' for even so much as a scrap o' soap."

Lelia shuddered, remembering that night when Angelina had been so desperate to bathe herself. "I'm so sorry," she whispered, tears threatening behind her eyelids.

"It's a miracle I lived. Men died around me like flies. If it weren't for my memories of you and the children, I have no doubt I would have given up and perished alongside them."

Lelia tightened her arm around her husband's chest and nestled her head on his shoulder, grateful he had entrusted her with a small portion of his experience. He put his arm around her, lying there in the darkness until they drifted off to sleep in each other's arms.

Chapter 7

The nurse's skirt rustled as she set down the oil lamp she had been carrying from one cot to the next. She sat next to the Lieutenant's cot. Squeezing the rag of its moisture, she blotted it across his fevered brow.

"Lieutenant Willoughby's fever seems to be climbing," she announced to the doctor as he approached with a questioning gaze.

"That chest wound was severe. Are you watching it for infection, like I asked?"

"Yes, Doctor," she affirmed.

"He's lucky to be alive. That last battle took a lot of our young men," the gentle doctor patted Elijah's leg, gave him a sympathetic look, and then moved on to other patients.

The nurse dipped the rag in the washbasin once more. She'd keep a close eye on him tonight.

He moaned under her ministrations, "Angel, angel," he muttered.

The nurse wondered if he was calling for someone or close to death. "Sh, sh," she whispered, "It's all right, I'm here." He settled down for a moment, as if her voice had soothed him, but another coughing spasm shook his frame. He gasped for air and she rushed to get him some water. When he finally lay back, he clutched her hand and wouldn't let go.

"I'm so sorry," he gasped. "I should have known what he would do. Please, forgive me." His grip slackened, exhausted by the effort of speaking.

She brushed his unruly hair back from his face. "It's all right," she murmured. "Rest now."

In his fevered state, Elijah's mind raced from one blood-curdling memory to the next. Interspersed amidst the scenes of war that plagued his mind stood only one reoccurring solace. A face flashed intermittently into his memory. With his smoldering temperature, he could not recall who she was or what she meant to him. Perhaps the beautiful girl with eyes as green as a spring meadow was an angel come to comfort him. But something told him she was mortal, for sometimes he held her close in his arms. He saw her eyes reflecting the moonlight as a violin played a waltz in the distance. At other times, he felt his heart racing in terror. She was in danger and no matter how hard he tried to reach her it wasn't soon enough.

His frantic mind searched to recall her significance, but he could not hold a single thought long enough to lay hold upon the memories. When the pains grew intense or the heat rose to dangerous temperatures, her face was the only thought he could pull to mind. He would dwell upon her silky complexion. He'd see her ruby lips moving as she spoke to him, but he could not discern the words. He looked around the open meadow surrounded by lush vegetation and then his gaze would return to her equally verdant eyes.

In this night's fitful dream, Elijah held her sleeping body against his chest, her golden locks spilling over his shoulders. He leaned down to look into her face, but was horrified to find her cheeks bruised and bright red blood trickling from her lip.

At the recollection, waves of guilt spread over him, guilt that had haunted him since that terrible night. The memories came rushing back in a flood as his brow broke into a cold sweat. He hadn't heeded his first instinct to follow Jacobsen outside. He'd remained curled up in the warm bed and told himself Jacobsen was only going to the outhouse and would return shortly. After all, it was the first decent night's rest Elijah had had in what felt like an eternity.

It wasn't until Jacobsen didn't return in a reasonable amount of time and the nagging feeling increased to an inescapable level that Elijah hurried into his boots, took no time to put on a shirt and rushed outside in search of his companion.

He heard the rustling of a struggle and discerned muffled cries coming from the barn. His heart raced as he turned in that direction. Just then, the moon broke through the clouds revealing the wicked scene transpiring in the barn. Evidently in Jacobsen's haste, he had not bothered to close the large barn doors. Elijah's heart hammered so hard against the walls of his chest that it felt as if it might explode. His chest rising and falling in anger and blazing indignation, Elijah reached for a board on the outer barn wall. With one powerful jerk, he ripped it from the structure. Without batting an eye or taking a second thought, he strode forward and slammed it across Jacobsen's head. An immediate swell of satisfaction and retribution pulsed through him as he watched Jacobsen's body teeter and plummet sideways into the straw. That feeling fled in an instant when his gaze redirected to the girl's terrified expression.

He rushed toward her, but she pushed him away. He pulled his flints from his pocket and lit a lantern that hung on the barn wall. In the light, his observation traveled the length of her, assessing the damage. Uncomfortable, he diverted his attention away from her torn nightgown, which revealed more than he should be seeing. His first instinct was to run to her, drape a blanket over her and stop the bleeding from the scratches on her throat and lip. He looked around to find something to throw over her, but saw nothing. With cautious steps, he started forward and winced when he noticed the bruises already forming on her cheeks.

Her frail yet firm command to remain where he was halted his motion. He tried to assure her that he meant no harm, but she looked as frightened as a horse startled by a rattler. Before Angelina realized it herself, Elijah knew that she would faint. He lunged forward, catching her just before she would have hit the floor face first. He scooped her up into his arms, her body limp and warm against his chest. Her head nestled near his throat, and her silken locks spilled over his bare shoulder.

Elijah paused for a moment to look into her face. She looked like a sleeping angel. So innocent and young, now violated and forced to face the ugly cruelties of life. Moisture threatened behind his eyelids as he thought of the beautiful spirited girl he'd seen that day. He recalled walking over her family's property with her, watching the soft breeze blow through her blonde hair. They'd sat together chatting and feeding apple pieces to her baby goat. He'd admired her graceful movements, his interest in her perhaps a little too obvious. He'd noticed her composure softening toward him and then stiffening when she obviously remembered that he was the enemy and not be trusted.

Would she ever be the same? Elijah let his face draw closer to hers and pressed his lips to her forehead, inhaling the sweet scent of her hair for just a moment before forcing himself to return her to her family.

He still recalled the pain he felt when Cal ordered him to leave her behind. He wanted to stay with her and help nurse her back to health. If only he could have stayed to learn the extent of her injuries, but after Cal shot Jacobsen, he didn't dare risk it. The expression in the boy's eyes had been cold as steel. Elijah had to admit that his response would have been no different if it had been Nancy attacked. He removed his ring from his finger and slipped it into her palm. He wanted her to know that he was sorry and that he cared about her. It was the least he could do for allowing her to come to harm. More than anything, he wanted her to remember him.

Elijah's eyes widened, staring up into the darkness of the hospital. He now knew who owned the beautiful face, but he also remembered why he could never be in her presence again. He could never return to Georgia and face Old Stone. By now, his friend would have learned of that wicked night and associated Elijah with it. Old Stone would not welcome his visit now. He'd want nothing to do with him ever again.

Chapter 8

Angelina sat under a hickory tree writing in her diary. She leaned back against the tree and closed her eyes, remembering the day her mother gave it to her, suggesting she might be able to vent some of her pain onto the pages. Her mother had been right. The practice had become therapeutic over the last several months.

"Care if I join you?" Angelina's father inquired as he came to stand beside her.

Angelina shut the diary and looked up at him standing there in his overalls. He rolled his shirtsleeves up to his elbows. "Please do," she gestured for him to be seated.

Everett sat on the grass facing her, "I figured I'd let Cal plow a while." He swiped his forearm to his forehead, wiping away the perspiration. The afternoon sun shone like a fireball in the sky, turning the humidity into a thick, suffocating vapor.

Angelina took a deep breath and spoke the words she'd never dared to speak before, "Daddy, I think I'm ready to talk about what happened." Her expression was serious, and she noted a flicker of surprise pass over her father's face and then disappear. Everett nodded his head and leaned toward her a little, resting his elbows on his knees as his hands twiddled a blade of grass.

Angelina began by telling of her descent from the loft to get a drink of water and proceeded through the night's events in a cool, almost detached manner, as if she were telling someone else's story. She knew she had to tell it that way or she wouldn't make it through it. Angelina surprised even herself as she let the story spill from her lips, revealing more than she ever had to anyone.

Only to her diary had she confided more. As she finished the last of the story with the Lieutenant pressing his ring into her hand and Cal ordering him to leave, she realized the process of writing in her diary must have given her the ability to confide in her father.

Angelina's eyes met Everett's. Moisture pooled in his. She looked away from him toward the field, swallowed back the lump in her throat, and tried to keep herself from breaking into tears.

She slipped her finger through Willoughby's ring that hung from a neckchain. After regaining her composure, Angelina summarized, "I really think Captain Jacobsen would have killed me if Lieutenant Willoughby hadn't come to my rescue."

"Willoughby?" Everett's voice held obvious surprise. Before this point, she had only referred to the two men as the Captain and the Lieutenant.

"Yes," Angelina replied, her gaze searching her father's unusual expression.

"What was his full name? Do you know?" his voice held urgency.

"Lieutenant Elijah Willoughby," Angelina replied.

"Hmmm," Everett stroked his chin, a far off expression in his eyes as he stared out over the fields.

"Why?"

Everett shook his head as if coming out of a fog, "Nothin', I – we should probably find some way to thank 'im some day." Everett took her hand and squeezed it.

"I just wish I could get past it and forget."

Everett sighed, "Look for the good, Sugar. Lean on the Lord, and look for the good." Angelina responded with a tip of her head, letting him know she understood. She stared across the field toward Cal who plowed a row in the distance. Moisture misted her vision as she watched Eleanor and Joseph play by an old stump on the other side of the field. She remembered how carefree the days of her own childhood playing with Cal had been. She missed those days and doubted she could ever feel that way again.

She closed her eyes and inhaled as the familiar ache churned in her stomach and quickened her heart's pace. "It's so hard, Daddy," she confided. "I try to concentrate on the good. I pray for help and comfort does come for a moment. But just when I think I'm doin' better, it all comes floodin' back, and I feel suffocated and helpless." Her protective fingers clutched her throat, the memories thick and heavy on her mind.

"You've got to let it go, Sugar. Count your blessings instead. Look," he took her hands in his. "You're healthy and intact. You're alive, and you have your family about you. He didn't take any of that from you. You're just as beautiful and smart as ever. You have your whole life ahead of you."

"But no one will ever want me now," she whispered, blinked back the tears, and dropped her gaze to her lap.

She could feel the crimson heat of embarrassment in her cheeks and the pounding of her pulse in her temples.

"Oh, Sugar," Everett put his palm to her cheek. "You can't believe that. You have so much to give, so much to offer a good man. Goodness knows there are several young men in town who'd be proud to call you their own."

Angelina grimaced, "I just don't feel anything for them. Paul Bennett came up here the other day, and I couldn't bring myself even to go for a walk with 'im. You know how I used to be so fond of 'im. Now I feel nothin'. I don't think I could ever feel anything for any man after what happened." Her fingers touched Willoughby's ring, "Except . . ." She shook her head side-to-side, brushing away the thought. The only man she felt anything for, the only man who might be able to capture her heart, would never want her. It had all been too embarrassing. She could never face him again, even if she knew where he was.

"It's gonna take some time to heal. Don't be rushin' yourself. When the time is right, you'll know it.

"But, I'm scared," she brushed a tear from her cheek. "What if I'm always scared? What if I'm always alone?" As terrified as she was of having a man touch her, she was even more frightened of spending her life alone – with no one to care for her, no one to protect her from harm. She looked at her father. He was her protector now, but even he could not live forever.

"I know you're frightened. It's only normal for you to be scared. But one day, you'll meet a young man and you won't feel the fear anymore. You'll feel safe with him, and then you'll know."

"How can you be certain?" her doubtful eyes met his.

"Because time heals all wounds, and when it's had its chance to do its work, the loving person you are and have always been will win out over the fear. You'll see. Love always conquers fear in the end."

Angelina put her arms around her father's shoulders and clung to him. "What would I do without you, Daddy?" she whispered into his ear and kissed his cheek.

Her father smiled at her gratitude and then cleared his throat, "You know, Sugar, I've been thinkin', and I think it's time you started buildin' a life for yourself."

Angelina's countenance fell. "What do you mean?"

"The town council is talkin' about gettin' a school started again in town. In our last meetin', we discussed lookin' for a couple of teachers. You were always top of your class, and well, I suggested we consider you."

"Me?" Angelina put her hand to her chest.

"You're more'n qualified."

"But, I – I'm not ready," Angelina shook her head negatively; her nerves making her feel sick to her stomach.

"You'd just be teachin' the younger children. Mrs. Simpkins would take the older ones," Everett took her hands again. "Ya can do this, Angelina. Ya *need* to do this for your own good. It'll take your mind off your troubles. Besides, your mama and I won't always be here to help ya. Cal's becomin' a man and will soon build a family of his own. Ya need to start facin' your fears."

"But," she began to protest.

"This is the easiest place to start," her father interrupted.

Angelina looked up at the blue sky, then closed her eyes and sighed, "Very well. But don't let the council give me special consideration over anyone else . . . just because I'm your daughter."

"Fair enough," Everett nodded and gave her hands an assuring squeeze.

~*~

In the fall, Angelina started working as a teacher at the little schoolhouse in town. She never would have agreed, but she trusted her father's judgment, and if he thought it was for the best, then surely it would be.

She didn't earn much for her time, just the produce and livestock the local townspeople could contribute, but it didn't take long for Angelina to be glad she'd followed her father's advice and taken the position.

Teaching kept her mind from wandering onto images of the past or from fretting over what seemed to be a bleak and lonesome future. She loved the children, and it helped that Joseph and Eleanor were among them. They were friendly faces cheering her on, letting her know she could do the job when self-doubts clawed at her confidence.

On the Friday of her third week teaching, she'd had a productive day, and a feeling of satisfaction swept over her as she remembered how she'd helped little Jeffrey finally figure out how to put letters together to form basic words. Smiling, she backed out the schoolhouse door and locked it. When she turned around and started down the stairs, Paul Bennett stood at the bottom. His hand leaned on the railing, his shirtsleeves rolled up to his elbows, while his other hand hung by his thumb on his overall straps. Paul rubbed one spit-shined boot on the back of his pant leg to bring it to a shiny luster. When his eyes met hers, a smile spread across his face, and he tipped his hat in greeting.

"Afternoon, Miss Angelina," his hazel eyes sparkled. He replaced his hat and smoothed down his blonde sun-streaked mustache.

"Afternoon, Mr. Bennett," she tipped her head, forced a congenial smile, and straightened her plain black skirt. She'd been practicing smiling even when she didn't feel like it.

"Was wonderin' if I might accompany ya home?"

Angelina's nervous heart began to pound. It wasn't the pounding she'd experienced three years ago when she'd been sweet on Paul. It was the nervousness one gets when she has to perform some worrisome task she'd rather not. It wasn't that Paul frightened her; it was just having to walk home on someone's arm, feeling uncomfortable with a man so close, hearing his breath, sensing his eagerness.

Besides, what could she say to him? She wasn't sure she was up to making conversation. Teaching was easy. The knowledge was in her head, and it was fun to watch the children's eyes light up when they gained understanding. But having to make small talk with a man didn't come natural. There was no knowledge inside her to pour out and fill the awkward lulls and voids Angelina knew would soon follow.

She could hear her father's voice coaxing her to face her fears. So she nodded her head in acceptance. "That would be most pleasant, Mr. Bennett," she offered in the most polite and accepting tone she could muster.

He took her satchel in one hand, and then extended his arm to her. She placed her hand upon it. Paul was a farmer like his father, and Angelina could feel the taut muscles beneath his sleeve. She'd always been thrilled by a man with brawny muscles; that was until she learned first hand how overpowering a strong man could be – how someone that powerful could take control of her and force himself upon her. Angelina's heart drummed in her ears as she remembered the suffocating helplessness, the complete inability to defend herself. She could feel the perspiration breaking upon her brow and without realizing it, her fingers tightened upon Paul's arm.

"You all right, Miss Angelina?" Paul's concerned expression turned to her. That instant, she loosened her grip on his arm and fanned herself with her free hand.

"I'm sorry, it's just a bit warm out here this afternoon," her fingers tugged at the collar of her blouse.

Paul looked around at the lush vegetation and the sunny September sky. Perhaps it was a little warm, but not enough to bring anyone to perspiration.

Gathering her wits about her, Angelina forced herself to think of Paul as the young boy she'd always known. She remembered how she and Cal had played in the Bennett's hayloft, and how Paul had protected her when the other boys pulled her pigtails. Paul had always been kind to her. There was nothing to fear.

Patting her handkerchief to her forehead, she soon regained her composure and did her best to make conversation with her companion.

As they passed a pasture full of grazing cattle, a broad grin spread across Paul's face, "'member that time Cal stepped in that pile o' cow manure, and his boot come off?"

Angelina smirked at the memory. "Took him nearly an hour to clean all that mess off before Mama would let him back in the house again," Angelina giggled.

"We had some fun times as youngins," Paul smiled, a far off look in his eye, apparently remembering cheerful days of youth.

"Things were easier before the war," Angelina noted.

"Sure were, but things will be good again. They're gettin' better all the time."

"Hope so," Angelina replied in a doubtful mutter.

"They will be. As Mama always said, 'this too shall pass.' Things are already gettin' better. Pa and I've just 'bout got our farm back in good workin' order, and we should get 'nuf out of this year's crop to pay the property taxes."

"That's good," Angelina smiled.

The walk home with Paul wasn't as laborious as Angelina had expected it to be. In fact, she rather enjoyed reminiscing with him and listening to his plans for the future. She'd forgotten how friendly and charming he could be. Now she remembered why she'd been so sweet on him, but things had changed. Try as she might, she couldn't muster those feelings for him anymore. She felt comfortable with him as a friend, but that was all. Feelings of friendship were a start though. It was more than she'd felt in some time. Perhaps she was starting to heal a little.

~*~

"Did Paul walk you home again this afternoon?" Lelia inquired as Angelina entered the door with a smile on her face several weeks later.

Angelina gave a positive nod of her head, still chuckling over a humorous comment he'd made just before they reached the house.

"I believe that boy wants to court you, but is just too shy to come out with it," Everett teased. He sat at the kitchen table, resting his elbow on the table and his chin in his hand.

"Oh, no," Angelina gave her head an insistent shake. "We're just friends."

"No man who walks a young lady as pretty as you home every day wants to be just friends," Cal interjected as he turned around from placing more wood in the stove for his mother.

Angelina's eyebrow creased with a twinge of worry as she looked to her father for his denial of Cal's observation.

"Cal's right, Sugar," Everett shrugged.

Angelina grimaced.

"Whatcha actin' all disgruntled about, Angelina? You come in smilin' every day after your walks. Paul's a good fella. He'd make ya a fine husband. If you'd dress a little nicer, stop wearin' those drab clothes and get your hair out of a bun, maybe he'd be assured you were interested," Cal retorted.

"There's nothin' wrong with the way I dress," Angelina adjusted the top button of her plain white blouse. "I don't see 'im that way, anyway," Angelina explained. "We're just friends."

"You may be just friends, but Paul's thinkin' marriage," Cal replied, and Everett bent his head in agreement.

"Oh, my," Angelina put a fretful hand to her bosom.

"You really should consider him more seriously, dear," Lelia interjected. "He's a sweet young man."

Angelina didn't reply, but climbed the ladder to the loft and took a few moments to lie down and rest a little while. She needed to think, but she didn't feel like thinking. Suddenly, she felt tired. Perhaps a light nap would help ease her mind.

~*~

He bent down to pet her goat, and when he stood, he moved closer to her, picking up the chain around her neck that held his ring.

"This ring is very special, just like you," his tender voice explained. The depth of his blue eyes was disarming, but she couldn't pull her gaze away. The warmth started at her heart and spread to her face as she looked into his eyes. "You're beautiful," he said, taking her face in his hands. His thumb caressed her bottom lip as if she mesmerized him. She leaned into him, wanting to feel his arms around her.

Sighing deeply, she breathed his name, "Elijah."

Before she could finish the last syllable, his mouth covered hers. She never thought it would be possible to feel this way. Surely such dreams were crushed in one violent night. But there he stood, his strong arms enfolding her, his kiss so exhilarating that when he broke the seal of their lips, she gulped in the life-giving air and sat upright in her bed.

Her pulse racing like a stampede of horses, Angelina looked down at her trembling hands, and then clutched his ring that still hung about her neck. She felt as if her spirit, which had been long absent, re-entered her body and jolted it back to life. She felt alive with electricity and a longing desire for – for him! And she knew it wasn't just for any man, only Elijah Willoughby could make her feel this way. The problem was that the last time he had seen her she was a battered victim of Jacobsen's attack. She'd be mortified to see him again even if she knew where he was. This was just a dream. In reality, facing him would be too painful and embarrassing.

Chapter 9

Thatcher Barrett lifted his hat, swiped the sweat from his brow with his arm, and plopped it back on his blonde head. He leaned his arm on the hoe and arched his back, stretching the soreness from it after a long morning's work. He leaned his arm on the handle as his eyes scanned the long-neglected Willoughby farm. As his attention moved south toward the red dirt road that ran along the edge of the property, he heard Happy's loud barking. The dog bolted across the field toward the road.

Thatcher noticed she was heading straight for a Union soldier. The swagger of the man's gait, his tall body, and the way he carried his tote across his broad shoulders left no room for doubting the man's identity.

Happy sped across the field, barking incessantly. As she reached the soldier, the man bent down and let the dog jump into his arms. Happy licked the soldier's face as the man wrapped his arms around the canine and buried his face into the collie's fur.

At the the sight, a smile spread across Thatcher's dirt-smudged cheeks. He turned toward the farmhouse and his deep voice hollered, "Nancy! Nancy, darlin', Come quick!"

Within seconds, a petite young woman with a rounded belly appeared in the doorway. "What is it?" she called out to him, her eyes narrowing as she stared at her husband and then followed his extended arm, out the length of it to his pointing index finger. Her eyes continued to travel in the direction he indicated until she saw the soldier.

"Elijah!" she gasped, her voice no louder than a whisper. She stepped off the porch and hurried across the yard toward the road. Thatcher cast down his hoe and ran to meet his wife. Together they hurried to the edge of the property just as Elijah and Happy stepped onto it.

Upon seeing his sister, Elijah dropped his pack and ran straight to her, throwing his arms around her, and kissing her cheeks. "Nancy, you sure are a sight for sore eyes!" he exclaimed as he stared into her face.

"'lijah! I've missed ya so!" she cried with tears of joy trailing down her cheeks.

"And I've missed you!" he released her and patted Happy's head. His eyes lowered to Nancy's belly. Slowly his gaze shifted toward Thatcher for the first time and the smile fled from his lips.

Thatcher fidgeted under Elijah's scrutiny. "We got married in February," he blurted, hoping that would slacken Elijah's stern expression.

"I'm sorry we didn't wait for ya, but when I didn't hear from ya for so long, I – we feared the worst," Nancy rushed to explain.

"We had no idea ya were alive until we got your letter last week," Thatcher added.

"That's all right," Elijah shook his head, a smile spreading across his face. "So I'm gonna be an uncle?"

Nancy nodded her head and placed a hand to her rounded belly.

"When?"

"January or so," Nancy smiled up into her brother's face, her hand reaching to brush a strand of long hair from his brow. "You need a good hair cut."

"Yeah, and a good bath," he chuckled.

"Well, come on inside and let's get ya cleaned up and fed," she laced her arm through his and turned toward the house. Thatcher ran down the road to retrieve Elijah's bag that he'd dropped and then caught up with the siblings just before they reached the house. Happy followed on Elijah's heels, up the stairs and into the house.

"When we got your letter last week, Nancy insisted we come out here and make the place livable," Thatcher explained. "I'm afraid it needs a heap o' work."

"Ya mean you two aren't livin' here?" Elijah inquired as his hands slipped in his pockets, and he looked around the cabin. His sister had cleaned and made new curtains for the windows.

"No, we've got a farm just down the road. You know the place I bought before the war," Thatcher pointed east. Elijah nodded.

"Sorry, we didn't get everythin' fixed up better before ya got here," Nancy apologized.

"That's all right. I'm just happy to be home! I don't care if I ever take another step out o' Knoxville again!"

"I've got some chicken and dumplin's cookin'," Nancy pointed to the potbelly stove in the corner. "It should be ready shortly."

"Smells delicious," Elijah smiled and patted his stomach.

"You're gonna have to let Nancy fatten you back up," Thatcher put a hand on Elijah's shoulder. "You're plum gaunt."

"Those military rations just can't hold a candle to Nancy's chicken and dumplin's, I'm afraid."

"Ain't that the truth!" Thatcher agreed.

"So how long have ya been home?" Elijah asked his brother-in-law.

"Got home in January."

"So you two didn't wait too long to see if I'd show up for the weddin'," Elijah teased as he pulled out a chair and sat down at the table. Nancy's sheepish eyes cast downward.

"That's my fault," Thatcher replied, coming behind his wife and slipping his arms around her waist. "I was skinnier than you when I got home. I got one whiff o' her chicken and dumplin's and begged her to marry me on the spot."

"You begged me to marry ya before ya even left," Nancy teased her husband.

"True 'nough," Thatcher replied, kissing her on the cheek.

"So have ya heard from any o' the others?" Elijah asked.

"Jerry and Lyle are back to work at the livery. Sam didn't come home. Shot at Vicksburg," came Thatcher's somber reply.

"Don't suppose there's any word from Doug?" Elijah held a hopeful breath.

Nancy shook her head negatively and Thatcher answered, "There's been nothin' but the letter the military sent his wife about 'im being missin' in action and presumed dead."

Elijah's head bobbed, and he released a slow breath as his shoulders slumped a little.

"I'm sorry 'Lijah. We all loved Doug so."

"Yeah," he nodded, running his hands through his long black hair. "Well," he stood up and slapped his hand to the wooden table. "I'm gonna go clean up. Reckon ya can round up a pair of scissors and cut this mop o' mine?"

Nancy smiled, "Be glad to, big brother."

"Good, cause it's drivin' me plum crazy."

~*~

Everett stepped into the mercantile in search of a new pair of boots. As he always did, he stopped to look at the board were Mr. Peters allowed folks to post items they had for sale or things they needed. One particular advertisement caught Everett's attention. The city of Knoxville, Tennessee was looking for a new school teacher. Everett scratched his head and his pulse quickened a little.

Knoxville made him think of Elijah Willoughby. His emotions where Elijah was concerned were mixed. On one hand he'd saved Angelina's life and probably saved Everett's, yet why hadn't he mentioned to Everett that he'd met his family? Why wouldn't he say anything when he knew how much Everett craved any word from home?

Was Cal right? Was Elijah just a filthy Yankee who would have gotten to Angelina if Jacobsen hadn't first? No. Everett shook his head as he stared at the advertisement and thought of the night Elijah brought him the orange. Had he been kind to Everett out of guilt? Was he just trying to compensate in some way for what happened to Angelina? Everett shook his head again. It hadn't been Elijah's fault about what happened. Angelina and Lelia were right. Elijah had saved Angelina. He was a good man.

Forcing the disturbing thoughts from his mind, Everett weaved through the aisles of merchandise until he came to the back wall where Mr. Peters kept the boots. As he searched for the ones he liked, his ears perked at the mention of Angelina's name.

The man's voice sounded familiar and heat rose to Everett's face as he discerned the man's words.

"That girl was just askin' for somethin' like that to happen to 'er – always runnin' around town with 'er yella hair blowin' in the breeze. Her mama'd no sooner tie it up than she'd have the ribbons yanked out, flauntin' herself for all to see. Shameful it was. I've no doubt she brought it on herself." The man's voice dripped with disgust.

Everett's fists tightened, and he took two determined steps toward Jeb Neilly whose voice he now recognized. Everett intended to give the man a piece of his mind, if not a piece of his fist.

Then Everett heard another man reply and immediately recognized Phil Davidson's voice. Would his friend defend Angelina? Everett listened intently.

"Now you've got no business talkin' about Miss Stone that way. She's a fine young woman. I don't care if she did like her hair down as a youngin. My own daughter didn't like hers bound up in braids. That don't mean she's wayward. And it's definitely no call for a man to do what he done to her. A gentleman knows restraint no matter how beautiful a young woman may be."

"Restraint? A Yank?" Jeb snorted.

"I just worry for her . . ." Phil's voice trailed off and Everett took a step closer, still waiting behind a stack of merchandise where they couldn't see him. "There's been talk 'round town and I'm afraid some folks wouldn't want their sons marryin' a girl who's been . . . a girl who's been . . ." Phil seemed to be stammering for the right word as he moved his checker piece on the board in front of him.

"Been what?" Everett barked, stepping out from behind the merchandise, facing the two men who sat at a checker table. "Damaged?" Everett's questioning eyes met Phil's and the man dropped his head shamefully. "Traumatized?" Everett continued, glaring now at Jeb Neilly. "Put through hell?" Everett gritted through clenched teeth, his chest rising and falling with indignation.

Jeb did not drop his self-righteous gaze, but met Everett's as he issued his single-word retort, "Sullied." Jeb said the word as if Angelina were nothing more than a saloon trollop.

Immediately, Everett stepped forward and slammed his fist into Jeb's jaw, knocking the man off the stool. Jeb's hand hit the checker board and the pieces pelted noisily to the floor. Before Everett could get in another punch, Phil pulled him back. Soon Mr. Peters, the store owner, had joined them. Jeb pulled himself to a standing position, ready to fight, but Mr. Peters, being a large man only had to put out a staying hand to Jeb's chest and the man slinked back.

"I'll have no brawlin' in my store. Didn't you two get 'nough fightin' outta your blood in the war?" Mr. Peters scolded.

"If I ever ... ever hear ya say another word 'bout my Angelina . . ." Everett threatened, pointing an accusing finger at Jeb.

"Stone," Mr. Peters interjected. "Cool yourself down."

Jeb snickered and Mr. Peters turned on him next, "And you, Jeb, you can get your useless, gossipin' self outta here."

"He can stay," Everett waved his hand. "I've had my fill." Everett gave Jeb a look that could maim, then turned on his heels.

"Oh, come now, Stone. What did ya come in for?" Mr Peters called after him.

"I'll get it later," Everett growled without turning back. When he reached the door, he snatched the Knoxville advertisement from the board and shoved it in his shirt pocket. If Angelina was ever to be happy, she'd need out of this gossiping town. Maybe this advertisement was just the solution.

~*~

"Angelina, when you finish with those dishes, let's go for a walk," Everett suggested.

Angelina looked over her shoulder as she reached into a cabinet to put away a stack of plates, "Sure, Daddy."

Her father stepped to the window. "Looks like a perty sunset." Angelina noticed her parents give each other a knowing glance and she wondered what her father wanted to talk with her about.

She dried her hands on a towel and removed her apron. Folding it over a chair, she joined her father and he opened the door, allowing her to walk out first.

They strolled a ways before he cleared his throat and spoke. "Angelina, are ya happy here?"

Angelina looked at him, puzzled by his question. "What do ya mean?"

"I mean in this town? With the people here?"

Angelina shrugged, "I don't know. I like teachin', but . . ." She hesitated. "I do feel like people are always starin' at me or whisperin' about me behind my back." She shook her head, "I'm sure it's just my imagination. I just . . ." Her eyes shifted toward the barn. "I just haven't been myself lately."

Her father stopped walking and faced her, taking her by the shoulders. "It's not your imagination, Sugar. The pastor's wife came and apologized to your Mama and me several weeks ago. She accidentally let it slip and well, these things do tend to spread."

Angelina could feel the tears welling in her eyes as her face grew crimson. She simply nodded and swallowed hard. She'd known it was probably something like that. It wasn't her imagination the way people stared and some refused to allow their children to attend school.

Her father let his hands fall to his sides and interrupted her thoughts, "Sugar, I'm thinkin' it might do ya good to get away from here for a spell."

"Get away?"

He reached into his pocket, pulled out a newspaper advertisement and handed it to her. "There's a teachin' position in Knoxville. It's a nice town and folks there wouldn't know about what happened. Ya could have some time to heal."

"But . . ." Angelina felt her chest tighten. "What about you and Mama, Cal and the kids? Would everyone go?"

Her father shook his head negatively, "No, we couldn't all go, but you could, Angelina. You could have a fresh start where ya wouldn't have to keep rememberin' what happened, and people wouldn't stare."

Something about his suggestion simultaneously thrilled and frightened her. She took the paper from his hands and read about the teaching position.

"It includes room and board. Ya'd have everythin' ya need," Everett pointed to the spot on the advertisement that spoke of compensation.

Angelina shook her head negatively, still uncertain about being completely on her own.

"Ya could just try it until summer. See if ya like it. If ya don't, ya can always come back home. Even a little break would help ya decide what ya want to do . . . whether ya want to marry Paul or . . ."

At the mention of Paul, Angelina's head came up, meeting her father's green eyes. She had been spending a lot of time with Paul. Was her father concerned about that? "Would ya rather I not see Paul anymore, Daddy? If this is about Paul, I don't even really feel . . ."

"No, Sugar, I like Paul. We all like Paul. But I can see ya hesitatin'. Ya're not over what happened, and I think this town . . . this farm . . ." He gestured toward the barn, ". . . isn't helpin' matters."

She stared at the ominous structure and nodded. It took every ounce of courage she could muster to milk Ol' Gerty because entering the barn brought back a torrent of images and odors from that evil night.

"I think perhaps you're right. But what about the town? It wouldn't be proper for me to leave 'em with no teacher in January . . . right in the middle of the school year." She pulled her shawl tighter around her shoulders

"That can be worked out. They can find someone."

"What about Joseph and Eleanor? They enjoy having me for their teacher," her mind kept filling with excuses, but she knew they were only that – excuses. She was terrified by the thought of leaving home, being alone, and parted from the family she loved.

"They'll be fine. They'll adjust." As if her father could read her mind, he put his hands on her shoulders again and his comforting gaze met hers, "It'll be all right. I'll take ya there, get ya all settled in, and make sure you're looked after."

"Ya talk as if I already have the position," Angelina chuckled, trying to lighten the moment. "Think of all the people who'd apply. What's the likelihood they'd even want me? It'd take a miracle."

"It's worth a try, though." Everett smiled. "Why not just give it a try?"

Angelina shrugged, "I suppose if I try and I don't get the position, I'll know I'm meant to stay . . . maybe consider marryin' Paul. And if by some miracle they want me, I'll know it's the best thing to go . . . that Paul and I aren't meant to be together."

Her father winked and patted her shoulder, "Pray about it, Sugar. It doesn't have to be long term. It might be just the break ya need to sort out how ya feel about Paul."

Angelina nodded and took the advertisement.

~*~

Elijah loaded a bushel of beans into the back of his wagon and looked out over his acreage, surveying his handiwork with great satisfaction. His eyes traveled from the cabin with its new roof and new front porch to the barn bursting with corn. His gaze traveled next to the corral with the fine horses he'd purchased for breeding. He put his fists to his sides and released a sigh. With a nod of his head, he pronounced it good and a far cry from the overgrown, weed-infested condition it had once been.

As his attention shifted toward the rolling hills and creek on the east side of his property he thought of Doug. Every glen and dale reminded him of rabbit hunting with his boyhood friend. He couldn't take a walk to the creek for water without remembering the hours they'd spent fishing.

The familiar pain needled his heart as old memories reminded him of his losses – his parents, his best friend. He'd kept as busy as he could in an effort to forget the past. Every day he rose before sunup and retired well past dark, spending his days plowing and planting, patching the roof and porch on the old homestead, clearing away brush, and repairing the stables.

Even amidst the flurry of tasks, his mind wandered to happier days with those he loved. Every now and then, his mind would reflect upon Old Stone and the stories he told of Angelina. He wondered what had become of her, how serious her injuries had been, and how severe the repercussions to her young heart. Working in the fields alone only seemed to give him more time to think of her. No matter how hard he tried to force her from his mind by day, she still haunted his memories by night.

He was thinking of the visit Angelina had made to his dreams the night before when he spotted Nancy walking up the road toward him on her way to the schoolhouse.

"Mornin', Nancy," he waved his hat in the air.

"How do, 'Lijah!" she called, resting one hand on her back and the other on her rounded belly.

"You're gettin' on out there, little sister," Elijah pointed to her bulging stomach. "Did the town council find a new teacher yet?"

"They've narrowed it down to a couple young ladies who could take my place. I hope they make a decision soon. It's gettin' awfully hard for me to bend over and help the youngins with their papers."

"I bet! How's Thatcher doin'?"

"Doin' fine, stayin' busy with the harvest. You two should team up and help each other. Four hands are always faster than two."

"You're right. If I could ever stop workin' long 'nough to go over there and suggest the notion," Elijah's smile reached his blue eyes and they sparkled in the morning sun.

"Then, I'll just have to suggest it myself!" Nancy winked and waved goodbye to her brother as she continued her journey down the road toward the school.

Elijah shook his head, pitying the new schoolteacher for what she would soon endure. The poor woman didn't know what she had ahead of her! It had taken Nancy long enough to tame the unruly bunch. Now, just when she had them under control, some new teacher would step in, and the rowdy troublemakers would torture her.

Chapter 10

The wind sent a few loose tendrils of Angelina's hair whipping into her eyes as she approached the post office. She smoothed them back with her hand and reached for the door to the building. As she was about to enter, Widow Glenn emerged.

"How do, dear?" the woman said as she tightened the bow of her blue bonnet and stepped out into the blustery afternoon. Her sympathetic eyes met Angelina's.

"Good, and you, Ma'am?" Angelina replied, self-consciously looking past the woman into the post office.

"Fair ta middlin'. Just my bursitis actin' up this week," her lips puckered as her wrinkled hands pulled her coat tighter around herself.

"So your bone spur's better, then?" Angelina replied, meeting the woman's gaze now.

"Why, yes it is, much better," the woman's sour expression brightened a little.

"I'm glad to hear it. Ya take care now," Angelina smiled and eased past the woman into the post office.

"You too, dear," the elderly woman replied, giving her gray head a sympathetic shake, then turned her attention to a piece of mail.

"Back again, Miss Stone?" Mr. Clements met Angelina with a friendly grin.

"Afternoon, Mr. Clements," Angelina greeted the stout, balding postmaster.

"Where's your usual escort?" he craned his stubby neck toward the door with an expression of expectation on his round features.

"I'm alone today," she replied.

"Again? What's gotten into that Paul Bennett, leavin' a pretty lady like you unescorted?" Mr. Clements could be such a tease, but Angelina liked him. The post office wouldn't be the same without his round head and rectangular spectacles peeking at her from behind the counter.

"Mr. Bennett's quite busy bringing in the apple harvest."

"I see," Mr. Clements nodded.

"Anythin' for me?" she inquired.

"There is. It just came in. I have it in the back if you'd care to wait a moment."

"I can wait," Angelina watched Mr. Clements disappear into the back room.

Angelina's mind turned to Paul. She was glad he wasn't with her. If what Mr. Clements had for her was what she thought it was, she didn't want to explain it to Paul today. Ever since Cal and her father mentioned that Paul wanted to marry her, her eyes had opened to the possibility.

The closer Paul came, the more she wanted to escape. So, when her father had shown her the out-of-town teaching position and suggested she apply for it, she'd mailed a letter with her credentials. She sent her letter and resolved to leave it in God's hands. If she obtained the position, then she would go and consider it a sign from heaven that she was not to marry Paul. If she wasn't hired, she would know that she should resign herself to matrimony. She'd cared for him once, she could care for him again. In spite of her resolve to remain detached from the outcome, each afternoon on the way home she stopped at the post office, hoping for a miracle.

"This what you've been waitin' for, Miss?" Mr. Clements inquired, stretching a long white envelope toward Angelina's trembling hand.

Angelina took the letter and stared at it for several long moments. Coming to herself, she lifted her gaze to Mr. Clements, "Yes, thank you, sir."

Mr. Clement's inquisitive dark eyes followed her as she turned and stepped out into the crisp autumn air. Still staring at the envelope, she started down the road for home. Now that she held her future in her hands, she wasn't sure she wanted to open it. All the excuses she'd raised with her father came rushing to her mind. She walked nearly a half of a mile toward home before a burst of resolution overcame her, and she broke the seal and pulled out the letter. Unfolding it, she began to read.

A smile spread across her lips and her heart raced with the realization that God had heard and answered her prayers. A torrent of opposing emotions battled in her mind as she realized she would be leaving the only home she'd ever known and the family she loved to venture off to a city she'd never been. She would know no one, but also no one would know her. The thought caused the corners of Angelina's lips to curl into a smile. There would be no pitiful stares from the women in Knoxville. Men would not tip their hats with sympathetic eyes, and young girls would not whisper about her as she passed.

The more Angelina weighed the prospects of starting a fresh life away from staring eyes, idle gossip and haunting memories, the faster her steps became. Her easy gait transformed into a brisk walk and finally into an all out run.

As she drew closer to home, she spotted Cal and her father carrying baskets of apples across the field. She waved at them and Cal called out her name.

"How do?" she waved, smiling and running toward them.

Cal and Everett quickened their pace until they met her in the middle of the field. "You look cheery this afternoon, Sugar," Everett grinned as he set his basket down at his feet and reached out to his daughter, giving her arm an affectionate squeeze.

"Whatcha got there?" Cal gestured his head toward the letter in Angelina's grasp.

She handed it to her father. Cal, still holding his basket, looked over Everett's shoulder.

"What's this about?" Cal's brow crimped into a worried furrow as Angelina leaned her hands on her knees catching her breath. "You applied to teach in Knoxville?"

Angelina nodded, an excited expression twinkling in her eyes. She shifted her hands to her hips and continued to catch her breath.

"You've got a position here. Why do you want to go to Knoxville?" Cal protested.

"Daddy suggested a change of scenery might be good. He found the position and I applied. Isn't it wonderful?"

"Daddy?" Cal gave his father a doubtful look. Everett handed the letter back to Angelina.

"I prayed about it, Cal. I prayed that if I should marry Paul that I wouldn't get the position, but if I shouldn't marry him, I'd get it," Angelina explained.

"That's no way to ask for answers, Angelina! Just ask if you're supposed to marry Paul. Don't go tanglin' it all up with leavin' !" Cal sighed in exasperation. Everett took his daughter into his embrace and gave her a big hug.

"It's the best thing for her, Cal," Everett said and then held Angelina at arms length. His hand patted her golden locks. "I'm so proud of you, Sugar!"

"But, what about us? Won't you miss all of us?" Cal prodded.

"Of course, I'm gonna miss y'all!" she assured, giving her brother a hug around his neck and a quick kiss on his cheek. "It's just for a little while – a chance to see a bit more of the world, to stand on my own two feet."

Cal shook his head. "I still don't like it," he grumbled.

Angelina leaned toward her brother. "Cal, I know you hold yourself responsible for that night, but I want you to hear me." She looked him straight in the eye. "It is not your fault and I don't blame you at all. You have to let it go, just like I did. This new teaching position will give me a fresh start and I think you should give yourself one, too. Forgive yourself, Cal." She reached up on tiptoe and hugged him again, more fiercely this time. "I love you, Cal."

He squeezed her tight, the tears forming in his eyes. "I love you, too, Angelina. Never forget that."

Angelina looked at her father who was wiping his eyes, "I'm gonna go tell Mama!" With that, she turned on her heels and ran toward home, leaving her brother and father to stare after her.

As Angelina's footsteps pounded up the steps, Lelia appeared in the doorway, "Heaven's child, what's this all about?"

"I got it," Angelina panted, waiving the letter.

"Got what?"

"The position in Knoxville," Angelina exclaimed.

"Really?" Lelia's anxious brow furrowed as she took the letter from Angelina's extended hand. She stared at it and turned her back to Angelina, walking toward the stove. She continued to study the letter as she stirred her pot of beans.

"Isn't it wonderful?" Angelina paced the room, her hands on her hips as she caught her breath from the long run home.

"Yes, yes it's wonderful," Lelia replied as she folded the letter, placed it on the table, and turned back to the stove.

Angelina watched her mother swipe a tear from her cheek. She put a gentle hand on her mother's shoulder, "Mama, we talked about this before I applied. I thought you'd be happy for me."

Lelia nodded affirmatively without turning her eyes from the stove, "I am happy for you, dear. I just . . . I just . . ." The next thing Angelina knew her mother's arms were around her and Lelia's head buried against Angelina's shoulder. "I'm just gonna miss ya so."

Angelina felt tears swelling in her own eyes as she hugged her mother tighter. "I'm gonna miss you too."

Suddenly, Lelia released Angelina and brushed the tears from her cheeks. "What am I thinking here?" she scolded herself. "We still have two months together."

"And it won't be forever, just until summer and then I'll be back."

"That's right," Lelia sniffed. "Before we know it, you'll be home again."

Angelina watched Lelia force a smile to her face. They would miss each other, but in her heart, Angelina knew this time away was a gift from heaven and precisely what she needed.

That evening, after the dinner dishes were done and the little ones in bed, Cal, Angelina and their parents sat outside on the front porch listening to the crickets and watching the moon and stars.

Everett and Lelia cuddled together on the porch swing as Angelina sat in a rocking chair. Cal rested on the porch steps, his back against the railing.

"I didn't think Eleanor and Joseph would take it so hard," Angelina's gaze went to her parents.

"They'll get used to it. It's hard, but we'll all get used to it in time," Everett assured.

"It's an inevitable part of life. Your father and I knew when you were babies that you'd grow up and go out on your own one day."

"And we knew that when that day came it wouldn't be easy," Everett added, a somber expression on his face.

"Well, we may get used to the idea, but what about Paul?" Cal's serious eyes went from his father to his sister. "You're gonna break his heart. He's in love with you, Angelina."

"He says he cares for me, but I don't know that he really does. He's offered his arm, but never so much as held my hand."

"That's because he's heard the rumors, and he doesn't want to scare you off," Cal replied.

Everett shot Cal a stern look.

"I don't think Paul knows," Angelina whispered.

"Of course, he knows," came Cal's blunt retort.

"He doesn't act like he knows. He doesn't look at me the way . . ." Angelina paused as her eyes met her brother's before finishing, "the way other people do."

Cal's expression grew more sympathetic as he whispered, "He knows, Angelina."

A painful lump caught in her throat. She rose to her feet and walked away from her family out into the yard. She stared out into the night. "All the more reason to leave," she muttered.

"But he doesn't care, Angelina," Cal insisted. "He knows and it doesn't bother 'im. He told me that."

Lelia rose from the bench, suddenly angry, "What do you mean he doesn't care? It doesn't sadden 'im? How can he know such a thing and not care that she was so cruelly treated? Has he no sympathy?"

"I don't want his sympathy," Angelina whispered to herself, but nobody else heard.

"I didn't mean it that way, Mama. I mean Paul doesn't hold it against Angelina. He doesn't care what people . . . " his voice lowered to a whisper, "say about her."

Lelia's expression darkened, "Angelina hasn't done anythin' wrong! What are people sayin'?"

"People talk, Mama," Cal whispered. "They say no man'll have her now that . . ."

Everett rose to his feet and whispered to his wife and son, "Angelina doesn't need to hear this."

"No, Daddy. I do need to hear this," Angelina turned and started walking back toward the porch. Everyone's eyes widened at her insistent response. "I needed to hear this to know that I'm right in leavin'. When Eleanor and Joseph got so upset, I almost decided I'd made a mistake. But now I know I'll never be seen as more than a thing of pity in this town – or worse!" Angelina's voice grew louder. "I'm just plain sick o' the whispers and the looks and the pity. I don't want people feelin' sorry for me anymore. It's over and done, and it appears as if the only way for me to keep one night from ruinin' my entire life is to get out of this town! The sooner I leave the better!" With that, she stomped into the house and slammed the door behind her.

Chapter 11

Two days later when Angelina saw Paul sauntering toward her as she came out of the schoolhouse, her stomach knotted into a queasy wad. She knew she had to tell him she was leaving before giving her notice to the town council. It wouldn't be right for him to hear it through the rumor mill.

He smiled and waved, and she forced herself to do the same.

"How do, Miss Angelina?" he inquired as he reached out his hands to take her satchel of books.

"Good, and you?" she handed it to him and took his arm as she descended the steps.

They strolled along making small talk about the weather and Paul's pumpkin crop until they reached the edge of town. There was a lull in the conversation, and Angelina took a deep breath, mustering her courage to speak.

"There's somethin' I need to speak with ya 'bout," she stopped walking, and Paul released her arm. He tucked her satchel under his arm and gave her an expectant glance.

"I wanted you to be the first to know. They offered me a teachin' position in Knoxville. I start in January."

Paul's brow furrowed as if he hadn't understood what she'd said. "What? Why? You've already a position here."

"I need to go, Paul. I need to do this." She looked across the fields, unwilling to meet his gaze.

Paul set her satchel on the dusty road and took her hand, gently forcing her to look at him. "You don't need to leave. You just need someone to take care of you – to love you."

Angelina closed her eyes against the lovelorn expression on his face. Cal was right, and the realization of it stabbed her heart.

"I love you, Angelina. Stay here and be my wife. I'll take care of ya and no one will ever hurt you again."

Angelina could feel the tears threatening behind her eyelids. When she opened them to look into his, a tear spilled down her cheek. He reached up and tenderly brushed it away.

"I can't, Paul," she shook her head. "I need some time away to forget the past." Her hands clasped her throat. "It's all around me here, smotherin' me, blockin' the light. Everyone knows. They talk, and they stare and whisper. If they don't pity me, they're sayin' awful, awful things about me."

"You don't need to leave. Marry me and it'll all stop. It'll all be forgotten when we're married," he insisted.

"I can't," she repeated. "I need some time away to sort things out, to forget the past. I just don't have it in me to give you what you deserve." Angelina looked into his sad eyes before continuing softly, "You needn't feel obligated to wait for me. I don't know when or if I'll ever be ready to give my heart to anyone."

Paul put his fingers to the chain that she always wore about her neck and lifted it, pulling its full length from where it rested inside her blouse. He held the ring up in front of her face. She stared at its silver intertwined rope design and thought about the man it represented.

Paul's voice grew low and thoughtful, "I think the truth is that you've already given your heart to a man."

"I don't know what you mean."

"Cal told me it belonged to that Yankee soldier." He paused, searching the astonished expression in her eyes. "You don't owe him anythin' for savin' ya from his captain. You certainly don't owe 'im your heart!"

She grew adamant, "You're wrong. How could I give my heart to a man I don't even know?"

"Then why is his ring always about your neck?"

"Because I want to remember to be grateful that the Lord delivered me. It reminds me to be grateful that there are a few good people in this world."

"If you're leavin' to forget the past, then why keep a constant reminder of it hangin' 'bout your neck?" Paul countered, letting the ring drop. She felt it bounce against her heart.

"I . . ." she stammered, unsure of how to reply and shoved the jewelry back inside her blouse.

"Forget I said anythin'," Paul slapped the air in defeat. "I hope ya find what you're lookin' for."

Angelina reached out and let her fingers take hold of his arm, giving it a gentle squeeze, "Maybe when I come back..."

Paul shrugged his shoulders, yet his chin dropped to his chest as he turned back toward town and left her to walk home by herself.

~*~

Fall soon became winter and it was time for Angelina to leave. After a teary farewell, she and her father set out on their long trip to Northeast Tennessee. As the wagon jostled over the dirt roads, the chilling January wind chapped Angelina's cheeks. Her teeth chattered, and she pulled the blanket tighter around her shoulders and adjusted the one that lay across her lap, tucking it under her legs.

"I hate to take you away from Mama and the children," Angelina said to her father, who sat beside her driving the team. "Cal could've taken me to Knoxville."

"No, this might be the last time we have much time to spend together."

"Why is that?" Angelina's eyebrows furrowed with concern.

"You're a woman now, startin' your own life. Who's to say when we'll have time to spend together again?"

"I'm comin' home in the summer," she assured him. "This isn't permanent."

"Well, you never know . . . one road does tend to lead to another," Everett patted his daughter's knee.

Angelina sensed that perhaps her father was right. Change was in the air. She could feel it deep in her bones and it settled deeper with every rut in the dirt road. Whatever she encountered in Knoxville would change her forever. She just hoped the alteration would rid her of the past so she could get on with the matter of living.

A tremor of worry surfaced in her mind, but she told herself that God had given her the new teaching position in answer to her prayers. Surely, God would not lead her somewhere that did not improve her life. She quoted her favorite passage from Proverbs 3:5-6, *trust in the Lord with all thine heart and lead not unto thine own understanding. In all thy ways acknowledge Him and He shall directy thy paths.*

The trip was long and arduous through dirt roads that cut through miles and miles of forest. They crossed over White Oak Mountain and were grateful that there had been no snow or sleet to make the trip treacherous.

Riding nearly thirty miles each day, they stopped each night, making camp. As they traveled, they witnessed the ravages of war, the burnt homes and destruction left behind. It prompted Everett to tell Angelina a little about the war.

As they settled down the fourth night, just ten miles outside of Knoxville, they built a fire, roasted rabbit and cooked cornbread in an iron skillet. As they sat by the fire enjoying their meal, Angelina turned to her father watching him tear a piece of meat with his teeth and chew it.

"So continue with what you were tellin' me earlier this afternoon about the Battle of Chickamauga," Angelina prompted.

Everett swallowed and nodded, "Oh, that's right. Where did we leave off?"

"You were tellin' me about how the Confederacy won that battle by a stroke of luck," she reminded, taking another bite of cornbread.

Everett's mind went back to the terrible three days at Chickamauga. He could almost smell the gunpowder thick in the air, and the forest around them reminded him of the woods in which he'd fought. "I don't think we could claim any credit for winnin' that battle." He gestured toward the trees, "The woods were about like this. It was next to impossible to tell where our men were. You'd just run upon the enemy anywhere and not realize it until it was too late. Men were shootin' each other at close range. It was nothin' but smoke and chaos."

He scratched his head and then continued, "I think I told you that we were tryin' to take control of Lafayette Road because it connected Chattanooga to Atlanta."

Angelina nodded her head in a gesture for him to continue.

Everett reached for a stick and drew the location of the troops in the dirt. "They really wanted to take Chattanooga because of the railroad. Anyway, the Union General, Rosecrans, had his men on the west of Lafayette Road and we had ours on the east."

"At one point, Rosecrans got his communication all messed up and accidentally moved a group of his troops over to fill a gap that he thought had developed in the Union line. The thing was, there wasn't a gap, but he made one when he moved his men. At that point, we saw our opportunity and marched through the openin'." Everett drew a line in the dirt, indicating where the Southern troops had marched through the opening in the Union line.

"Ah," Angelina's eyes widened with understanding.

"We drove the Yanks back, most retreated, but Thomas and his men refused to budge from Snodgrass Hill. We fought there until the North commanded Thomas' men to retreat."

"So you won because Rosecrans accidentally left a gap in his line?" Angelina clarified.

"Right, if Rosecrans hadn't've made that mistake, who's to say who would've won that battle."

"Where were you durin' it all?"

Firelight danced in Everett's eyes as his expression grew somber. "I was over at Snodgrass Hill." The bloodcurdling screams accompanying amputations in the little Snodgrass cabin would echo in Everett's memory for a lifetime. He shook his head in an effort to jar the memory.

"What happened next?"

"General Bragg took our men into Chattanooga and I ended up atop Lookout Mountain. They called it the 'Battle above the Clouds.'"

"Sounds romantic," Angelina noted.

"Yeah, well, it wasn't. We were outnumbered nearly ten to one. It was anythin' but romantic!"

"Mmmm," Angelina shook her head, her lips turning into a somber frown.

"A lot of people thought we should've gone after Rosecrans' retreatin' army and got 'em while we had 'em because they ended up receivin' tens of thousands of fresh troops. In the end they beat us at Chattanooga and our commander even resigned."

"He resigned? You mean Bragg?"

"Yep, the other officers wanted rid o' him, so I guess after that humiliatin' defeat, he decided to oblige 'em."

"Is that why some people speak so poorly of Bragg?" Angelina asked.

Everett nodded and then shrugged, "But I think people are too hard on the general. We were as rag tag as the Union when we left Chickamauga. It was a miracle we even won that battle. To ask us to go after Rosecrans' men and destroy 'em at that point would've been foolishness. Bragg did the best with what he had."

"I've heard the men in town say that Bragg was mean to his men."

"Oh, he was strict, stern, but I wouldn't call 'im mean. He made us do things with precision and by the book. In most cases, his strictness kept us alive. Just some jealous officers directly under 'im questioned 'im so much. They didn't like bein' ordered about or bein' held to regulations."

Angelina leaned her arms on her knees. "So you don't agree with those that say Bragg was a bad general?"

"No, I liked 'im, but I like things to run efficiently. I think he rubbed a lot o' people the wrong way because he wasn't free with his flattery or praise, but he didn't allow others to praise him either. He was devoted to his duty, not one for socializing, and I guess a lot o' fellas thought him too stiff and demandin'. But at least you knew where you stood with 'im."

Angelina nodded. "How did you end up in prison?" she asked as she cut herself another piece of cornbread.

Everett ran a hand through his hair and his mind shot back to the impossible conditions atop Lookout Mountain. As if to punctuate his feelings, he snapped the twig in half and tossed it into the fire. "I got shot in the leg at Lookout Mountain." His hand gripped his right thigh. "They patched me up a bit and transferred me to Rock Island Prison on the Mississippi River, up near the Iowa-Illinois border. There were 468 of us taken there from Lookout Mountain. It was a newer prison, and we were the first to go there. Thousands came later . . . over 8,000 prisoners at one point."

Everett's gaze shifted toward the last remnants of the evening sun, now only a thin blanket of pink lying across the mountainous ridge and covered with a river of mournful blue.

"What was it like?" she whispered.

His gaze fell to the fire before him. He lifted another stick and poked it into the coals, watching the orange flecks sputter and float into the air as wispy ash. "Awful," his voice matched her own in volume, and he hesitated. "It was filthy. Cold. Dark." He punctuated each word with a pause. "Men died of smallpox and influenza or just plain malnutrition and neglect."

"How horrible for you," Angelina reached for her father, laying a comforting hand on his arm.

"I watched my friends carried off to the pest houses, never to return. They just dumped 'em all in unmarked graves."

"Oh my," Angelina's fearful eyes widened and he could tell she was visualizing dead bodies toppling into dirt pits – at least that was what he saw in his own mind.

"It's a miracle I survived," he added.

"Mama prayed for you every mornin' and night. We all did."

Everett placed his hand over his daughter's, giving it a gentle squeeze, "I know, Sugar. And I'm sure it was all your prayers that brought me home safe and sound . . . that and the guardian angel the Lord sent to watch over me."

"Guardian angel?"

"Well," Everett winked with a humored turn of his lips. "Not a *real* angel. He was mortal 'nough, but I pro'bly would've died if it hadn't been for him. He snuck food to me – you know, greens and jerky, the occasional apple. One time he brought a blanket, another time, even an orange!" His smile grew more pronounced, "I'm not sure where he got that, but it was like eatin' a bit of heaven while trapped in the pits of hell."

"Who was he?"

Everett's eyes met his daughter's and his smile lessened. He paused for a few moments deciding whether to answer her question. His eyes rested upon the ring dangling from Angelina's necklace. He reached out and took it between his fingers, letting his thumb trail over the silver. "Just a Union soldier who remembered that we're all countrymen, and children of the same God."

~*~

That very night in a little cabin in Knoxville, Elijah sat in a rocker holding his niece by his sister's bedside. He bent over, kissed the baby's chubby cheek, and traced his finger through the downy red fuzz atop her head.

"She's such a pretty little thing," he winked at his sister who lay in her bed.

Nancy smiled proudly, and Thatcher put a hand on his wife's shoulder, "She takes after her mama."

"I believe you're right about that, with this carrot top." He let the baby's hand slip around his finger. "But she's got a mean grip, like her pa," Elijah lifted his finger a little to demonstrate the baby's tenacious grip.

"Now it's your turn, 'lijah," Nancy prodded. "Time for you to give little Rachael a cousin to play with."

"Slow down, Nancy," Elijah chuckled. "Last I heard it takes a wife for such things."

"What about Bonnie?" Thatcher suggested. "She's a pretty young woman."

"And you two get along so well," Nancy added.

Elijah looked as if he were considering the notion and then shook his head, "No, I couldn't."

"Yes, you could," Thatcher insisted, but Elijah continued to shake his head negatively.

"Why not?" Nancy coaxed.

"It . . ." Elijah paused. "It just wouldn't be right."

~*~

Everett and Angelina arose early the next morning, prepared their breakfast and set out on the last ten miles to Knoxville.

"It's bitter cold, quite the miracle we've made it the whole way without rain. Don't ya think?" Angelina observed, her green eyes studying the cloudless blue sky.

"'Tis unusual for January," Everett jiggled the reins. The team accelerated to a slight gallop as they neared the city. Angelina glanced at her father. He'd been oddly quiet since they'd broken camp that morning. His anxious eyebrows remained scrunched and the corners of his mouth drew downward. She wondered what had caused him to become so withdrawn and feared she'd pressed him too much about the war. He'd related more than she had ever heard him say before. Perhaps it had dredged up old memories that caused his gloomy mood.

As they came into town, Everett headed for the livery and pulled the team aside. "I'll be right back," he said as he hopped down from the wagon.

Angelina pulled her blanket around her tight and shoved her hands under her arms. She could see her breath in the mid-morning air, and she enviously eyed the vibrant orange flames that licked the rim of a metal barrel by the blacksmith shop. She almost hopped out to warm herself by the fire, but decided she better not wander off. There were some unsavory looking men milling around the tavern. Hopefully, whatever business her father had in the livery wouldn't take long. She assumed he'd stopped to ask directions.

Soon he returned, and they were rolling along down the main street and turned down a quaint avenue lined with homes, one of which had a sign out front that read "Bonnie's Boarding House." The school board had arranged for Angelina to stay at the widow Crestworth's boarding house. Angelina imagined Mrs. Crestworth as a petite elderly woman with silvery white hair – someone who could represent her mother while she was far from her own.

Angelina's eyebrows rose with surprise when an attractive woman in her mid-twenties greeted them at the door. Smiling, the patroness brushed a strand of brown hair from her chestnut eyes and opened the door wider.

"You must be the new school teacher?"

"Yes, ma'am, I'm Angelina Stone and this is my father, Everett Stone."

"Bonnie Crestworth," she extended a hand. "Good to meet you both and glad to have you here at the boardin' house, Miss Stone."

Everett carried Angelina's trunk in behind her while Angelina eyed the fine furnishings and English tea set in the parlor.

Bonnie noted Everett's heavy load, "Let's show you up to your room so your father can set down your things."

Angelina smiled as she followed the woman's slender form up the stairs to a bedroom at the front of the house. Definitely not a plump widow, Angelina thought. She couldn't have been more erroneous in her assumption of a matronly boarding housekeeper.

"Here's your room, Miss Angelina," Bonnie opened the door and motioned for them to enter. "And here's your key."

She handed Angelina the key and went further into the room. "You should have plenty of room for your things here in the armoire and the dresser." She moved to the dormer window. "You may store your trunk under here." She pointed to a small door leading to a storage area inside the dormer. "And you have a beautiful view over here and a desk for gradin' papers and such."

"It's perfect," Angelina smiled as her eyes examined the accommodations adorned in forest green draperies. A handmade green and navy quilt lay across the bed. "What a beautiful room!"

"Thank you, dear. I'm glad you like it. If you'll come along with me now, I'll show you the kitchen and dinin' room." Angelina and her father followed Bonnie back down the stairs. The wood creaked beneath their feet, but the house was sturdy and in good repair. Bonnie showed them an elegant parlor at the front of the house, a dining area and the kitchen in the rear.

"Two meals each day are part of your accommodations. We serve breakfast at seven and supper at six. Be prompt, because I can't guarantee there'll be leftovers with the crowd we keep around here," she smiled.

"Yes, ma'am."

"And for heaven's sake, stop callin' me, ma'am! I'm not that much older than yourself," Bonnie placed a hand on Angelina's arm and smiled. "Just call me Bonnie."

"Very well, Bonnie," Angelina agreed. She decided right then that she was going to like it here at Bonnie's Boarding House. She'd expected to find a surrogate mother or grandmother, but instead, she decided she'd found a future friend. And being new, Angelina knew she could use all the friends she could find.

"Mr. Stone, could I interest you in some tea and cookies?"

"Well, don't know. I do have a little business here in town I need to tend to 'fore I head back."

"Oh, you come along now. You've had a long trip," Bonnie motioned for Everett and Angelina to follow her into the parlor.

They did so and Bonnie served each of them tea from a floral serving set. Their conversation was casual as they enjoyed their refreshment. After popping the last of his cookie into his mouth, Everett rose to his feet. "Well, ladies, this has been delicious, but I must be on my way."

A plummeting rock sank to the pit of Angelina's stomach. She stood, "Can't you stay just a bit longer?"

He put both hands to her shoulders, "I best be goin'. Got to make use of daylight while I can. You're in good hands here with Mrs. Crestworth."

"I know. I'll just miss you," Angelina's sad smile tugged her lips.

"You write us now, ya hear? And if you need anythin', you let us know immediately, and I'll come as quick as I can."

Angelina embraced her father, and swallowed the uncomfortable lump in her throat. Then he was gone. She watched him climb into the wagon until Bonnie came to the window and laced her arm through Angelina's. "Don't you fret about a thing now, Angelina. I'll see that you learn your way around town and such. Ask me anythin' you need to know."

"Thank you," Angelina smiled into the beautiful woman's eyes. She wanted to know how Bonnie had become a widow, but she answered the question for herself. Bonnie must have lost her husband at war.

Chapter 12

Everett pulled scribbled directions from his pants pocket. *Go five miles north of the outskirts of town, at the fork in the road veer left, and look for the third farm on the right.* He followed the directions, turned down the dirt road and followed it nearly a half a mile before he came to the farmhouse with the cedar shake roof. The afternoon's sun had warmed the air a little – enough to knock the chill off. But it wasn't enough to keep Everett from feeling just a bit jittery. He'd almost decided not to come. At the fork in the road, he almost turned around and went home, but decided for Angelina's sake he better press on.

He stopped his team, climbed from the wagon, and strode toward the porch. He gave the front door two sound taps and waited. No one came. He remained a little longer, and then deduced no one was inside. He stepped off the porch and started around toward the barn. As he drew closer, he noticed movement inside. In the shadows, he could see a bale of hay fall from the loft. Rubbing his hands together for warmth, he quickened his pace a little.

When he reached the barn door, he looked up into the loft. The man bending over to toss another bale of hay glanced over his shoulder at Everett.

"How do? You come to look at the colt?" the man called as he let the bale drop and went for another one.

"No, not the colt," Everett replied.

"Needin' eggs?" the man asked as he continued his work.

"No, not come to buy anythin'."

The man stood upright, and even though Everett could not see his face, he could see the tension in the man's shoulders and neck as he stood still as death for what seemed like an eternity. A sick, nervous dread seeped into the pit of Everett's stomach. Perhaps this had been a mistake. He took a wary step backwards before the man slowly turned around and his somber gaze fell upon Everett.

Finally, a smile tugged at the corners of the man's lips and his eyes twinkled, "Old Stone? Is that you?"

Breathing a sigh of relief, Everett put both hands in his pockets and shook his head, "It's me."

Elijah Willoughby backed down the ladder and came to stand in front of Everett Stone. He stretched out his hand. Everett took it, and then pulled Elijah into a jovial embrace, slapping his back three times.

"Just look at you! I hardly recognized you! You look as strong as a mule!" Elijah smiled holding Everett's shoulders at arms length to examine him.

"You too. Farm life's put the color into your cheeks."

"Yeah, well, it'll do that. Looks like it's done the same for you!"

"How've you been?" Everett inquired.

"Good, doin' good, especially now that the farm's runnin' smooth again," Elijah hesitated, his pensive brows furrowing. "I've worried about you, Stone. I wasn't sure you'd make it out of there."

"Well, I did. And much of the thanks goes to you for that."

"Ah," Elijah waved a bashful hand. "Was the good Lord lookin' after ya."

"True . . . that's most assuredly true," Everett agreed.

"So what in the world brings you up here?"

"Droppin' off my daughter in town. She's stayin' at Bonnie's Boarding House."

The color drained from Elijah's face. "Your daughter?"

"Yep, Angelina's teachin' school up here now. I gave her a ride, and I remembered you lived up in these parts. So I asked around."

"Really? Well, I'm glad you came to see me."

The two men stood and smiled at one another, and Everett sensed that Elijah was as unsure about what to do next as he was. Everett had dreaded the meeting, half-expecting that seeing Elijah's face would dredge up old memories too painful to withstand. But, seeing Elijah had the opposite effect. It was a calming sensation. Shaking hands with the man who had once guarded him in prison gave a peaceful closure to the past.

Elijah draped his arm around his friend's shoulder and turned him toward the house. "Well, let's get in out of this chill and tell me what you've been up to."

The two men sat in Elijah's house, sipping cocoa and talking about their lives. Everett went into one of his descriptions of his farm and family. It reminded him of those nights Elijah had kept him company. Everett felt proud to sit in freedom and warmth with his friend and to tell him things had worked out just fine.

After an hour's visit, Everett rose to his feet and stood by the fire. "Would you be willin' to do me a favor, old friend?" Everett asked, his gaze still watching the fire.

"Just ask, and it's yours," Elijah agreed.

"Would you keep an eye on my daughter while she's here? Just make sure she's safe. She's a pretty thing and, well, you know how men are in a big city."

Elijah shook his solemn head, then rose slowly from the rocker, and stepped toward the fireplace. Leaning his elbow on the mantel, he looked at his friend and took a deep breath. "Stone, there's somethin' I need to tell ya." He looked down as if he were trying to muster the courage to speak.

When Elijah's eyes next met his friend's, a single tear had escaped the outside corner of Everett's eye.

"I know, Willoughby, I know," Everett whispered and closed his eyes, releasing a slow breath. He'd gone there wanting to make Elijah admit the truth, but now he didn't have the heart to torture the man.

"You know about that night?"

Stone nodded.

"Then she told ya? About Jacobsen? About me? About what happened?"

"Most of it."

Elijah leaned the heels of his hands on the mantel and hung his head in silence. After several long moments he muttered, "You must hate me."

"I won't lie to you, Willoughby, I was awful sore at ya at first."

Elijah took a deep breath, "I'm so sorry I didn't stop it sooner, Stone. I should've gotten up earlier, should've gone and checked to see what Jacobsen was up to." He turned toward Everett, "I stopped it the minute I saw what was happenin', but I should've gotten there sooner."

Everett's confused eyebrows furrowed. What was this? He hadn't heard anything about this.

Elijah continued, "I know I'll never forgive myself for what happened. So I don't 'xpect that you ever could."

"What are you talkin' about, boy?" Everett's eyes narrowed.

Elijah quickened his pace, retelling the story as if he'd practiced it a hundred times. "I was there, in your house . . . in the bed you should've been sleepin' in . . . all lazy and warm. I heard Jacobsen get up. The thought crossed my mind that I should check and see what he was up to. He'd been drinkin' some that night and he was always stealin' from people, up to no good. I should've checked on 'im sooner. If I had, it wouldn't 've happened, or I could've stopped it sooner." Elijah's blue eyes clouded over with moisture.

"Boy, you're carryin' an awful heavy load aren't ya?" Everett put his calloused hands to Elijah's shoulders, "Lookee here, young man. Nobody blames ya for that. We're just grateful you were there to stop it. If I was angry with ya for anythin', it was for not tellin' me about my family while I was in prison. You know good 'n' well that word from home would've been priceless to me in those days."

Elijah's head hung again, and then he gradually lifted his gaze to Everett's. "I'm sorry, Stone. I didn't even piece it together that it was your family until that last night when you gave me directions to your place. I figured it out when I was walkin' out of the buildin'. But then I remembered that awful night, and I knew if I told you about it, it'd kill ya. Those sweet dreams of your family were all that you were hangin' onto. It would've crushed ya to hear about what happened to your daughter."

"I know . . . I know . . ." Everett whispered. "I'm not mad at ya anymore. I figured that was why ya didn't say anythin'."

Elijah's glistening eyes filled with hope, "So you don't hate me?"

"Of course not."

Elijah breathed a sigh of relief and his broad shoulders relaxed, looking as if they'd just shrugged off a heavy load that had been burdening him for ages.

"Thank ya, Stone. Thank ya for that."

"No. Thank *you*."

The two men embraced, and Everett asked once again, "So will ya check on my Angelina every now and then?"

"Are you certain you want me to do it? I mean, you might forgive me, but I might bring back some awful memories for your daughter." Elijah's wary gaze held Everett's.

"She needs to face the memories. That's why when I saw the teachin' position open here, I suggested she apply for it. She hasn't been the same since that night. I think she needs to face the past, and I think you're just the man to help her do it. I think it was God openin' up this position for Angelina so she could see you again."

"I don't know," Elijah replied with a doubtful gesture.

"If anybody can help her get past it, you can. Help her through it so she can get on with her life. Give her the resolution that we've given each other here today."

A smile started at the corners of Elijah's mouth and Everett believed he was starting to warm up to the idea.

Everett continued, "She's got a young man waitin' to marry her back home, Paul Bennett. She's just too obsessed with the past to move on and let herself love 'im again. She did once, but that night killed somethin' in her. I really think if she can just face her demons, and you can help her make peace with the past, that she can come on back home and marry the man she loves."

Elijah bit his lip and the twinkle that had been in his eyes a moment before vanished. "I – uh," he fumbled, turned his back to Everett and crossed to the stove to stoke the fire. "I'll check on her . . . make sure she stays safe, but I can't guarantee I'll be able to do anythin' about the past."

"Well, just do the best ya can. I'm sure the Lord'll take care of the details." With that, Everett bid his friend farewell and left, relieved in knowing he'd made his peace with Elijah and left his daughter in good hands. Even though Elijah didn't look like he wanted the responsibility of looking after Angelina, Everett knew he could trust him. Angelina would be safe and that's all that mattered now.

~*~

After settling in upstairs, Angelina decided she'd go for a short walk in town to familiarize herself with her surroundings. She changed from the riding dress she'd been wearing into a green one that matched her eyes. She slipped her arms into her coat and started downstairs.

Angelina poked her head inside the kitchen, "Bonnie, I'd like to walk to town, maybe look around the General Store I saw. Could you please give me directions?"

Bonnie told her how to get to town and asked her if she'd mind picking up a sack of flour while she was there.

Angelina agreed, slipped the money into her purse and went on her way. She strolled away from the boarding house down the road until she reached the center of town. She turned right and headed toward where she'd seen the General Store earlier in the day.

The temperature had risen since morning. The afternoon sun had melted any frost on the ground and its soothing heat felt good as it sank through her coat, warming her shoulders.

As she approached the store, she noticed a man wearing a heavy beard coming toward her on an old gray mare. The poor animal had most definitely seen better days. She looked every bit as ragged and worn as the man sitting astride her. When he steered the mare around a wagon, Angelina noted that the shabbily dressed man was missing a leg. His right leg went only to the knee, and he'd cropped off the pant leg and tied the opening with twine. It was odd to see a man with only one foot in a stirrup. Angelina imagined that might make for difficult riding.

She tried not to stare, but she felt so sorry for him! How horrible to have but one leg, especially for a man who would need to earn a living and be a provider for a family. Of course, this man didn't look as if he'd have a family. He looked more like a drifter, a man without a regular place to lay his head.

His dusty bearded face turned in her direction and his eyes seemed to peer through the forest of hair to meet hers. She withdrew her gaze from him, embarrassed that he'd caught her staring at him.

Angelina often attempted to discern a person's story just by looking at them. She really needed to discontinue the practice, for she knew firsthand that one could not look at a person and know their secrets. She turned and stared in the window of a dress shop, noting her reflection in the glass. No one could know her story by looking at her! That was certain. She examined her golden locks curling around her shoulders. She'd left her hair down to keep her warmer as they traveled. She noticed it made her look very young and innocent. Here she was nineteen and looked more like a girl of fifteen. No one would ever guess that she had been disgraced and violated. The corners of her lips tipped downward.

Pulling her thoughts from the past, she reminded herself that she'd come here to forget all that. She glanced to her right and watched the man ride down the road. Her gaze lowered to her black boots. At least she had two good legs! That was something for which to be grateful!

As she resumed her stroll toward the General Store, Angelina's mind turned back to the drifter. She couldn't recall ever seeing a beard that long and scraggly. It had jostled against the middle of his chest with the swagger of his old mare. He must've been growing that thing for several years! Angelina's mind set to wondering what would drive a man to wander aimlessly like that. Perhaps he'd returned from war without a leg and found his family killed. Or maybe his wife had spurned him when he came back crippled. But what kind of woman would do such a thing? She thought of the man's dark brown eyes, almost as black as coal, yet there was something kind and sad about them. A woman wouldn't send away a good-hearted man like that just because he was missing a leg. She might want to shave off all that hair to find the face she loved! But she wouldn't turn him away.

Angelina's thoughts turned to Lieutenant Willoughby. What she wouldn't give to see him again! She wouldn't care if he had no legs at all and a beard down to his boots, she'd still be happy to see him and thank him for what he'd done for her.

Angelina stepped inside the General Store, strolling through it and taking time to examine its wares. She let her fingertips run along the red, green and blue bolts of fabric, her hand pausing on the lovely shade of blue. It reminded her of a painting of the ocean she'd seen in Bonnie's parlor. She reached for a comparable shade of thread and held it up to the cloth, contemplating the possibility of making a dress. She thought upon it for several moments, but then the practical side of her took over. She replaced the thread, deciding she better hang onto her funds until she settled in and determined what her expenses would be.

She'd gotten so caught up in her thoughts of making a dress from the lovely material, she almost forgot all about Bonnie's flour until her eyes fell upon the sacks of sugar, flour and corn meal arranged in a tidy corner display. She decided to look around a bit more and wait to pick up the sack of flour when she was ready to leave. Noticing the bins of dried commodities: jerky, corn, pinto beans, coffee beans, pipe tobacco and chewing tobacco, she moved in that direction. Angelina loved the smell of coffee beans. She didn't care much for the flavor of the beverage itself, but she leaned toward the coffee bin, inhaling deeply, and sighing with pleasure at the rich aroma.

Moving along, she strolled toward the clerk's counter and her eyes widened at the shiny assortment of jewelry. There were gold rings, gold and silver chains and even a strand of pearls. She paused, lifting a set of silver combs to admire them. She'd love them for her hair.

She noticed the price tag threaded to the combs and raised an eyebrow. Such a purchase would be out of the question with her limited funds. She'd have to settle for pulling her hair back with hairpins as she usually did.

She approached the counter facing the balding clerk, "Good afternoon, sir."

"Good afternoon, Miss, what may I do for you?"

"I need a sack o' flour, please."

The merchant walked to where the flour sacks were stacked on a wooden pallet. He lifted one over his shoulder and brought it back to the counter, letting it fall with a thud on the wood.

"You must be new here," he remarked as he took her coins and made change.

"I am. I'm Miss Stone. I'm here to teach at the school," she accepted the coins and watched his chubby cheeks get even fatter with his smile.

"Ah, so your Nancy Barrett's replacement?"

"Yes, sir," she nodded and reached for the sack.

"Well, well. I wonder how those older boys will ever be able to concentrate on their studies with a pretty young thing like you as their teacher."

Angelina's cheeks flushed, "I . . ." She wasn't sure what to say to that. "I assure you that I am an experienced teacher, Mr. ..." She paused, realizing she did not know the man's name.

"Mr. Rivers," the man extended his pudgy hand in greeting. "I'm sure you are, Miss. The town council thought long and hard 'bout Mrs. Barrett's replacement. I didn't mean to embarrass ya."

Angelina took his hand in a friendly gesture. "You didn't." She lifted the sack of flour and wrestled for a good grip on it.

Mr. Rivers reached out helping her adjust the sack.

"Thank you, sir," Angelina's face still flushed a little.

"Welcome to town, Miss Stone," he called out when she turned to leave. She nodded with a smile and carried the heavy sack toward the front door. Fortunately, a gentleman was coming in when she was going out, and he held the door for her long enough for her to exit.

Angelina looked down at the burdensome sack, wishing she'd taken time to look at more of the city before she'd weighed herself down with it. She'd have to cut her window-shopping short now and lug it home.

Chapter 13

Elijah studied his reflection in the hand mirror and straightened his collar one last time before leaving his house. He went to the stable, saddled his horse and mounted. Nudging the animal's sides, he headed toward town. As he rode along, he considered upon the evening ahead. His stomach churned a little with nervous expectation. If it hadn't been for the invitation, Elijah would have postponed facing Angelina Stone for a month or two. Everett had brought up his hopes one minute – telling him that God brought Angelina to Knoxville, and more importantly to him. Just when Elijah dared to believe that the angel of his dreams was here for him, Everett ripped the prospect from his reach by telling him he wanted her to marry this Paul Bennett fellow.

Elijah felt as if an ornery mule had kicked him in the stomach. He was just a demon Angelina had to face. Once he'd accomplished that task, Elijah's job was to send her home to marry another man. It didn't make him feel very good about himself, that's for sure. Not to mention he'd thought so much about the girl since he'd met her, he couldn't stand the thought of being this close to her and not finding a way to make her his own. She had the school year to finish anyway, he reasoned. Why make her face her demons now?

As he rode along, he thought of his promise to Bonnie. He'd already accepted her invitation. In fact, it was a standing one. Two Fridays each month he ate supper at Bonnie Crestworth's boarding house. Bonnie expected him there. She'd passed him in town the day before and asked him about supper. He'd agreed to be there for her delicious fried chicken, mashed potatoes and gravy, and famous apple pie.

Nobody in their right mind would pass up Bonnie's apple pie. He'd been enjoying it for years, ever since she and Doug first married and invited Elijah over to eat. The habit of spending two Fridays each month at the Crestworth's started long before the war. When Elijah returned but Doug didn't, Bonnie insisted that the tradition continue. It was her way of celebrating the life she once shared with her husband, her way of anchoring herself in a drastically altered world.

A little before six, Elijah arrived at the boarding house. He didn't bother to knock, but walked right in. Nobody ever knocked on the front door. Tenants were always coming and going, and so no one stood on formalities. Elijah's boots tromped across the wooden planks, back toward the kitchen where Bonnie stood over a hot skillet frying chicken.

"Hmmm, smells good! Need some help?" he grinned and winked as he entered the room.

"'Lijah!" she exclaimed, wiping her hands on her apron and stepping toward him, giving him a hearty hug.

Angelina, who stood nearby peeling and dicing carrots, looked up from her work. Her jaw dropped, and her eyes grew wide. A smile instantly spread across her lips at the man before her and instinctively she stepped toward him as well. But as quickly as her excitement came, it fled when she watched the man she'd most recently seen in her dreams joyously embrace Bonnie. For a fleeting moment, she'd been so excited and grateful to see him. But the emotion collapsed, leaving jealousy instead of gratitude. Simmering irritation soon replaced what should have been joy.

"Oh, Angelina, you must meet my oldest and dearest friend, Elijah Willoughby!" Bonnie turned toward Angelina, her arm threaded through his. Bonnie smiled as if the sun, which had long been hidden behind wintry clouds, had suddenly made an appearance. Angelina's back teeth ground against one another.

"'Lijah, this is Miss Angelina . . ."

"Stone," Elijah finished for her and cordially outstretched his hand toward Angelina.

Angelina extended her hand, which still held a paring knife.

Elijah glanced down and chuckled. "The war's over, Miss Stone. We can put our weapons away now."

"You two know each other?" Bonnie's quizzical gaze bounced between the pair. Angelina slipped the knife into her apron pocket and extended her hand to Elijah.

"We've met," Angelina answered dryly, brushing back her loose locks and wishing she'd taken the time to pin her hair up properly.

"Good to see you again, Miss Stone," Elijah took Angelina's hand in his gallant grip and pressed it to his lips.

"Good evening, sir," Angelina's reply was cool, but her fingers felt like they'd been touched by fire when they met with Elijah's hand. She withdrew her hand quickly and turned to Bonnie. "I best set the table. Where do you keep your silverware?"

"Right over yonder," she pointed.

Angelina immediately went to work retrieving the utensils and carried them past the pair, into the dining room, out of their presence. She needed to get away. She felt like lashing out at both of them. Why hadn't Bonnie mentioned anything to her about Lieutenant Willoughby? They'd talked for hours while cooking that day, and yet Bonnie had never mentioned him. She'd never even said a word about a guest joining them for supper. It was obvious Bonnie was fond of him – quite fond of him. Embracing each other like that, it was more than Angelina could stand to watch! Angelina gripped the fork in her hand until its hard silver shook in her trembling hand.

Her heart pounding, she looked down at the utensil, forced herself to loosen her grip, and lessened the tension in her jaw. What was she thinking? She took a deep breath and scolded herself. She had no right to feel this way. In reality, there had never been anything between her and Lieutenant Willoughby. It was all in her dreams -- dreams that often replayed in her waking imagination. In those scenes, it was she he held in his strapping arms. He directed his smile and winks to her, not Bonnie Crestworth! Angelina fought to bring herself back to reality. The pair had done nothing wrong. It wasn't their fault that they cared for one another. Neither of them knew of Angelina's harbored dreams. Willoughby had not betrayed her, and neither had her new friend.

Angelina stood over the box of silver that set on the dining room table and put her hands to her cheeks, attempting to cool her emotions. While she'd never expected to meet Willoughby again, she certainly never dreamed that if she did, he would belong to someone else! She had seen it all so clearly in her mind's eye, convincing herself that he would sweep his protective arms around her and kiss her as he always did in her dreams. She knew now that it would never happen. It had all been just silly dreams, nothing more.

~*~

"You know her?" Bonnie whispered, her expression quizzical.

He shook his head. "Met 'er during the war when I passed through Chattanooga into Georgia."

"She said her father fought for the Confederacy."

"Uh, hmm," Elijah leaned his hand on the counter.

"She doesn't appear too fond of you," Bonnie smirked.

"No, she probably wouldn't be," he shrugged, the corners of his mouth turning down into a scowl.

"What happened?" She retied the bow of her apron behind her.

"I'd rather not discuss it," he replied dryly.

"Jiltin' hearts 'cross Georgia, then?" Bonnie teased with a twinkle in her eye.

"Hardly," Elijah rolled his eyes, picked up a tray of chicken and briskly carried it into the dining room.

When he set the platter of chicken down on the table, Angelina's back was to him, and she was still working on setting out silver.

Lost in thought, she did not notice Elijah's presence. As she backed toward the next place setting, she ran squarely into his chest. Jumping with fright, she released a small cry.

His hands caught her waist "It's all right," he whispered into her ear. "It's me."

Angelina spun around to see with whom she had collided. When she did so, she looked up into his handsome face. With his strong hands at her waist, Angelina's fright melted into a warm dreamy sensation, as if she sat by a cozy fireplace roasting chestnuts. The heat spread to her rosy cheeks.

Her breathing became shallow, and she fought for control. In one second, her heart hammered, remembering the last time she'd seen him. He had pressed his ring into her hand, and she'd been too traumatized to say anything. But now, their eyes met for a lingering moment, and the same thrilling sensation from her dreams charged through Angelina's entire body. When Bonnie entered the dining room carrying a bowl of mashed potatoes, Angelina abruptly stepped out of Elijah's reach.

"I'm sorry, so clumsy of me. I didn't see you there," she muttered and hurried through her arrangement of the last place setting.

Bonnie lifted a single eyebrow in Elijah's direction and her mouth drew into a teasing smirk. Angelina's heart fell when Elijah shook his head and frowned.

At that moment, Angelina heard the happy chatter of four females and their noisy footsteps bouncing down the stairs. They entered the dining room together.

"Good evenin'!" a buxom brunette called with a happy smile. Her eyes widened, and she stepped toward Elijah. "'Lijah!" she exclaimed and gave him a hug, kissing his cheek in welcome.

"That's right, it's Friday!" a curly-headed blonde chimed as she, too, rushed to Elijah and embraced him with a kiss on his cheek. Angelina's eyes widened as the next two women in turn put their arms around Elijah and kissed his bearded cheek. Again, she felt agitated. Elijah seemed well acquainted with many women and it seemed as if each one enjoyed the pleasure of his embrace but her. On the other hand, perhaps she had misread the encounter between Elijah and Bonnie if everyone greeted him in such a manner. The possibility washed over her leaving hope in its wake.

"Angelina, these are the Forrester sisters," Bonnie introduced, gesturing to the four women who all appeared to be in their twenties.

"I'm Dot," the tall brunette said, extending a hand to Angelina.

"I'm Lucille," the woman straightened a crease in her elegant dress and inclined her curly blonde head in greeting.

"I'm Edna."

"And I'm Thelma."

"A pleasure to meet you all," Angelina smiled as each woman took a seat around the table and left one end for Bonnie and the other for Elijah. Bonnie asked Elijah to bless the food and just as his prayer concluded, Dot reached for the potatoes.

"Like I was sayin', I had supper out at the Merriweather place the other night, and I swear it was the best supper I ever did eat! Why, they served the most delicious pot roast. You could cut it with a spoon, I declare! And those roast taters and carrots, in a scrumptious broth with salt and pepper, sweet milk and that yummy peach cobbler for dessert – simply divine, I say, just divine!

Angelina smiled at Dot's theatrical way of describing a meal. She didn't believe she'd ever heard anyone itemize the contents of a supper down to the salt and pepper. She looked to Bonnie who smiled with a wink, indicating that she may as well get used to it for Dot did not stop chattering all evening long. It was as if the sound of her own voice was the air she breathed. For everyone else, it was like the tablecloth upon which the meal was placed. It was there, constant, continuous, and relentless; but also something you didn't take time to notice.

Everyone else simply continued their conversations on top of it.

"And it was just the loveliest day. The sun was shinin'; the birds were singin'. Nothin' like you'd expect for January . . ." Dot wove on.

"So 'Lijah how was your week?" Edna cocked her red head toward their handsome guest and raised an eyebrow with the question.

"Good . . . good, the mares are expectin' in spring and . . ." Elijah described the successes upon the farm while Dot continued:

"Oh, my! And that youngest Merriweather baby! He is just the funniest child. We sprawled him out there on a quilt and watched 'im stick his toes in his mouth. It entertained us for hours . . ."

"And how was your week then, Edna?" a humored smile tugged at Elijah's lips.

"Oh, I've been workin' on a new quilt. Material can be so hard to come by these days, but Mrs. Johnson down the street brought me a sack full, so I've made some wonderful progress."

"Now, Edna," Lucille tossed her blonde curls in superiority and paused to tweak a piece of lint from her dress. She sighed, then continued her condescending reprimand, "I've been meanin' to tell ya that material of Mrs. Johnson's simply won't do for the quilt you're workin' on. The material doesn't match. And it's just makin' an atrocious lookin' thing."

"I think it looks good," Edna defended.

"That's simply because you don't have a lick o' taste, dear," Lucille relayed the criticism as if it were as obvious as the stripe on a skunk's back.

"Yes, I do." Edna's eyes misted.

"No, dear, you don't," Lucille stated in a matter-of-fact tone. "Everyone thinks they have good taste, but everyone couldn't possibly have good taste or there wouldn't be so many frumpy things in this world."

Tears started to trickle down Edna's cheeks.

At this point Thelma interjected, "Now, Lucille, how do ya know it's not *you* who has bad taste? Maybe Edna's the one with good taste, and you just don't know it."

"Have you *seen* the thing?" Lucille's eyes grew wide. "She's got navy squares, bright red ones mixed in with pink, bright yellow and lavenders. It looks like somethin' exploded on a weavin' loom, for heaven's sake!"

Meanwhile Angelina sat there dumbfounded, listening to Dot's continuous outpouring of meaningless drivel and what was now swelling into a full-blown argument.

Her eyes studied Elijah, and he caught her glance, giving her a wink. By now, Bonnie had entered the conversation, attempting to keep Edna — who had risen from her chair and claimed she was full — from departing.

"Now, Lucille, quilts don't always have to be perfectly arranged. Especially not in times like these when material's so hard to come by. Edna's quilts are always so warm and cozy, and that's what's most important." Bonnie patted Edna's hand. "Please sit back down, Edna, and enjoy your supper. We'll find somethin' else to talk about."

Dot, who still chattered on about the oddness of seeing a bluebird in January, seemed oblivious to the hothouse of emotion spilled out like hot coffee upon her tablecloth of monotony.

Angelina couldn't help but smile, her eyes widening as she turned her head away from Edna and Lucille toward Elijah. My! He was handsome! Sitting there in that white shirt, his sleeves rolled up a couple turns exposing his strong arms, his suspenders and navy pants doing little to hide his muscular build. And he was smiling at her now, those blue eyes twinkling, communicating his own amusement with the eccentric Forrester sisters and his complete understanding of how it felt to be an outsider thrown into the midst of them.

As much as she'd wanted to be mad at him and guard herself from possible pain, right now, the frosty shell she'd placed around her heart melted like an ice cube on a sweltering summer afternoon.

Chapter 14

The rest of the evening continued as bizarrely as it began. By the time the women gathered in the parlor and Bonnie and Elijah settled into the kitchen to clean up, Angelina needed to escape. Excusing herself, she stepped out on the front porch for some fresh air. It was cold out, but she could only handle so much confusion in one sitting. She wondered how she'd ever survive staying at the boarding house.

"So what do you think of Bonnie's henhouse?" Elijah's deep humored voice broke the silence of the night.

Angelina glanced toward the door and smiled, "That's a good description for it."

He drew closer to her. "They aren't always this bad," he assured.

"Really?"

"No, sometimes they're worse," he laughed.

Angelina giggled.

"They can be kind of lovable once you get to know them."

Angelina didn't say it, but she wasn't sure she could tolerate them long enough to get to know them that well.

"They're like a bad batch o' soup. Individually, they aren't that bad, but mix 'em together and their flavors clash," he released a humored sigh. "Well, of course, except Dot . . . she's the same no matter who she's with."

Angelina giggled again. It felt good to laugh.

As she faced the yard, leaning her hands on the railing, Elijah leaned his hand next to hers and drew a little closer. She closed her eyes and sighed, berating herself for having let her imagination get so carried away over the last year. She really hadn't expected ever to see him again, yet here he stood so close to her that she could barely think straight.

"It really is good to see ya again, Miss Stone," he paused, and Angelina glanced toward him. "I mean . . . to see ya looking so well. I'd worried about what had become of ya."

"Well, as you can see, you needn't have worried about me," her reply was stiff.

His voice lowered, "I'm truly sorry for the circumstances under which we met and upon which we parted company."

Angelina forced an anxious swallow. He stood so close she could smell the alluring masculine scent of him, that clean leathery, intoxicating Lieutenant Willoughby aroma that she remembered from the day they'd walked in the fields and fed little Wilma apple wedges.

"Will you please forgive me, Miss?" his eyes were so sincere. How could she deny him her forgiveness? There was really nothing to forgive in Angelina's mind. She'd already forgiven him for entering their home. After all, he wouldn't be such a mysterious and captivating part of her life if he hadn't. And without him, Jacobsen surely would have killed her.

"There's nothin' to forgive, Lieutenant Willoughby," she whispered. "After all, you *did* save my life."

"Thank you, Miss Stone. Thank you for that," he inclined his head, leaned his elbows on the porch rail, and stared up at the full moon.

"Thank *you*," she whispered.

His hand, which rested beside hers on the railing, moved atop her slender fingers and embraced them. Startled by his touch, Angelina looked up into Elijah's compassionate face. In his eyes she saw his remorse over what had happened to her, gratitude for her forgiveness, and something else she could not quite pinpoint. Was it respect? No, it was more than that. It was almost reverent hope, as if he were assuring her that the future would be brighter than the past. Did he see something of worth inside her that would make it so?

Even though she could see their breath lingering in the frigid, dimly lit air, Angelina felt warm, safe, even a bit flushed.

"My heavens! It's plum freezin' out here. You two'll catch your death!" Dot exclaimed as she poked her head outside the front door.

Angelina's head shifted toward Dot, but Elijah seemed not to notice the woman. His gaze remained intent upon Angelina's face. Even though her eyes were directed at Dot, her entire attention riveted on the hand that Elijah still covered with his own. She felt as if her entire being had climbed into that single appendage. Her heart beat there. Her lungs breathed there. Elijah Willoughby's warm calloused hand, which lightly caressed hers with his thumb, held all Angelina's thoughts, wishes and hopes.

"Bonnie wants you to come eat this last piece o' pie, 'Lijah," Dot called, motioning dramatically for him to come inside.

Elijah squeezed Angelina's hand a little tighter and then released it. He crossed to the door, and Angelina followed a few steps behind, her eyes lingering upon her hand that still tingled sweetly from his touch.

~*~

One week later

A sharp prick stabbed the back of Angelina's neck. She slapped her hand to the spot and rubbed it to soothe the familiar sting, then spun around on her heels.

"All right, who did it?" she gritted her teeth, her angry eyebrows scrunching. Her gaze moved from one pupil's innocent-looking face to another. Fourteen kids in this classroom and not one of them would admit to shooting peas at her!

Her attention focused on Harry Todd who sat twiddling his thumbs on his desk, looking up at the wooden rafters of the schoolroom as if he were as innocent as an angel. Her accusatory glare shifted to his brother Freddy. He had his freckled nose in a book, and Angelina thought he looked a little too interested.

She stepped toward the two boys, standing in the row between them.

"Are you enjoyin' that book, Freddy?" she queried with as much sweetness as she could muster.

"Yes'm, it's really good."

"I bet it would be even better if you turned it right side up!" she put her palm to the book and twisted it around to the correct position.

142

The classroom broke into giggles, and a smirk tugged at the corners of the fourteen-year-old's thin lips.

Angelina thrust out her open palm, "All right, hand it over."

"What?" came Freddy's innocent retort.

"You know what I'm talkin' about - the pea-shooter. Hand it over."

"I don't have a pea-shooter," the lanky teen scurried to his feet and turned his trouser pockets inside out, revealing their emptiness.

Angelina's eyes narrowed at him. She couldn't prove it, but she just knew he was the culprit. It was either him or his brother. She shifted her attention to Harry, and Freddy quickly slipped back into his seat.

"Let's see your pockets, Harry," Angelina motioned for the twelve-year-old to rise. The boy sifted his slender fingers through his dusty brown hair, his brown eyes darting toward his brother for instruction.

Freddy gave him a subtle nod. On cue, Harry rose from his seat and emptied his pockets, pulling out an assortment of marbles, jacks and rocks. Angelina raised a single eyebrow, wondering how the boy managed to keep his pants up with so many trinkets shoved into his pockets.

His cupped hands placed the heaping contents of his pockets onto his desk. The moment he released them, marbles and rocks went rolling in a dozen directions, pelting the floor and scattering under desks. Chuckles and snorts filled the classroom.

Angelina rolled her eyes, "Pick it up." She exhaled a heavy sigh, "Help him, Freddy."

"Why?" Freddy groaned.

"Just do it, Freddy," Angelina barked and then bit her lip. She was letting them get the better of her. This day was progressing from bad to worse. Softening a little, she squatted down to pick up the marbles and rocks strewn around her feet. She stood and handed them to Harry who shoved them back into his pockets.

Giving up for the moment, Angelina turned and went back to the chalkboard. At this rate, she'd never get through her math lesson. When she got to the board, she looked around in her chalk tray, but there wasn't any chalk there. She turned to search her desk, then her eyes scanned the floor.

"Lost somethin', Miss Stone?" Jeremiah Abrams called from the back of the room and the class erupted into another round of giggles and snorts.

She leaned her clenched fists on the desk, "Just go." Her head gestured toward the door. "Go eat your lunch and come directly when I ring the bell."

The words were no sooner off her lips than desks went scooting and scraping, and students' feet scrambled like a herd of cattle. Within seconds, Angelina stood alone in an empty room.

Lord, help me. What have I done? She'd traded a sweet and well-mannered class back home for this unruly bunch, and she'd swapped a loving home with her family for the henhouse of emotional females at Bonnie's. There was no one to go home to, no Daddy to tell her troubles to, no Cal to make her laugh, no Joseph and Eleanor to hold down and tickle until they giggle-cried for mercy. She was so lonely, frustrated, and downright angry! Maybe she should just quit and go home and get her old position back before it was gone for good.

No, I can get through this. I'm not gonna give 'em the satisfaction of drivin' me off this easily! She stamped her foot, took a deep cleansing breath and grabbed her lunch pail.

She unwrapped her meal to find a slimy wet toad looking up at her.

"Ribbit"

"Aaheeeahhhahh!" she screamed, jumping back from the desk, tripping over her chair and landing on her backside with a bone-jarring thud. She scrambled to her feet, standing clear of the amphibian.

"Ribbit, Ribbit"

"Oh, be quiet!" she shook her head, gritting her teeth, her lips drawn into a tight line.

With stiffened arms, she grabbed the sides of her lunch pail, carrying it at arm's length out the schoolhouse door and tossed the contents over the side of the step railing. She spun on her heels, ignoring the giggles, and re-entered the building. She slammed the door shut, pounded the pail down on her desk, and stood there several fuming moments. Finally, in defeat she slumped into her chair, buried her head in her hands and fought back the tears. She had to pull herself together. The last thing she wanted was to see the smug grins on those boys' faces if they came back in and saw her eyes swollen and bloodshot.

Blinking back the tears, she resolved to persevere and face her fourteen Goliaths. She buried her head in her hands and prayed for help. *Show me what to do. Please show me how to get through to these children. Some of 'em really want to learn. I can see it in their eyes, but there's those few who make it impossible. I don't know what to do. Please help me!*

Upon concluding her prayer, Angelina's stomach rumbled, reminding her that her lunch was gone. She sighed, determined to make constructive use of the time, and reached for her Bible. She opened it on her desk, letting it fall wherever it may. It landed open to 2 Timothy

1:7, *"For God hath not given us the spirit of fear; but of power and of love and of a sound mind."*

Angelina stared at the words. Was she afraid? She thought about it for a moment. She was frightened of many things. But was she afraid of a classroom of children? She had to admit, there was some fear there. Not that she thought they would actually harm her, unless relentless pelting with peas could cause some kind of brain damage. Nevertheless, she did fear she'd never bring the class under control. At the rate things were going, it didn't look promising. What if the children who really wanted to learn, like Maggie Stevens and Lizzie Folsom, fell behind in their studies because of the disruptions? What if the town council let her go because she couldn't do the job?

It was silly, really. What was the worst thing that could happen? She'd have to go home to Georgia. That wasn't so bad. She missed her family. What she wouldn't give for her Daddy's consoling words and a comforting hug right now! The bad thing was that if she lost this position, she'd have to live with the humiliation of knowing she'd failed. She'd go home like a mutt with its tail between its legs. Her family wouldn't shame her for it, but Angelina had a measure of pride. She didn't like appearing the fool, especially not in such a publicly humiliating way!

Then again, only a handful of boys caused most of the trouble. If she could just win over Freddy and Harry Todd, it would make a big difference, but she felt powerless to have any effect on those two. Angelina read the verse again. If God wasn't giving her the spirit of fear, who was? She snickered to herself and muttered, "The devil with a handful of help from some rowdy boys!" She read it again and thought, *God's spirit gives power, love, and a sound mind.*

Angelina rolled her eyes at the sound mind part. She certainly didn't feel like she had a sound mind, especially not today. She decided she would have to ponder on this verse a little longer because evidently she was missing some main ingredient in the recipe.

Chapter 15

A few hours later, Angelina watched the last young woman leave the schoolhouse, released a sigh of relief and slumped in her chair. It had been a long, long day – and an extremely long week.

Teaching these teenagers was a stark contrast to her class back home. She knew why they were acting this way. They were evidently disturbed to lose Nancy Barrett as their instructor, and they were taking their frustrations out on her. Angelina rubbed her neck. She'd lost count of how many peas had pelted her this week. She felt like a pincushion. No matter how many pockets the boys emptied, they still managed to hide their weapons. She mused that if the North had put this classroom of youngsters on the front lines, the war would have ended much sooner, and spared her precious Georgia the ransacking fires.

Angelina wondered if Miss Barrett had experienced as much trouble from them when she first started teaching. Probably not. Most likely, they treated Angelina this way because they perceived her as one of their peers, she being so close to their own age.

Angelina rose from her chair, gathered her belongings and headed for the door. The last week had been difficult, but she'd survived through Friday, and it felt good to know she would have a few days to rest.

She stepped out of the schoolhouse, locked the door and started south. The school was on the Main Street of town. Her route home took her past a tavern, the livery, and the blacksmith shop. Opposite them stood the general store.

As she drew near the tavern, she noticed two inebriated men scuffling about and bellowing loudly outside the door. Tightening her coat around her, she looked both ways and crossed to the other side of the street. Her departure did not deter the two men. One whistled loudly, and the other called out a lewd remark.

Angelina's heart raced, and she burrowed her head into her scarf, quickening her pace. She hoped that if she paid no heed to their remarks, they would forget about her. Instead, through her peripheral vision she saw them following her across the street. Terrified, she ran toward the general store, yanked the door open and rushed inside the building. Brushing past aisles of merchandise, she escaped deeper into the mercantile until she reached the back of the store. Quickly she stepped toward a display of material and hid behind the upright bolts. Her pulse drummed in her ears as she lowered her head and let her fingertips run along a silken bolt of fabric. From her position, she could not see the door. So she couldn't be certain whether the men followed her, but she did hear the bell above the door chime another time after she'd entered. Angelina closed her eyes, praying the men hadn't followed her.

Suddenly, she felt a hand on her arm, and she jumped, nearly knocking over the bolt of material in her hand. Her frightened eyes lifted toward Elijah Willoughby's concerned expression. Instantly she breathed a sigh of relief.

"Are you well, Miss?" he inquired.

"Oh, I – uh . . ." she stammered and shook her head. "Those men at the tavern . . ."

"Did they hurt you?" he blurted, his voice husky with emotion.

"No," she shook her head. "I just . . ."

"This isn't the safest route home. It may be the shortest, but it isn't the safest." His voice was filled with concern. "Are you sure they didn't hurt you?"

"I'm sure. I just didn't know that wasn't a safe route. It's broad daylight for goodness' sakes." Her hands were trembling and Elijah took them in his own.

"You're freezin'," he said, rubbing her hands slowly within his own.

Instantly Angelina's cheeks flushed, and she pulled her hands away before he read the emotion in her face. "I'm fine, really. Thank you for checkin' on me."

"May I show you a better way home?" he asked, a small smile playing on his lips.

She nodded affirmatively, still trembling and her heart still racing, whether from the incident or from his touch, she couldn't tell.

"Do you have some business to tend to in here?" his head motioned toward the bolts of material.

"No, I just came inside to get away." Her voice sounded less shaky and it gave her confidence.

He took her arm, "You were wise to come in here." Leading her to the front of the store, they exited the building into the freezing afternoon that was already starting to grow dark. They stepped onto the boarded sidewalk in front of the general store, and Angelina's eyes darted warily toward the tavern, but the men were gone.

"Are you in a hurry for home? Because if you are, we'll take the shorter route, and I can show you the safer way on Monday."

Angelina quickly weighed her options. On one hand, she would enjoy his company home again on Monday. On the other, she did not want to appear rushed because at this moment she craved his soothing presence for as long as she could hold it. As odd as it was, this ex-Yankee soldier who once invaded her home was the most familiar person she knew in this town.

"I'm in no hurry," she replied.

"Me either, but it's rather nippy out this afternoon. We'll go the faster way, and Monday I'll meet you at the school and show you the safer one."

"That is very kind of you, sir, but I wouldn't want to inconvenience you on two occasions. Perhaps you could just tell me the safer route."

"It's no inconvenience. I have business in town on Monday afternoon."

Propriety would have demanded that she protest more. However, Angelina dared not do so. Knowing that Elijah Willoughby would escort her home on Monday gave her something to look forward to at the start of the week and would alleviate some of the dread in returning to the classroom.

As they strolled along Main Street, Elijah carried her satchel. While one of Angelina's hands rested on his arm, the other gripped the folds of her skirt as she attempted to control her nervous tremor. The encounter with the men outside the tavern had shaken her more than she realized.

In an effort to divert her mind, she stopped to admire a burgundy gown hanging in a dress shop window. Her eyes met Elijah's, and she dropped her gaze, sure he could read her very thoughts. As her eyes fell, they rested on Elijah's military boots. The events of the day overwhelmed her as the scenes from the summer she'd first met Elijah flashed into her mind – Jacobsen's lascivious glances, his lurid remarks, and Elijah appearing in the barn wearing those exact boots!

Suddenly, the sickening memories came flooding back, and Angelina was no longer standing on a Knoxville street corner, but back in the barn being attacked by Jacobsen. Without realizing what she was doing, Angelina's body began to quake with an uncontrollable shiver. Her head began to spin and her vision dimmed. Elijah's face swam before her eyes.

He dropped her satchel to the ground and took her by the shoulders. "Are you sure you're all right?"

Her eyes closed and opened languidly as she swayed side-to-side, feeling darkness closing in, "I just . . ." Her frightened eyes met his and then she collapsed. Immediately, Elijah caught her, lifting her into his arms and carrying her toward the boarding house, leaving her satchel laying in the middle of the sidewalk.

Elijah's heart raced, fearing for Angelina's well-being. He'd seen the McNeal brothers coming after her and had intercepted them before they reached the General Store. He suspected they had caused her no physical harm, but he could only guess at the mental anguish this episode must have aroused in her.

He'd just entered Bonnie's yard when Angelina awakened in a startled condition.

"Put me down!" she cried, pushing at his chest. "What are you doing?"

"You fainted, Angelina," he soothed. "You had a scare back in town, and I guess it caught up with you."

She continued to push on him, squirming in his arms, making it difficult to hold her. "Those men, they were after me. I had to get away . . ."

"It's all right, Angelina," he held her tighter, speaking in soothing tones. "I'm here. I'm here."

"It can't happen again. I can't go through that again," she cried and shoved her fists into his chest, attempting to extricate herself from his arms.

He held her calmly, drawing his head closer to hers. "Sh – Sh," he whispered into her hair. "It's fine. I'm never gonna let anybody hurt you again. Never." His eyes met hers with determination. "Never. Do you understand me, Angelina? Never."

His words seemed to calm her. She nodded with understanding and leaned her head against his shoulder. He carried her up the front porch steps and shoved the door open with his shoulder.

Whisking her to the couch, he set her down there, helped her lie down, and pulled an afghan from the back of the couch. He knelt beside her and draped it over her. Tucking it into place, he leaned over her, meeting her gaze.

"How do you feel now?" He pushed a strand of hair back and searched her face anxiously.

"I don't know. What happened?" she asked, closing her eyes.

He put his palm to her pale face. "You fainted. I think I should go get the doctor."

When he started to rise, her eyes flew open and she grabbed his arm. "No, please stay," she begged. "I don't want to be alone right now."

He looked at her panicked face and changed his mind. "Very well, I'll stay. Everythin's gonna be all right," he soothed.

He knelt beside her for a minute, lightly stroking her hair, then noticed that Bonnie had her usual pot of peppermint tea sitting on the serving table. "Perhaps a little tea would make you feel better. Would you like that?"

Angelina nodded and then leaned her head back, closing her eyes as Elijah got up and poured her some. He returned to her side and handed her the cup and saucer. Her hands trembled so violently that the cup clanked noisily against the saucer. She pressed it to her lips, rattling the dishes as she did so. Elijah knelt beside her and steadied her hand with his own. For an instant, her eyes met his gratefully and then she closed them and took several sips.

"Thank you," she whispered. As he took the cup and saucer from her and placed them on the coffee table, Bonnie entered the room.

"My stars, what on earth has happened?" she exclaimed upon finding Angelina pale and prostrate with Elijah hovering over her.

"She had a run in with the McLean brothers and . . ."

Angelina shot him a silencing look. "I missed lunch and I suppose it made me weak," she explained.

"She fainted," Elijah added.

"Oh my! Let me go get you some warm blankets. That afghan's too porous for warmth." Bonnie darted from the room.

"Why didn't you eat lunch?" Elijah inquired, standing and going to the serving table once more.

"There was a frog in my lunch pail," she replied sheepishly.

"I suppose Bonnie didn't put it there," he handed her a cookie with his smile.

"No, I'm sure Bonnie did not."

"They're givin' you a hard time, aren't they?" he observed, sitting on the edge of the couch beside her.

"Uh-hmm . . . a bit," she admitted and took a bite of her cookie.

"If truth be told," he lowered his voice and leaned toward her, resting his hand on the couch beside her as if he were confiding some great secret. His face drew so close to hers that he could smell the sweet scent of her hair. "They were a handful for my sister as well."

"Your sister?"

"Yes, Nancy Barrett . . . my sister . . . they made her work hard for her money when she first started teachin'."

"It did get better, then?"

"After a year or two," he affirmed.

"Oh my!" Angelina rubbed the back of her neck. "I don't think I can tolerate two years of pea pelting!"

"Pea-shooters – eh? Devils!" Elijah scowled, but then a twinkle captured his blue eyes, "It needn't take you as long as it did Nancy."

"Why is that?"

"Because you have me," he pointed a thumb to his chest and mischief glimmered in his eyes.

Even in her shaken condition, he couldn't resist teasing her a little. Elijah felt encouraged when indeed his remarks brought a wash of color to Angelina's face.

"I – I don't understand," she stuttered nervously.

"I was away at war when Nancy started teachin' that bunch. When I got home, I gave those oldest Todd boys a talkin' to and once they saw the light, well, the rest of 'em fell right in line. Never were a bit of trouble again. It looks like they just need a little instructin' from someone who can speak the language they'll listen to."

"Oh, I – uh . . ." Angelina stammered, "I couldn't ask you to fight my battles for me, Mr. Willoughby."

Elijah put a hand over hers. "Miss Angelina, I think it's 'bout time I fought a battle on your side o' the line," he said softly, his serious eyes meeting hers for several silent moments before continuing. "It would be the least I could do."

"I, uh," Angelina stammered. Elijah thought her cheeks looked even rosier. "What . . . what would you say to 'em? You wouldn't hurt 'em, would ya?"

"Of course not," his eyebrows crinkled at her preposterous notion. "I won't hurt 'em. Trust me. I know what to say to 'em."

Angelina paused, meeting his gaze. Elijah felt the air in the room suddenly turn tense. He watched the emotional conflict brewing like a storm in her green eyes, her feelings raw and exposed. "Give me another week," she whispered.

He knew their conversation was about more than the Todd boys. In his heart, he knew she was telling him that she needed more time. "You just say the word, and I'll be there." He gave her hand a gentle squeeze just as Bonnie re-entered the parlor carrying two large quilts with Edna trailing behind her with a third.

"Bonnie said you had a run in with the McLean boys!" Edna's voice carried through the house as she flung her hand to her bosom. "How frightenin' for you! They are the roughest, nastiest pair that ever slithered upon the earth."

"She was smart 'nough to run into the general store before they could get to her," Elijah added, taking a blanket from Bonnie and putting it over Angelina.

"Good for you, Angelina," Bonnie's grave expression confirmed the danger of the situation had not simply been Angelina's imagination. "You have to be careful around that tavern."

"I told her I'd show 'er a safer way home on Monday," Elijah rose from the couch beside Angelina, preparing to leave while Bonnie and Edna put the two remaining blankets over Angelina.

"Oh, I could show you the way, Angelina. It's not hard," Edna offered.

Bonnie's eyes issued a silencing command toward Edna and interrupted, "You're not leavin' already are you, 'Lijah?"

"I probably should get goin'. I've got some more work to do at home before sunset. I'll stop by the doctor's house on my way and ask 'im to check in on Miss Angelina."

"That's a good idea," Bonnie agreed.

"Thank you for your help, Mr. Willoughby. You've been too kind," Angelina looked a bit embarrassed about all the fuss made over her.

"'Twas nothin'. I'll see ya Monday after school then?"

Angelina's head gave a timid nod and Elijah left.

Bonnie went to the serving table and poured tea for Edna and herself. Edna received hers and sat in a wingback chair on the opposite side of the coffee table from Angelina. Bonnie sat down in a matching chair nearby.

"You seem to have a little more color to your cheeks now," Bonnie noted.

"Yes, I'm feeling quite a bit better," Angelina sat up a little on the couch and reached for her tea. She took several sips before replacing it on the table beside her.

At that instant, Elijah stepped back in the front door of the house and slipped Angelina's satchel onto the floor by the door. He smiled and nodded in her direction then closed the door behind him.

Angelina listened to his footsteps descend the stairs and then Bonnie intruded upon her thoughts of him. "He's sweet on you, you know." She stated it as if it were an obvious fact.

Angelina's eyes widened self-consciously for a split second before they furrowed into an expression of denial. She motioned negatively. "He's simply being kind."

"Kind would be seein' you home today. Sweet on you would be dotin' on you as he's done and offerin' to see ya home again on Monday," Bonnie replied.

Edna's eyes widened with understanding. "Bonnie's right. After all, I did offer to show ya the way."

"It's only because he promised to do so earlier. He was only bein' a man o' his word," Angelina protested, yet secretly a part of her hoped the women were right. She swept the notion aside, telling herself that she simply felt drawn to Elijah because he always seemed to be coming to her rescue.

"He is a handsome one, isn't he?" Bonnie smiled at Angelina, coaxing a reaction.

Angelina could feel her lips involuntarily rising, then bit the right side of her lower lip, forcing it to stay down. "I hadn't noticed," she lied.

"She hadn't noticed. You hear that, Edna? Angelina hadn't noticed how handsome Elijah is."

"We better ask Doc Miller to examine her eyes while he's here," Edna pretended a worrisome expression, but a teasing glimmer in her eyes betrayed her mirth.

"I think you're right. It won't do for a schoolteacher to lose her eyesight like that," Bonnie shook her head as if Angelina were in grave danger of losing her vision.

"It's frightenin', it is!" Edna affected urgent concern. "She could lose her teachin' position over somethin' like that."

"That's true! Destitute and blind! It would be a sad state o' affairs, it would," Bonnie added.

"Oh!" Angelina sat up on the couch, placing her feet on the floor and tossing the blankets aside. "You two are awful. Do you know that?"

"You're not blind, then?" Bonnie pretended mock relief.

"Of course I'm not blind, but that doesn't mean anythin'. He was simply bein' nice."

"And you're simply enamored with him," Bonnie added.

Angelina lifted her chin, tilting her nose in the air "I won't even dignify that with a response." She rose to her feet, draped one of the blankets around her shoulders and started to walk away.

"Now, lie back down, Angelina. We were just teasin'. Don't go strainin' yourself," Bonnie cautioned.

"I think I'd prefer lyin' down in my room for a while. After all, I do have lessons to prepare." With that, she gathered her satchel and started up the stairs. Bonnie and Edna were silent, evidently making sure she ascended the stairs safely. Just as she reached her bedroom, Angelina heard the women break into giggles.

Angelina shut the door behind her and plopped on the bed, letting her satchel fall to the floor with a thud. She leaned back on her pillow and thought about Elijah. She most assuredly found him attractive, and he did make her insides twirl in a flutter, but she couldn't forget that long ago night. He'd rescued her from Jacobsen, carried her to safety and pressed his ring into her hand. She could still remember how he looked that night when his blue eyes misted with anguished remorse. Instinctively her hand went to her neck and pulled the chain from beneath her dress. She lifted the ring, examined it, and let her finger slip through it.

Her face drew into a scowl. He'd also seen her beaten and her dress torn. How much had he seen of her that night? Her gown had been nothing but a shredded rag. Crimson heat rose to her cheeks as the memory dredged up humiliation, fear and utter embarrassment. How could he look at her and not remember that night? She could hardly look at him without thinking of it. Whenever they met, did he remember her beaten and exposed?

If he did, he did not show it. Elijah seemed confident and relaxed in her presence. Angelina forced back a faint smile. In spite of it all, she wanted to be near him. She felt drawn to him, somehow more secure in his presence. After all, in the most horrifying moment of her life, Elijah Willoughby had come to her rescue, and he seemed determined to keep doing so.

Chapter 16

When Elijah reached the schoolhouse door on Monday afternoon, he stood there silently watching Angelina. She held her head in her hands, leaning her elbows on the desk and staring down at the wood grains. He knew that today hadn't gone any better, and he felt sorry for her. Maybe now she'd let him intervene on her behalf.

He watched her take several deep breaths and press her fingertips to her eyes, forcing back tears. He tapped at the door lightly, and she looked up at him with an expression of surprise.

"Did ya forget I was comin'?" he asked, stepping inside the building.

"Actually, I did," she lifted her shoulders apologetically, sighed and repositioned a few loose strands of blonde hair into her bun.

"Rough day?" he observed.

She inhaled a deep breath and released it slowly, "Afraid so." She put her hands to her desk, pushed her chair backwards and rose to her feet.

"Do ya need some more time?" he offered. "I'm in no hurry."

"No, thank ya. I'm ready to go." She gathered her books into her satchel and joined him at the door.

"Here," he took her satchel from her, and she locked the building.

"Do ya wanna talk about it?" he asked.

"Oh," she leaned her head to the side and shook it slightly.

"I'm a good listener," he offered his arm as he stepped from the schoolhouse steps onto the dirt pathway.

"Well," she took his arm and they started toward Main Street. "I'm just havin' trouble gettin' 'em to behave." She shifted her lunch pail so that it rested in the crook of her arm. "I tried makin' 'em earn their recess time with good behavior, but that didn't work. They just turned the whole class into a circus instead!"

"What did they do?"

"Oh, you know, just gettin' up and walkin' around the class while I'm teachin', throwin' things across the room, hidin' my chalk, puttin' critters in my lunch pail. If it wasn't for Bonnie's hearty breakfasts and dinners I'd be wastin' away. I don't think I've been able to eat a single lunch for a week! I should just stop bringin' 'em." She lifted her empty lunch pail in the air by the handle, indicating its uselessness.

"I'm sorry to hear that. You really need to be eatin' your lunch. We can't have you faintin' again," Elijah felt like putting an arm around her and consoling her. She looked like she needed a hug, but he didn't figure they were close enough for that.

She held up her thumb and forefinger, less than an inch of space between them. "I was this close to tryin' Dot's idea."

Elijah could only imagine what Dot would tell her to do, "And what was that?"

"She told me to just stand at the front of the class and belt out in song!" Angelina shook her head. "She said it would take 'em by such surprise that they'd behave. I told her I wasn't much of a singer, and she said it didn't matter. She said that the worse I was, the better it'd be. I could threaten to keep singin' until they behaved!"

Elijah's smile grew even broader, "I can just see you standin' at the chalkboard beltin' out *Battle Hymn of the Republic!*"

Angelina laughed, "No, *Dixie!*"

"That's right, *Dixie!*"

He steered her to the left down a side road that bypassed the main part of town and the tavern in particular. They walked for several moments in silence, periodically their eyes meeting and then breaking into chuckles again at the thought of Angelina serenading her class.

Finally, Elijah broke the humored silence, "I should've asked ya earlier. How's your family? Your mama and the children?"

"They're good. Daddy came back from the war safely. He's well as are Mama and the children." Her lunch pail slipped to her fingers and she let it swing slightly as she walked.

"I'm glad to hear it. You have a very nice family." He looked toward the field they passed and shifted her satchel in his hand.

Angelina gave him a doubtful look. "I'm a bit surprised you'd think so." She paused, her face growing somber. "You weren't treated too cordially."

He looked at her again, giving her an apologetic smile. "I didn't deserve to be. I wasn't exactly an invited guest."

Her head cocked to one side and gave a slight nod, evidently unwilling to disagree with him on that point.

"I hope your brother doesn't hate me too terribly," he added when Angelina made no reply.

"Oh, he doesn't hate ya," she insisted. "He was just very angry that night."

"As he should've been," Willoughby agreed, his expression serious.

"But you saved my life. He shouldn't 've treated you so. And he knows that now."

"I'm not such a hero," Elijah replied softly as he exhaled.

Angelina paused in walking, "Pardon me?"

Elijah turned to face her and took a deep breath, "I need to apologize for what happened." He looked past her for a moment noticing an old barn standing in the field. It reminded him of that night and her lying there beaten and her gown in shreds. He closed his eyes, shutting out the memory, and drew in a deep breath.

"You've already apologized. It wasn't your fault."

"Ah, but it was." He opened his eyes, looking into hers remorsefully. "I was layin' there all comfortable when I heard Jacobsen get up. The thought occurred to me that I should follow 'im to see what he was doin'. He was always up to no good. But I didn't. I was too tired and lazy, and so I ignored the warnin' voice in my head." Elijah felt sick every time he had to admit this, but he knew he owed her an apology. If he could get through the entire story this time, it would be the last time he'd have to speak of it. "If I'd gotten up when I first thought to, none of it would have happened." He paused, "So, you see then, it's partly my fault."

She stared at him for nearly a full minute, expressionless. Elijah began to worry that she hated him now for his negligence.

Finally, she spoke, "You can't blame yourself for that." She put her hand lightly on his arm, "You did come, and you did save my life."

"I just wish it had been sooner." Elijah hung his head, his eyes lingering on her fingers that rested on his arm.

Angelina retrieved her hand, turned and resumed walking. After a step or two, he heard her mumble, "So do I."

Elijah felt his heart stab. He had let her down. He knew it, and she knew it. It was then that he resolved to take matters into his own hands with the Todd boys. He wouldn't bother asking her permission. He'd just fix things and that would be that.

~*~

Tuesday morning when the students came trailing into class and taking their seats, Angelina noticed Freddy Todd rubbing his arms, trying to warm himself with the friction of his hands. She wondered why he didn't wear a coat. He wore only a red flannel shirt. Did he even have a coat? She couldn't recall ever seeing him with one.

Had she actually never noticed that Freddy didn't wear a coat to school? Had she been so engrossed in her own problems that she missed a child in her class lacking such a basic necessity? She felt sick. What kind of teacher was she? Even more, what kind of Christian was she?

She crossed to Freddy's desk and stood over him, "Freddy, would you mind stoking the stove with a little more wood for us please?"

"Yes'm," he readily rose from his seat and went toward the wood-burning stove. He lifted a log from the pile, opened the iron door and shoved the wood inside. He held his hands in front of the orange glow and then added another log.

A lump formed in Angelina's throat as she thought of the frigid winter they'd been having, and here Freddy had been coming to school without a coat! She started to ask him about it, but decided she shouldn't embarrass him with the question. Instead, she'd have to find some way to remedy the situation.

After school, Angelina took the back road that Elijah had shown her that led to Bonnie's, but then turned and went toward town to stop by the general store. It was a long way to go to avoid the tavern, but she didn't dare get near it again.

The heat felt heavenly as she stepped inside the toasty mercantile. She rubbed her gloved hands together and crossed to the fireplace. Three old men sat at a nearby table playing Rummy. They met her with a nod and continued their game. She stepped cautiously around them. She still wasn't comfortable around strangers. As she stood in front of the fireplace, enjoying the heat, she noticed a large shadow fall on the hearth and felt a presence beside her. She looked to her right, and met the charcoal eyes of the one-legged man. Her heart accelerated a little, unnerved by the big hairy vagabond. She thought his lips turned up under his heavy beard, but she couldn't be certain. His head inclined toward her.

Angelina forced a tight-lipped smile and turned her gaze back to the flame. He stretched out his left hand, raising it to let the heat penetrate it. Angelina noticed the dingy rag that wrapped around his palm. She expected he wore it to keep himself warm since he wore no glove. His fingers remained unwrapped, and Angelina raised a single eyebrow, a bit surprised to see what appeared to be a gold wedding band on his ring finger.

She tried not to look at him, but she was curious about this man. What was his story? And how did he manage to stand on only one leg? She tried to observe him through the corner of her eye, but couldn't be certain how he stood erect. His left arm retracted, and he stretched his right hand toward the fire. It was then that Angelina noticed he wore a second ring. This one looked so familiar. Her eyes widened and reflexively she put her hand to her chest. Her fingers fumbled with Elijah's ring that hung from the chain beneath her dress.

The man's ring looked identical to Lieutenant Willoughby's! It was the same intertwined rope design! Her mind darted with the possibilities. It was such an unusual ring. She wondered how this drifter would come to possess one just like it.

When the man turned and headed for the bin of beef jerky, Angelina glanced over her shoulder watching him hobble away. He'd made a crutch from a piece of oak, and his right hand leaned on the rung of it. The top of the crutch disappeared up into his long black coat that draped over his broad shoulders and fell to his knees. He certainly was a formidable looking fellow. Even with one leg, no one would dare call him a cripple.

She imagined that even a healthy man would regret meeting the man's charcoal eyes and large form in a back alley. He would have frightened Angelina, except that both times her eyes had met his, she had seen only a kind sadness. He may look menacing to the world, but Angelina sensed something gentle in him. Deep down she felt certain the drifter owned a good heart.

She watched Mr. Rivers step back a little as the man placed a large rag-wrapped hand on the counter. The portly mercantile owner's eyes shifted nervously. He named the price of the beef jerky and took the money the drifter offered.

Angelina moved to the coats, but kept her eyes on the dark stranger as he left the building and turned up town. Her gaze went to Mr. Rivers whose stiff shoulders seemed to wilt with an exhaled sigh of relief. He went back to his work straightening items on the shelves behind him, and Angelina concentrated on finding a coat for Freddy Todd.

She looked at several of them, holding them up to her, trying them on to find the one that would be about Freddy's size. He was taller than she was, but thinner. Mr. Rivers came to stand by Angelina just when she'd settled upon a black coat that would fit Freddy and would be warm enough.

"Those are the men's coats, Miss. Our lady's line is over yonder," Mr. Rivers pointed to his left.

"I know; I'm just tryin' to find a coat for someone I know."

"Aha," Mr. River's gave her an insinuative nod, his eyes lighting with a mischievous gleam.

"It's not like that," Angelina retorted.

"It's none of my business who you buy a coat for, Miss," Mr. Rivers raised his palms in the air as if he had no intention of pressing her, but that he knew she must be buying it for a male friend.

Angelina rolled her eyes and sighed, "How much is it?"

When Mr. Rivers named the price, Angelina's heart sank. She didn't have that kind of money. She might in a few months, but by that time, Freddy Todd would catch his death of cold.

She hesitated for several moments and then pushed the coat into Mr. Rivers' arms. "Would you mind holding it for me until tomorrow? I don't have any money with me right now."

"Certainly," Mr. Rivers' satisfied smile spread across his round face. He folded the coat over his arm, and his mirthful eyes followed Angelina as she left the building.

Chapter 17

Angelina took slow, methodical steps as she started down the street and turned toward home. How was she going to come up with enough money for the coat? She fastened the top button of her coat and pulled her scarf tighter around her neck. Her knuckle brushed against the hard silver ring beneath her dress. The ring would bring enough money for a coat for Freddy Todd.

Angelina shook her head. No, she couldn't sell the ring. It belonged to Elijah Willoughby, and she had no right to sell it even if it was for a charitable cause. The thought occurred to her that she should really give it back to Elijah, but she hated to part with it. It gave her hope – hope that someday he could be hers, in spite of all that had happened.

She shook away the notion. She needed to concentrate on a solution for Freddy, not get lost in daydreams of Elijah! When she stepped inside the boarding house, an idea came to her. She waved a greeting to Edna who sat quilting in the parlor and scurried up the stairs. She unlocked her bedroom door, tossed her satchel on the floor by her desk and headed for her cedar chest.

She opened the hinged lid and pulled some clothes from the top. There it was - the log cabin quilt her mother made her. She ran her hands along the beautiful pattern of vibrant colors, and then lifted the fabric to her face, inhaling the scent of home. Images of her mother flooded her mind. She could almost feel her mother's arms wrapped around her and smell the sweet scent of her hair.

Angelina spread the quilt out on her bed to examine it one last time. A twinge of regret shook her heart. She couldn't part with this quilt! Her mother had made it just for her! Then she remembered the image of a lanky teen rubbing his frigid hands on his sleeves for warmth. She folded the quilt and bundled it under her arm. She'd do it quickly before she had time to change her mind.

Hurrying down the stairs, she waved at Edna again, "I'll be back in time for dinner." She carried the quilt straight to the store. The bell rang as she stepped inside.

"You back already?" Mr. Rivers greeted.

Angelina headed directly to the counter behind which the stout man stood. "I was wonderin' if you might be interested in a trade. I have this quilt that my mama made for me. She unfolded it a little for him to see the pattern. "It's beautiful and surely it would be worth as much or more than the coat."

Mr. Rivers' eyebrows furrowed a little as he examined the quilt. He opened it more and spread it out on the counter. "It is a fine quilt, but are you sure you want to part with somethin' your mama made for you?"

Angelina's shoulders slumped, "It's the only thing I have that would be worth that much."

"Well," the man scratched his bald head, then opened his cash register. "I can give you the coat and this in trade." He extended a silver piece to Angelina.

"I'll take it," she took the coin and slipped it into her drawstring purse while Mr. Rivers reached under the counter to retrieve the coat.

"Could you please wrap it up in brown paper for me?"

He gestured affirmatively and set about wrapping the parcel while Angelina folded the quilt. She put it to her face one last time, inhaling her mother's familiar scent, and then gingerly placed it on the counter.

"Now if you manage to come up with the money in the next few days, you come back in and buy it back. I'll try to hold it for ya for a little while, just in case."

"That's very sweet of you, Mr. Rivers," Angelina smiled, but doubted there was any way she'd come up with the money that soon.

She watched him tie twine around the brown paper. Angelina cleared her throat. "By the way, who was the man here earlier with the missin' leg?"

Mr. Rivers' eyes narrowed, "Some new fella, don't know much about him."

"Do you know his name or where he's from?"

"Why?" Mr. Rivers' brows lowered.

"Oh, I don't know," Angelina shrugged nonchalantly. "Just wondered who he was."

"His name is Jack. That's all I know. He's a drifter."

"Ah," Angelina dipped her head in understanding.

"Kind of a menacin' lookin' fella, don't ya think?" Mr. Rivers confided.

"He is rather large and hairy," Angelina's lips tipped up humorously. "But he has kind eyes."

"Hmmm . . . hadn't noticed," Mr. Rivers handed her the parcel and thanked her. She thanked him as well, and started back to the boarding house. She wished she could get the coat to Freddy that night so he'd have it for the morning, but she didn't even know where he lived. Besides, she really didn't want him to know that she was the one giving it to him. She wanted it given anonymously. *"Let not thy right hand know what thy left hand doeth,"* came to her mind.

When she re-entered the boarding house, Edna met her at the door. "Where have you been traipsin' in and out to this afternoon?"

"Oh, I just had a purchase to make," Angelina tried to act as if it were only a trivial item and wrapped her arms around her purchase as she stood in the foyer.

"What did you buy?" Edna pointed to the package.

"Well, uh," Angelina didn't want everyone in town knowing she'd be giving the Todd boy a coat. "Just somethin' for one of my students."

"Oh?"

"Could I trust you to keep a confidence?" Angelina whispered and looked around to make sure no one else was around.

"Certainly," Edna agreed.

"Come upstairs with me," Angelina tugged on Edna's sleeve and then started up the stairs. Edna followed Angelina to her room. Once inside, Angelina shut the door.

"Do you know where the Todd's live, by any chance?"

"Sure, their house is just a few streets over."

Angelina grew excited. "Would ya feel up to making a delivery?"

"Ya mean this?" Edna pointed to the package.

"Yes, I need this to be delivered to the Todd's, but I don't want them to know where it came from. Could you sneak it to their door, then maybe knock and run?"

Edna's lips slid up into a sly grin, "Oh, this sounds fun!" She rubbed her hands together excitedly.

"So you'll do it?"

Edna agreed, and Angelina went to her desk and wrote *"For Freddy"* on the brown paper. "Make sure they don't see you."

"What is it?" Edna took the package and squeezed it a little.

"It's just somethin' he needs," Angelina replied. "And I don't want anyone to know that I'm the one who gave it to him."

"All right," Edna tilted her head to one side and lifted her shoulders. "When do you want me to deliver it?"

"The sooner, the better. Right now, if you have time."

"Sure, why not?" Edna tossed a hand haphazardly in the air. "I'll be back in a little bit."

"Thank you, Edna," Angelina squeezed the young woman's hand gratefully.

"You're welcome."

Angelina watched Edna open the door and slip out of the room. She hoped she'd be able to deliver the package without anyone seeing her.

Edna returned a short while later, tapped on Angelina's door and then stepped inside, quickly shutting the door behind her. Angelina sat up on her bed, and Edna came to sit beside her.

"How did it go?" Angelina asked anxiously.

"Went well. I put it by the front door, knocked and then ran to hide behind a bush. I waited a little while to watch and make sure they got it. Mrs. Todd came outside and got the package and carried it inside callin' Freddy's name."

"Good, so they didn't see ya?" Angelina asked.

"No. I did wait a little longer and saw Freddy and Mrs. Todd step back outside and look around. But they didn't see me. Finally, they gave up and went back inside. Then I came on back home."

"Thank you so much!"

"You're welcome. It was fun," Edna giggled.

"I'm glad you enjoyed yourself," Angelina smiled at Edna.

"So are you gonna to tell me what it was?" Edna prodded.

"You promise not to tell a soul?"

"I promise," Edna crossed her heart with her index finger.

"It was a coat. He didn't have one." Angelina said, letting out a breath. "I just couldn't imagine him goin' all winter without one."

"Oh, how sweet of you!" Edna put a hand on Angelina's shoulder.

Angelina shook her head negatively, feeling a little embarrassed. "He needed it."

"You're a good teacher, Angelina. Those kids are lucky to have you."

"Well, I don't know about that," Angelina didn't feel like a very good teacher, but she was starting to care a lot more about her students.

~*~

The next day, Angelina watched Freddy proudly enter the classroom wearing his new coat. Several of the young women commented on the fine material and his friend Jeremiah Abrams remarked how warm it looked.

175

When they asked him where he got it, he just tossed up his palms and said it was a gift . . . probably from his Aunt Mabel.

Angelina couldn't help but smile at him, thrilled to see him so happy and knowing that she had played a part in his happiness. As the day progressed, there were no peas shot at her neck. No one stole her chalk and the students stayed in their seats when she taught. There were still a few giggly girls, but the Todd boys behaved like angels. Their good behavior seemed immediately to spill over onto the other students – especially the boys.

Angelina wondered whether they had perhaps observed Edna dropping off the coat and linked the gift back to her. Why the sudden change? Then again, she was trying some new creative teaching techniques, and she did genuinely care more about them.   Maybe they sensed her growing fondness.

Later that afternoon when she stepped out of her schoolroom, she locked the door and turned around to descend the wooden staircase.

A deep male voice startled her, and she looked to find Elijah Willoughby. She caught her breath. Every time she encountered him, it was almost like the first time. His handsome features nearly took her breath away, and with each meeting, she remembered less of that eventful night. She smiled, "Mr. Willoughby. What a pleasant surprise. I hadn't expected to see you today." Angelina ran a hand over her hair and met him at the bottom of the schoolhouse steps.

Elijah leaned his hand on the banister and flashed his engaging smile, "I was in the area and thought I'd walk ya home . . . that is if it's acceptable to you."

Angelina could feel her cheeks turning a rosy red. "That sounds lovely, Mr. Willoughby."

Elijah took her satchel and extended his arm, "Please, call me Elijah."

"Very well," she acquiesced and took his arm, thrilled to be on a first name basis with him. The familiarity made her heart accelerate like a raging bull kicking on the walls of its stable stall.

"How was your day?" he looked down into her eyes with a dimpled grin, then turned toward Main Street.

"Much better. I think things are finally beginnin' to turn around."

"So they're behavin' themselves?" he raised an eyebrow.

"Yes, they were much better today."

"I'm glad to hear it," he smiled satisfactorily.

They continued walking toward town for several moments in silence, but Angelina's mind was not silent. She'd felt an odd mixture of emotions upon hearing Elijah's confession on Monday. What if he'd heeded his first prompting? She could have been spared the horrific encounter. Then again, if only she'd stayed in bed. If only she hadn't let Sam get hold of the chicken bone, he would have been alive to protect her. If only she'd gotten Cal, or Cal had awakened when she'd left the house. She'd blamed herself a thousand times and in dozens of ways for what happened that night. She'd finally concluded that she couldn't blame Elijah anymore than she could blame Cal or herself. She felt sorry for this man who had come to her rescue, for she knew what it felt like to blame oneself for something that could never be undone.

She knew it was Elijah's guilt that led him to give her the ring that still hung about her neck. Ever since seeing the stranger with the same ring, she'd been contemplating giving it back to Elijah. She knew she should. Yet, she did't want to part with it. It was as if as long as she possessed the ring, she owned a piece of Elijah. They turned onto the side road to bypass town, and she put her hand to her blouse, feeling the metal beneath the cloth.

"Mr. Willoughby," she began hesitantly.

"Please, it's Elijah."

She smiled nervously. "Elijah," she inclined her head slightly and reached for the chain at her neck. She withdrew her hand from his arm, brought the chain out from under her blouse, and unfastened the clasp. Slipping the ring from the chain, she held it in her palm.

"Here, I want you to take this back."

Elijah stopped and turned to face her, a scowl on his face. "Why?"

"Because it's not right that I should keep it."

"Why not?"

She studied the expression in his eyes. He almost looked as if she'd hurt his feelings, so she rushed on. "I know you only gave me the ring because of what happened that night and because you felt it was partly your fault. But it wasn't your fault."

She took his hand that rested at his side and pressed the ring into his palm. "You should take it back, and please . . . please know that I don't blame you in the least for what happened that night. On the contrary, I am most grateful."

Elijah stared at the ring in his palm for several moments before finally slipping it onto his right hand.

They resumed walking and Elijah fiddled with the ring the way she remembered him doing. It was better to see it on his hand again and witness the nervous gesture once more. Angelina smiled, "Where did you get the ring? It is very unusual."

"My father made it for me. He was a blacksmith."

"Really?" her eyes widened in surprise. "Did he make more than just that one?"

Elijah stopped and faced her again, "One other. Why?"

"Because there's a man in town who has a ring just like yours."

"There is?" Elijah put his hands to her shoulders and shook her a little. "Who? Where?"

Angelina looked down at her shoulders, surprised that he was being a little rough with her. Instantly, he released her. "I'm sorry, I just need to know who you're talkin' about."

"There's this drifter in town. Mr. Rivers says he's new in these parts and goes by Jack. He has one leg and an extremely bushy beard that nearly covers his entire face except for his dark black eyes. He looks more like a wolf than a man."

Elijah raked both hands through his hair and quickened his pace in the direction of Bonnie's. He went so fast that Angelina had to jog to catch up to him.

"Do you know 'im?" she inquired when she reached him.

"I'm not sure, but my father only made two of those rings."

"Who did he make the other one for?"

"My brother," Elijah answered numbly.

"Your brother?"

"Well, not my real brother, but he may as well 've been my brother. We were inseparable. My father said there was a tie between us . . . just like the ropes on this ring." Elijah held up his ringed hand.

"Then maybe it was him?"

"It couldn't be him." Elijah shook his head negatively.

"Why not?" Angelina was a little winded from their speedy pace.

"He died at Gettysburg."

Angelina's face fell, "I'm so sorry."

Elijah walked a little slower and continued in pensive silence.

"Perhaps this fellow in town knew your friend?" she offered.

"Maybe. More likely he stole the ring off his body."

Angelina grimaced.

"Where did you see this man again? I'd like to find 'im and ask 'im a few questions. Maybe he knows somethin' about what happened to my friend."

"I've only seen him twice. Once when he was ridin' into town on an old gray mare and the next time was in the general store. Mr. Rivers seems to know a bit about 'im. Maybe he could help you locate 'im?"

"All right," Elijah' face grew serious. "I'll stop by and see Mr. Rivers."

Elijah was usually the one who carried their conversations, but now he was quiet and looked to be a million miles away. They walked on in silence, and Angelina strolled along beside him without retaking his arm. She tried not to stare at him. Instead, she concentrated on the houses they passed, but she couldn't help looking over at him every now and again. She loved the set of his jaw, especially when it stiffened as it was now with him being lost in thought.

Finally, after nearly ten minutes, they reached Bonnie's street. Angelina lightly touched his arm. "Are you gonna be all right?" she whispered.

He turned to her as if suddenly awakened from a dream. He put his hand over hers and extended his arm for her to take it once again, "I'm terribly sorry. I'm afraid my mind has been in the past when it should have been here with you."

"That's all right. I understand." She gave him a small smile as they turned into the gate. "Thank you for seein' me home, Elijah." She stopped at the door.

He smiled, "Thank you for the . . . the ring." He held up his hand and twiddled it around his finger.

"I hope you find 'im and get the answers you're looking for."

Elijah started backing down the steps, evidently anxious to be on his way.

"I'd ask you in for some tea, but you're probably anxious to get to town."

He smiled with a nod, "Thank you. Perhaps another time." With that, he turned around and started on his way. Angelina stood on the front porch watching him as his pace quickened, and then transitioned into a full sprint toward town.

Chapter 18

Elijah ran the whole way to town. His heavy black boots stomped noisily up the wooden steps to the general store. He burst through the door and marched straight toward Mr. Rivers. Leaning both hands on the counter, he inhaled and exhaled several times, trying to catch his breath. The cold air had caused his lungs to burn, and stepping inside the toasty store had made his face feel hot.

"Mr. Rivers," he panted. Several patrons in the store stopped to stare at him.

"Slow down there, Elijah. Catch your breath," Mr. Rivers chortled and patted Elijah on the shoulder.

Elijah put his hand to his side and breathed in and out several more times until he gained control of his lungs.

"Mr. Rivers, there's a new man in town I'm tryin' to find." He panted once more. "He's got only one leg, a big bushy beard and dark black eyes. Goes by Jack."

"Yes, he's been in here a couple times," Mr. Rivers bobbed his shiny bald head.

"Do you know where he's stayin'?"

"I think he's got a room over at the tavern. Either that or he's a heavy drinker 'cause I see him comin' in and out o' there a lot."

"Thanks," Elijah offered the man a slight wave and started for the door.

"Whatcha want with the fella?"

"I just think he may know a friend o' mine."

"Well don't cross 'im. He looks awful big an' ornery to me. One leg or not, he could be dangerous."

Elijah waved at Mr. Rivers without turning to face him. "I can hold my own."

He walked briskly toward the tavern, dodging a horse-drawn buggy, and stepped inside. His eyes scanned the dimly lit establishment. Three men sat at the bar drinking whiskey shots. There were two tables full of poker players. The other tables were empty.

Elijah went to the bar and sat on a stool in front of the bartender.

"What's your poison?" the lanky man quipped.

"I'm not thirsty," Elijah replied.

"Lookin' for some female companionship then?" the man snapped his fingers and instantly a voluptuous blonde in a bright red dress appeared at the man's side.

Elijah's eyes left the woman and concentrated on the bartender. "No, I'm just lookin' for somebody."

The bartender frowned, and the woman came out from behind the bar.

"I don't kiss and tell, darlin'," the woman cooed as she came to stand directly behind Elijah. She put her hands on his shoulders and let them slide the length of them. He flinched when she ran her finger flirtatiously around his ear.

Elijah bent his head away from her and tried to shrug her hands off him. He directed his next comment to the bartender. "I just came in here to look for someone."

"Maybe it's me you're lookin' for, darlin'?" the woman whispered in his ear and then pressed her shockingly crimson lips to his cheek.

"No, I'm lookin' for a fella that might be stayin' here. A big bushy-bearded fella who's missin' a leg."

"Oh, him," the woman stood up straight and grimaced as if she'd just taken a bite of lemon rind.

Elijah directed his anxious gaze to her, "You know where I can find 'im?"

"He's upstairs. Room three," she replied.

She'd no sooner given him the room number than Elijah was on his feet and heading toward the staircase.

"I'll be waitin' here for ya when you've finished your business. Perhaps then we can engage in a little business of our own?" she called out.

Elijah ignored her and trotted up the stairs, in search of room three. He hadn't gone far when he found it on the right. He rapped on the door and waited. No answer came. He knocked again, but still nothing. He looked around in both directions. If he went back downstairs, he'd have to face the saloon girl again. It took him no longer than a second to make his decision. He leaned his back against the wall across from room three, slid down and sat on the floor to wait.

He extended his fingers in front of him and examined the ring. Doug Crestworth was the only other person he knew with the same ring. Elijah still remembered the day his father finished them and gave them to the two boys. They were only fourteen at the time. Knowing the young men planned to become blood brothers, Mr. Willoughby suggested they forego the pain and possibility of infection and make their vow of brotherhood with the rings instead of cutting themselves with a blade. The boys accepted the rings and promised to wear them always to remind each that he had a brother he could count on until death. Two years later, Elijah's parents passed away with influenza and two years after that, the young men joined the Union. Elijah joined a regiment that went south and Doug went north. That was the last time Elijah saw his friend.

If Elijah hadn't received word from Bonnie that Doug was missing and presumed dead, he never would have let the ring off his finger. That night at the Stone farm when he decided to give it to Angelina, it seemed only fitting. Doug had been gone for nearly a year, and Elijah wanted the young woman to have something to remind her that there was one person in the world who cared about her.

If he'd never given Angelina the ring, he wouldn't be sitting in this hallway. Perhaps this drifter could give him the final piece that would finish Doug's story. Then Bonnie could move on with her life, and Elijah could lay Doug to rest in his own mind.

The thought did occur to Elijah that this drifter could be Doug. Perhaps he hadn't died at Gettysburg, but Doug would have come home to his wife. He wouldn't let Bonnie suffer this way. He loved her too much for that.

Elijah sat there thinking for nearly an hour until he heard *stamp – thud – stamp – thud – stamp – thud – stamp* coming from the direction of the stairwell. Elijah quickly snapped to his feet and turned toward the sound.

Soon he was face to face with the large bushy man. Elijah thought he looked more like Moses climbing up Mount Sinai than Angelina's description of a wolf. His hair stood out from the top and sides of his head as if he'd been frightened by a ghost.

Elijah's gaze traveled down the man's black coat. He noted his crutch and one black boot that came up to the man's knee. He met the man's wide eyes. The whites of them seemed even more prominent than a normal man's would be, probably because of the dust and hair covering his face.

Elijah squinted, perplexed. There was something familiar about the eyes. He looked to the man's hand that braced along the crutch. There was the ring.

"Excuse me," the man muttered as he lowered his head and started to pass Elijah.

Instead, Elijah shifted over, squaring his broad shoulders and widening his stance, not letting the man pass.

"Excuse me, my room's here," The drifter bent his head toward the door.

"I know it's your room. I'm here to speak with you."

"I don't wanna speak with you," the man wedged himself between Elijah and the wall.

Elijah turned and put his hands on the man's shoulders, and tried to stare him in the eyes, but the drifter cast his gaze to the floor.

"Doug?" Elijah whispered, his heart thumping like a drummer's call to battle. "Is that you?"

"The name's Jack," the man corrected and then took advantage of Elijah's startled condition to push past him to his door. He quickly unlocked it and started inside. He tried to slam the door, but Elijah wedged his foot in the way and pushed inside, knocking the man back until he lost his balance and fell on the floor.

Elijah entered, shut the door and extended his hand to the man. "I'm terribly sorry. Didn't mean to knock ya down." While he suspected it could be Doug, he wasn't positive.

What little bit of the man's face that was exposed grew red. Reluctantly and evidently with great humiliation, he took the proffered hand. He rose to his feet, went to the washstand, poured himself a drink of water, and guzzled it down.

"I want ya to leave," the man said in a deep voice.

Elijah ignored him and came to stand before him, staring into his eyes, searching his face. "Is that you under all that hair, Doug?"

"The name's Jack," the man growled.

Elijah pointed to the ring on the man's hand. "Then where did you get Doug's ring?"

The drifter straightened his fingers while resting his thumb on the crutch. He looked at the ring as if it was something unfamiliar. "I won it playin' poker."

"You don't play poker."

The man looked at Elijah as if he were crazy.

"You were always lousy at cards. Remember the time Marty Jules beat you so bad you lost your favorite aggie? And then you snuck inside his tree house the next day and stole it back?"

"He cheated. He always cheated," the man grumbled and turned his back to Elijah.

"Doug? It's really you, isn't it?" Elijah came around to stand in front of him and put his arms around him, pulling him closer, tears of joy misting his eyes in knowing that his friend was alive.

Doug stiffened uncomfortably. "Go home, 'lijah. Forget you ever saw me."

"Where on earth have you been for the last two-and-a-half years?" Elijah stepped back from him, suddenly irritated.

"Around," Doug shrugged.

"Around? Around where?"

"Here and there?"

"Here in town," Elijah pointed to the floor, getting angrier by the minute. "You've been to town before now?"

"A few times over the years, to check on Bonnie."

"You mean Bonnie knows you're alive?" Elijah stepped back in shock.

"No, and she's not gonna," Doug barked.

Elijah curled his fist and slammed it into Doug's jaw, sending him falling on his bed. Elijah stood over him, inhaling and exhaling angry, labored breaths. "You mean you've been in town and haven't come to see Bonnie? It's bad 'nough that you haven't taken the time to see me, your own blood brother, but Bonnie! Of all people, you should've seen her! Do you realize the hell you've put that woman through?"

Elijah raised his clenched fist ready to give Doug another pounding, but Doug raised an arm in defense.

"Wait," he pleaded and raked his other shirtsleeve over his bleeding lip.

"Why? I should beat you to a pulp for what you've done! Do you realize Bonnie's never believed you were dead? She still has her Friday dinners, still invites me to come, just hopin' that one day you'll walk through her door and sit down to a plate of her fried chicken and apple pie!"

"I don't want Bonnie to know I'm here," Doug's voice was coarse and emotional.

"Why?"

"Bonnie doesn't need me."

"Bonnie loves you, Doug. You can't just leave her mournin' like this for the rest of her life. She needs to know her husband's alive and well."

Doug snickered, an irritated, angry chortle. "Alive and well!" He pointed to where his shin should be. "Look at me! Do you think Bonnie can love this?"

"I never thought I'd say it, but you, Doug Crestworth, are a lily-livered coward!"

Doug gritted his teeth angrily, leaned over to grab his crutch and hoisted himself to his feet. "Get out o' here. I don't need you makin' me feel even worse than I already do." Doug turned his back to Elijah and walked to the washbasin for a towel. He pressed it to his face, absorbing the blood.

As Elijah watched him, his heart softened and his anger began to subside. He lowered his voice, "You are a fool. You don't even know what you've got. You're blinded by that injury of yours and can't see that Bonnie's not gonna care about your leg. All she's gonna care about is that her husband's alive."

Doug shook his head negatively and dabbed at the moisture in his eyes before he turned to face Elijah once more. "I don't have anythin' left to give 'er."

"You've still got arms to hold her," Elijah put a hand on Doug's shoulder. "And somewhere under all those horrible whiskers are some lips to kiss her."

Doug just rolled his eyes and looked at Elijah as if he'd lost his mind.

"I know Bonnie. I married her, 'member?" Doug thumped his thumb to his chest. "She'll take me back, and then I'll be a burden to her, a millstone about her neck.

She's too young and beautiful to be saddled with the likes o' me."

"You're wrong. You won't be a burden to her. She loves you. Don't ya know anything about the woman you married? She's all alone now. She does well with the boardin' house. She doesn't need a breadwinner; she needs the man she loves to hold her at night instead of cryin' herself to sleep."

For an instant, Doug looked as if Elijah's logic was getting through to him, but then his eyes clouded over. "Doesn't matter what you think, 'lijah. You can talk 'til you're blue in the face, but I'm not goin' home."

"Then at least come to my place. You can clean up and have some good food, and . . ." Elijah paused, rubbing his beard and remembering his father's blacksmith tools. "I think I might have an idea for that leg of yours."

Doug looked down at the appendage. "What?"

Elijah shook his head negatively, "You've got to come with me to find out."

"Will you make me some of your flapjacks?" Doug asked, and Elijah could see the old glimmer of hope flickering in his eyes.

Elijah nodded, "Just like Mama made 'em."

Doug slapped Elijah on the shoulder, "You are a sight for sore eyes, brother."

Elijah choked back the lump in his throat and blinked his burning eyes. Perhaps Doug didn't want to go home just yet, but Elijah determined he'd find a way to reunite him with Bonnie somehow.

After they'd rounded up all Doug's belongings and stepped into the hallway, Elijah looked left and right. "Now, is there some way to get out o' here without runnin' into that brazen saloon girl?"

Doug pointed to the bright red lips on Elijah's temple, "Looks like you already ran into her."

"What?" Elijah put his hand to his face, rubbed it, and then held out his hand to examine the red smudge. "Good grief! Why didn't ya tell me sooner?" He pulled a handkerchief from his pocket and wiped away the rouge.

Doug just tossed his head side to side and started toward the stairs.

"No wonder you kept lookin' at me like I was crazy," Elijah called after him and then caught up to him.

"No, the lip rouge only made it difficult to keep a straight face. The part 'bout you bein' crazy is just a simple fact," Doug quipped and eased his crutch onto the next step.

"Isn't there another way out o' here?" Elijah whispered.

"Not if I don't want to have to pay for another night. I've got to check out and turn in my key."

Elijah groaned and waited patiently for Doug to hobble down the stairs. He would have offered to help him, but knew that would be the wrong thing to do. The only way Doug would return home to Bonnie would be if he was convinced he wouldn't be a burden.

Once they reached the bottom of the stairs, Elijah put a hand on Doug's shoulder, "I'll meet ya outside."

Doug's beard jiggled on his chest with his laugh. His charcoal eyes followed Elijah around the room as he darted past people and dodged tables in his frantic sprint from the tavern.

Doug sighed with a shake of his head and came to stand before the bartender. He tossed his key on the counter. "I'll be checkin' out now."

"All right," the man took the key. "Good evenin' to ya, sir."

As Doug turned to leave, he heard Lilly, the saloon girl, murmur, "Glad to be rid of 'im. There was no seducin' that one."

"Would you 've really wanted to?" the bartender quipped sarcastically.

Lilly broke into giggles, "No, I guess not!"

Doug clenched his teeth and exited the tavern. "My horse is at the livery," he pointed across the street.

The men retrieved the horse and Doug rode while Elijah walked alongside him back to Elijah's place. It had already grown dark, but the moon shone bright in the crisp evening air, lighting their way.

When they arrived, Elijah motioned for Doug to have a seat at the table while he fired up the stove and made them some ham and eggs.

"You've done a lot of work around here," Doug noted, his eyes surveying the cabin.

"Been workin' hard. The place was run over by weeds when I got home and the roof had to be replaced."

"When did you get home?" Doug asked, drumming his fingers on the kitchen table.

"June," Elijah replied.

"And you still haven't found a wife yet?" Doug's eyebrows rose.

"Haven't had time." Elijah raised the wick on the lamp that sat in the center of his kitchen table, illuminating the room a little brighter.

"What about the Harris girl you were so sweet on?"

"Married," Elijah turned back to the stove, scooped up a plate of ham and eggs for Doug, and set them in front of him.

Doug wasted no time and began to eat. After a few bites, he leaned back in his chair. "So, how did ya find me, anyway?"

"The ring," Elijah pointed to Doug's hand and then turned back to the stove to fill his own plate. "A friend saw you wearin' it and told me."

"A friend?"

"Yeah, a friend. I do have other friends besides you, ya know," Elijah said as he placed a bowl of ham and eggs on the table.

"I know. It's just that I made a special effort to steer clear o' anyone you knew."

Elijah gave him a perturbed expression and tossed his plate noisily on the table. It still aggravated him to know that Doug had been hanging around town avoiding him and Bonnie. "Well, you don't know her so you wouldn't think to hide from 'er." Elijah sat down at the table across from Doug.

"Her?" Doug raised a single accusing eyebrow, "So you haven't been too busy after all?"

Elijah rolled his eyes, "It's not like that. She's the daughter of a man I met when I was a guard at Rock Island prison. He asked me to keep an eye on 'er while she's up here teachin' school." He put a forkful of ham and eggs in his mouth.

"Oh, got yourself a pretty little school teacher to watch over and protect? Sounds like a gratifyin' task," Doug teased.

"What makes you think she's pretty? She could look like a buck-toothed beaver."

"If she looked like a buck-toothed beaver, your cheeks wouldn't be blushin' such a lovely shade o' pink," Doug countered dryly, waving his fork in Elijah's direction. "Besides, I think I know who this school teacher is. Does she have wavy golden hair and big green eyes?"

"That would be her," Elijah replied.

"I should've known you'd attach yourself to the prettiest unmarried girl in town. Should've known to steer clear of her."

"I'm not attached to her," Elijah defended and poured himself a glass of water from the pitcher on the table.

"Oh, yes you are. You forget who you're talkin' to," Doug teased.

"Just drop it, Doug." Elijah retorted curtly. "Why don't we talk about somethin' more useful, like where you've been for almost three years?"

Doug's lips straightened into a line, "Here and there."

"Well, that sure clears it all up," Elijah retorted.

Doug only stared at him and then shoveled some eggs into his mouth.

"When did it happen?" Elijah gestured toward Doug's stump.

"Gettysburg. I was left for dead. Woke up several hours later and dragged myself to a house I'd seen when we'd marched into the area. The family that lived there took me in. They tried to care for my leg the best they could, but the gangrene set in and a local doctor sawed it off."

Elijah winced and wondered at how Doug could relate the encounter so emotionlessly.

"I stayed with the family 'til I healed over 'nough to leave. They were kind 'nough to give me these clothes and that ol' mare so I could be on my way. Since then I've just been driftin' here and there, mainly tryin' to stay out o' the way o' the fightin'.

"If you have no intention of goin' back to Bonnie, why did you come back to Knoxville?"

"Cause I wanted to see her, even if it was just through the window or when she went out to hang laundry. I had to know she was all right."

"Wouldn't you've wondered that sooner?" Elijah retorted, still irritated with his friend's indifference to Bonnie's suffering.

"I've been here before. I've checked on her every six months or so. Every other time, I've camped just outside o' town, but this time it was just too blasted cold. I thought I'd risk the tavern. Never figured on you havin' spies 'round town keepin' a lookout for me."

Elijah rolled his eyes and ladled more eggs onto each of their plates.

"I should've known when that schoolteacher batted her thick eyelashes at me that she was up to no good," Doug teased.

Elijah's face turned into an irritated frown, and he could feel the heat rising under his collar.

Doug laughed and slapped Elijah on the arm, "You are a jealous fool. You think a pretty little thing would be battin' her eyelashes at the likes o' me?"

"How did we get back to this subject?" Elijah grumbled.

"Because that's the way o' women. They get under our skin, and we just keep comin' back around to 'em until we get ourselves into a pickle – a pickle like I'm in right now." Doug's expression darkened, then he muttered more to himself than to Elijah, "I should've been more careful."

"No, it was time ya came home."

Doug groaned.

Elijah scratched his chin as he stared across the table at his friend. "I think I can help ya, but I need to know one thing first."

"What's that?" came Doug's cautious reply.

"If you were convinced that you wouldn't be a burden to Bonnie, would ya let me take ya home to her?"

"That would take a miracle," Doug muttered.

"Don't worry about how it would happen, just answer me. Would you go home if you were convinced you weren't gonna be a burden to Bonnie?"

Elijah noted the formidable man's eyes get misty. Doug tipped his head affirmatively then leaned his forehead in his hands with his elbows on the table.

Elijah stood up and placed a consoling hand on Doug's dejected shoulder, "Then leave the rest to me."

Chapter 19

The next morning, Elijah rose before sunup to search for the perfect piece of oak. He believed he had something in the woodshed that would work. He had his father's carpentry and blacksmith equipment in a workshop out back by the barn. He was glad his father was a bit of an inventor and had taught him some skills before he passed away. Elijah knew enough about using the tools that he believed he could make a wooden leg for Doug that would look almost as real as his other.

Before long, he'd found the piece of wood and went to the workshop to begin. He lit a couple lanterns and hooked the wood up to his father's lathe. He'd taken the opportunity to measure Doug's leg and boot size the night before while he slept. Elijah decided he'd get the process started and then show it to Doug later when he was ready to make the final fitting. He'd need Doug's cooperation to shape the prosthesis to the stump.

Elijah's mind set to planning the design while he shaped the wood into a tapered piece that could pass for a leg. When he finished, he removed it from the lathe, and held it up to admire it. Next, he sanded it smooth and carried it to the workbench. He would need to get the right fittings and shape something for Doug's leg to fit into to hold the prosthesis in place. Elijah rummaged around the workshop looking for the right bolts and screws, but realized he didn't have exactly what he needed. He'd have to go into town for that later.

He worked for several hours, losing track of time until he heard Doug hollering from the house, "Hey, you baited me out here by promising me flapjacks! Where are they?"

Elijah waved his hand out the door, "Sorry! Forgot! Be right there!" He set down the piece he'd been working on and left the workshop to return to the house and make Doug breakfast.

Elijah not only started cooking flapjacks, but he also put a large kettle of water on the stove to heat for Doug's bath. He'd need to get him cleaned up and make a plaster cast of his damaged leg so that he could create the best fit.

Doug sat down at the table and Elijah put a plate of food in front of him. "We'll eat, and then I'll get your bath ready so you can clean up." Elijah made himself a plate and sat down.

"Are you tryin' to tell me I stink?" Doug quipped.

Elijah's head bent to the side a little. He wasn't going to lie. Doug didn't smell too fresh, and he wanted him bathed before he went to work on his leg. "I need you to clean up so I can take some measurements and get a cast o' that leg."

"What for?"

"I've made quite a bit o' progress on a wooden leg for ya. It's out in the workshop, but I need to build something to fit it to your leg."

Doug raised an inquisitive eyebrow, "You really think that'll work?"

Elijah leaned back in his chair. "If I do it right, you should be able to walk around and no one'll be able to tell the difference except for a limp."

"Really?" Doug raked a hand through his bushy hair.

"I think I can do it," Elijah assured. "But I'll need your cooperation."

"You've got it," Doug dropped his hand to the table, letting it fall with a slap.

After breakfast, Elijah dragged the tub inside the house and filled it with well water.

"Now before I put the hot water in there, let's cut back some o' that hair so ya don't look so much like Angelina's wolf man."

"Oh, no you don't! I'm not givin' up my disguise until ya prove to me that that leg is gonna work," Doug protested, stroking his long black beard. He backed away from the tub and stood by the front window of the cabin.

"Well, at least let me cut your hair a bit and trim up the beard," Elijah propped his fist on his side.

"No. I know you. If I let you near me with scissors, you won't quit until I'm clean shaven."

"Come on, now. You know I'm not a liar. Just let me trim ya up a bit so I don't feel like I'm livin' with a wolf!"

"You promise?"

"Promise. I'll just cut your hair to your shoulders and trim back the unruliness of your beard a bit. Ya still won't be recognizable. Plus, where would you be goin'? You can just stay here until you're ready to go home."

"All right," Doug sighed and reluctantly sat in a chair at the kitchen table with his back to Elijah.

Before long, there was a mound of jet-black hair on Elijah's kitchen floor and an attractively groomed, but still bearded Doug sitting in a chair. Elijah went to his room, retrieved a hand mirror, and held it out in front of Doug's face. "What do ya think?"

"Hmmm.. not bad."

"And ya didn't trust me," Elijah teased. "Now, let's get you that bath." Elijah poured the hot boiling water from the stove into the tub. "Give me those clothes, and I'll wash 'em good. I'll get ya some o' mine to wear."

Elijah left the room to find clothes for Doug and when he returned, Doug was sitting in the steamy water scrubbing his back with a soapy brush.

"Feel good?" Elijah smiled.

"Heavenly," Doug replied, scrubbing under his arms.

Elijah smiled, "Well, take your time and enjoy it. Here's some clothes for ya." He set the long johns, pants, socks, and a flannel shirt on the kitchen table and went to the door. "I'm goin' back out to the workshop. I'll come back in later, and we'll make that cast."

~*~

After making the cast of Doug's leg and ascertaining all the items he would need to complete the project, Elijah left Doug at his house and rode into town. Normally, Elijah enjoyed walking to town, but today, he didn't want to waste any time. The sooner he got that artificial leg made, the sooner Doug could go home to Bonnie.

If everything went smoothly, he might even be able to get it done in time to take Doug to Bonnie's the next evening for Friday dinner. Elijah smiled as he thought of Bonnie's elated expression. He could just picture how she would react upon seeing her husband standing before her once more. He rode a little faster with the thought of it.

When Elijah reached the store, he went straight to the hardware section and rummaged through the screws, nuts and bolts, selecting those he'd need for the project. Next, he went to the boots, and selected a pair of knee high ones in Doug's size.

After finding the right pair, he scratched his beard and looked around the store. He needed something soft to line the prosthesis where it met Doug's leg or it would chafe. Elijah headed for the quilt section. As he felt the different quilts and blankets, searching for just the right consistency and thickness, Mr. Rivers came over carrying a quilt and hung it up on a rack near Elijah.

"That's an awfully nice quilt. Edna Forrester didn't make that did she?"

Mr. Rivers snorted and shook his head, "No, Edna didn't quilt this. Look at the fine pattern and the coordinated colors."

"Well, I thought she'd sure improved if it was hers." Elijah grinned. "Whose work is it, then?"

"The schoolteacher's mother made it for her."

"Why would Miss Stone part with a quilt her mama made her?"

"She didn't have the money for somethin' she wanted to buy, and this was the only thing she had that would cover the cost."

"What did Miss Stone need so bad that she'd trade somethin' like this for it?" Elijah stepped closer and examined the pattern.

"Well," Mr. Rivers drew closer to Elijah and whispered. "She swapped it for a coat."

"A coat? Miss Stone has a good coat. What did she need with another one?"

"Oh, it wasn't for her. It was a man's coat. Must be a small man, but it was black like that one over yonder," Mr. Rivers pointed toward a rack of garments.

Elijah's eyebrows narrowed, and then they rose in understanding. Freddy Todd had worn a coat like that Tuesday night when Elijah stopped by his house to talk to him and Harry. He'd pulled them aside and spoke with them about their misbehavior at school. He'd told them that Miss Stone had endured a hard life and that she was a good young woman and a fine teacher, deserving of far better than they'd been giving her. He let them know that he'd be awfully disappointed in them if they didn't start acting better for her. He'd be so disappointed that he wouldn't need their help on the farm the next summer like he had the last. The boys agreed to behave better and scurried off inside the house.

So Angelina traded her mama's quilt for a coat for Freddy Todd? Elijah smiled to himself, thinking that she was an angel in more ways than one.

"I'll take the quilt along with these things," Elijah lifted another soft blanket, set the boots and the hardware on top of it and carried the items to the counter.

"I hung onto the quilt for as long as I could. I wanted to give 'er time to come back and get it, but I could only wait so long," Mr. Rivers explained as he leaned his hands on the counter.

"Speakin' of Miss Stone, I'd rather you didn't mention to her that I bought the quilt," Elijah replied. "You think you can keep that to yourself?"

"Of course, I can," Mr. Rivers looked a bit offended. "What do you think I am? The town gossip?"

Elijah had to bite his lip to confine a smirk. Mr. Rivers told everyone just about everything he knew. Elijah hoped this time the merchant could keep his mouth shut, at least for a little while.

Elijah returned home around noon and other than milking his cows and tending to his animals, he spent the remainder of the day working on Doug's artificial leg. Friday he rose early and continued with the project. Around four o'clock Friday afternoon, he stepped proudly inside the house carrying the completed leg with a boot on the end of it.

Doug was sitting in a rocker near the fireplace reading a book. His eyebrows rose as he saw Elijah enter with the leg in his hands.

"Ready to try it on?" Elijah asked.

Elijah drew closer to where Doug sat and helped him fit the leg into place and strapped it on. Carefully, Doug rose to his feet. He shuffled forward a little, teetered, and Elijah took his arm. "It might take a bit of getting used to." Elijah shoved a coffee table out of Doug's way with his boot.

"Here," Elijah released him, "Can you stand there for a moment on your own?"

Doug shook his head positively and Elijah trotted off to the back bedroom. Quickly, he returned with a cane. "This was Pa's. Maybe you could use it for a while until ya get used to the leg."

Doug took it and carefully eased forward, then hobbled around the room. It wasn't as easy as Elijah had hoped it would be. "I know it will take some gettin' used to, but what do you think?"

Doug nodded, "I think maybe it'll work . . . eventually anyway."

"The great thing is that you can stand and walk around and no one would ever know you're missing a leg.

They'd just think you had a limp. But a limp is better than no leg, don't ya think?"

Doug agreed and then walked a few more steps.

"Better go easy on it at first; you don't want your leg to get sore." Elijah watched his friend shuffle from the fireplace to the kitchen and back. "So," Elijah rubbed his hands together excitedly. "How 'bout we clean you up and take ya home to Bonnie? She's got some fried chicken and apple pie waitin' for us tonight."

Doug shook his head negatively. "Not yet."

"Oh, come on, Doug! You'll get used to the leg. Why put off bein' with her any longer?"

"Not until I can get around like a man," Doug plopped down in the rocking chair once more and rubbed his leg.

Elijah tossed his hands in the air, "Suit yourself you stubborn ol' mule. I'm gonna go get cleaned up for dinner." He stomped off to the bedroom shaking his head.

After Elijah had changed clothes and headed toward the door to leave, Doug called out to him, "What time do ya usually start home?"

"Around nine o'clock," Elijah looked toward Doug who still sat in the rocker with a book open on his lap.

"I think I'd like to see Bonnie tonight."

"Great! Get ready and come along with me."

"No, I don't want to go to dinner with ya. I don't want her to see me yet, but I'd like to catch a glimpse of 'er. If I ride out later, do you think you can get her onto the front porch or at least by the front window after supper? Maybe around eight?"

Elijah bent his head in agreement, "All right. I'll do my best."

Chapter 20

Angelina started down the stairs. She'd finished grading tests earlier than she expected and decided to help Bonnie prepare the Friday night supper. Her mind kept returning to Elijah Willoughby. He would be coming to dinner that night, and she was looking forward to seeing him again.

As she thought about him and the week she'd had, she smiled, anxious to tell him how well the last few days had gone. She'd tried some new creative ideas for occupying her class, and they seemed to be responding. She congratulated herself, happy that she hadn't had to resort to belting out *Dixie*. No one had shot a pea at her since Tuesday, and there had been no critters in her lunch pail. She felt proud of her resourcefulness in bringing the class under control.

She recognized the change as an answer to her prayer. Even with the new methods, their shift in behavior was nothing short of a miracle. She was actually starting to like them, even beginning to see good qualities in the Todd brothers. She'd been praying for each child by name, picturing them in her mind as she did so. Love was gradually conquering the fear in her heart and giving her power to teach in a way that got through to her students.

Most of all, Angelina couldn't wait to ask Elijah about the one-legged man and find out why he had a ring like his.

As Angelina approached the closed kitchen door, she stopped, put her hand to the door and started to push, but paused when she heard familiar voices on the other side.

"So, when do you plan to officially start courtin' our Angelina?" Bonnie wiped her hands on her apron and reached for another potato to peel.

"What in blazes are you talkin' about, Bonnie?" came Elijah's irritated retort.

Angelina's heart drummed forcefully. She moved her hand away from the door and stepped aside, then leaned her back against the wall and listened intently.

"It's obvious you care for 'er," Bonnie coaxed.

"I care for 'er, but not in that way," he replied.

"Oh, stop denyin' it, 'Lijah; we all see it," Bonnie insisted.

"You're seein' what you want to see 'cause you don't understand."

"What don't I understand?"

"I – I let her get hurt durin' the war, and I won't let that happen again. I'm just tryin' to protect her and make sure she's safe. That's all – just makin' up for things. Just makin' sure she has what she needs and that people treat her right."

"What she needs is a good man," Bonnie argued.

"Well it won't be me."

Angelina felt hot tears stinging her eyes, and she swiped away one that trickled down her overheated cheek. Swiftly she turned on her heels, rushed through the parlor, and up the stairs to her room. She felt as if Elijah had punched her in the stomach. Here she'd finally begun to believe that he cared for her. Her mind replayed the afternoon she'd fainted, and his tender care of her. She thought of their walks together after school and the way he would touch her hand and look at her. Had she misread him so completely?

Now, to discover that he only saw her as a child to be protected left her feeling deflated. All this time, even though she'd denied her feelings to Bonnie and Edna, she'd hoped there was something more. Now she knew there wasn't. He only spent time with her out of guilt. She flopped down on her bed and buried her head in her pillow.

His words ran through her mind *Just makin' sure she has what she needs and that people treat her right.* It suddenly dawned on her that the reason her class had behaved that week was because Elijah Willoughby had spoken to the Todd boys! Hurt transformed into indignation. It wasn't her teaching methods at all! It was that big oaf interfering in her affairs! What right did he have? She'd specifically told him not to speak to the boys. The more she thought about it, the angrier she became.

"But you do care for her," Bonnie prodded Elijah as she leaned against the kitchen counter.

"Of course, I care for her. I just said I did," he shot her an impatient glare.

"And she is beautiful."

"Of course, she's beautiful," he barked.

"And you'd love to court her."

"Bonnie, it doesn't matter whether I want to court her or not. I couldn't if I wanted to."

"Why? It's very simple. You're practically courtin' her already. You just say . . ."

Elijah turned toward Bonnie, squaring his broad shoulders. "Her father asked me to keep an eye on 'er and see that she comes home safe. She's supposed to marry some fella back home," Elijah blurted. He hadn't meant to say it. Instantly he felt guilty for it. He had no right to be spreading rumors about Angelina's private life, but he was tired of Bonnie's relentless matchmaking. Her needling pricked his heart and left him feeling helpless. And Elijah Willoughby couldn't stand to feel helpless. He was the kind of man who made things happen, who stepped into the fray and protected the defenseless or devised a means to make hopeless situations work. But he couldn't this time. No, Everett wanted Angelina to go home to marry this Paul fellow. His own feelings for the girl couldn't distract him.

"Are you certain about that? She's never said a word about him," Bonnie's eyebrows rose in surprised doubt.

"Well, it's true. Maybe she just didn't want you meddlin' in her affairs!"

Bonnie clamped her mouth shut, her lips straightening into a thin line. She turned back to peeling her potatoes and worked alongside him in silence.

Elijah felt bad for barking at his friend that way, but she was like a dog gnawin' on your favorite shoe. Ever since they'd been teenagers and she tagged along with him and Doug, she'd always managed to needle him just where he was most sensitive. He supposed he had it coming to him for all the times he'd teased his little sister.

Several long awkward moments passed between them.

"I'm sorry I snapped at ya," Elijah's deep voice whispered as his arms lengthened in strokes, peeling the carrots.

Bonnie's eyes turned to him apologetically, "I'm sorry I meddled."

~*~

"Angelina, supper's ready," Dot called from the other side of Angelina's door.

"I'm not feelin' well. I'll not be down," Angelina replied.

"Are you sure? Would you like me to save you a plate?" Dot offered.

"I suppose so. Maybe I'll feel like eatin' later."

Everyone sat around the table when Dot entered the dining room. "Angelina's feelin' poorly so she won't be comin' to dinner. It was probably that mutton we had last night. I told you, Bonnie, that there was an odd taste to that mutton."

"The mutton was fine, Dot," Lucille interjected, rolling her eyes.

"I thought it was delicious," Edna added.

"Well, some people just can't handle mutton, and Angelina must be one of 'em 'cause she's up there in her sick bed just wastin' away without supper, poor girl."

Elijah rose to his feet, "Maybe I should go get Doc Miller?"

"Did she say she needed a doctor?" Bonnie asked Dot.

"No, no, but I didn't think to ask her."

"Just sit back down, Elijah, and enjoy your dinner," Bonnie put a hand on Elijah's arm. "I'll go up and check on her."

Elijah remained standing until Bonnie left the room. When he heard her footsteps on the stairs, he reluctantly took his seat.

Bonnie put her hand on the door, "Angelina, dear, do we need to fetch you a doctor?"

"No, I'm not that ill. I just feel a little queasy and tired and dare not eat."

"Are you certain? Elijah's offered to fetch Doc Miller if you think you need a tonic or somethin'."

"No, no, don't send for the doctor. I'll be fine. I might come down a little later and eat somethin'."

"Very well. I'll save you a plate."

"Thank you."

"She doesn't want the doctor. She's just feelin' queasy and tired. Those children have probably run her ragged again," Bonnie explained as she walked around the dining room table and took her chair.

"She said that they've been better lately. Said they'd turned into regular little angels all of a sudden," Edna explained.

Elijah smiled, happy that he could make something better for Angelina.

~*~

Everyone sat around the parlor after dinner. Edna and Dot worked on a quilt while Lucille and Thelma cross-stitched. Bonnie sat relaxing by the fire, unwinding after the big dinner she had prepared, while Elijah read the newspaper. When the grandfather clock chimed eight, Elijah lowered his paper a little, looking over the top of it at

Bonnie. He folded the paper neatly and set it on the table in front of him.

"Bonnie, would you feel like steppin' out on the front porch with me? I feel like a little air."

Bonnie leaned her hands on the chair, pushed herself up and joined him. He opened the door for her and then stepped out on the porch. Elijah looked around trying to spot Doug, but didn't see anyone. He hoped he was out there somewhere.

He leaned on the porch railing and motioned for her to join him. When she came to stand beside him, leaning her hand on the rail, he asked, "So, how are things going for you? Do you have everything you need?"

"Things are good," Bonnie nodded.

"You seem to have a full house these days."

"Yes, business has been good," she agreed.

"What about the house? Is there anythin' around here that needs fixin'?"

"Not that I know of," she shook her head as she leaned her elbow on the porch rail.

"What about the roof, is it holdin'?"

"It's fine."

"You know I'm happy to make any repairs you need," he assured.

Bonnie put a hand on Elijah's arm, "I know that I can always count on you. Everythin's in good order, really."

"You'd tell me if you needed help now wouldn't you?"

"Of course, I would." Bonnie pushed a strand of hair back.

"'Cause I'm here to help."

"I know," she smiled and patted his arm.

He pointed toward the shed. "How do you stand on firewood? You looked a little low."

211

"I suppose I could always use a little more," she smiled with a shrug.

"All right, before I leave tonight, I'll make sure your firewood's stocked. Anything else?"

"Can't think of anything. You really are a sweet one, 'Lijah," Bonnie stood on her tip toes and kissed his cheek. "Thank you for lookin' out for me," she patted his hand and then rubbed her arms. "It's chilly out here. I think I'll go back inside now."

Elijah hoped their short conversation on the porch had given Doug enough time to catch a glimpse of his wife. He could only imagine how difficult it would be not to be able to touch or speak to the woman he loved. At the thought, he felt a twinge of disappointment that Angelina hadn't come down to dinner.

~*~

Angelina drifted off to sleep and when she awakened, the sun had set. She wasn't sure of the time, but her stomach growled and grumbled, unhappy that her pride had denied it of one of Bonnie's Friday night feasts.

She could still smell the lingering meaty aroma of chicken and gravy, sweetened with the scent of spiced apple pie. She sat up in bed and adjusted the wick on her lamp to bring more light into the room. She slipped her feet into her shoes and went to the mirror that hung on the wall above her dresser. Yawning, she stared at her reflection. She still wore her green dress, but her hair had started to come loose from its bun. She removed the pins and let it cascade around her shoulders. She fluffed it a little. Angelina disliked wearing her hair in a bun, but it was part of her efforts to look older and more authoritative for her students.

She couldn't hear voices or noises from downstairs, so she assumed by this time of the evening everyone would have retired. She quietly opened her door, so as not to disturb anyone and carried her lamp into the hall to light her way. As she started down the stairs, she could see the light streaming from the parlor lamps and a fire glowing in the hearth. Evidently, it wasn't as late as she thought. Bonnie was probably still in the kitchen making her shopping list for the next day.

As she passed a window at the front of the house, she caught a glimpse of a shadowy figure standing on the lawn, leaning against a tree by the woodshed. Frightened, Angelina stepped backwards away from the window. She extinguished her lamp and set it on a nearby table as her mind darted back to another dark evening, another shadowy figure. Her hands grew clammy as the dreaded memory replayed upon the stage of her mind.

When she heard footsteps tromping up the porch steps, she froze, her heart palpitating at an anxious rate. The doorknob jiggled ominously, and she could hear the heavy weight of a man's shoulder thump against the door. Coming to her senses, she stepped back into the shadows. The door flew open, and a cold burst of wind entered along with a man carrying an armful of wood. Quickly he stepped in and kicked the door shut with his boot.

"Angelina," he whispered, his eyes widening in surprise as they met hers.

"Elijah," she choked, her pulse racing, and her palms perspiring even more. She'd assumed he'd left. *Figures,* she thought to herself. Figures she'd do without supper all evening long and then be forced to face him alone now.

He tromped toward the fireplace. "You feelin' better?" he inquired as he set the armful of wood down beside the hearth.

She stepped into the parlor, drawing closer to him so that no one would be awakened by their conversation.

"Yes, I'm feeling better."

He turned around and swiped his hands together several times to eliminate the stray particles of bark and moss.

"You look like you've got a little color to your cheeks," he smiled. His gaze traveled over her face and shoulders, and she knew he was looking at her hair. She shouldn't have taken it down.

Why did he have to look at her like that? Why did he have to make her feel this way? He had absolutely no intentions toward her, yet his eyes certainly conveyed intentions. Was she that inept at understanding men? The more his eyes twinkled in the firelight and the more the grin played upon his lips, the more his gaze sent her insides quivering, and the angrier Angelina became.

"How was your week?" he inquired.

"Good," came her curt reply.

He raised a single eyebrow at her hostile delivery of the word.

"Then again, you already knew that," she snipped.

His eyebrows lowered questioningly at her obvious irritation.

"Don't act as if you don't know what I mean, Mr. Willoughby. You obviously spoke to the Todd boys."

Elijah tossed his palms in the air, "They needed it."

"I think that was for me to decide." She stared at him like a terrier defending its territory.

214

"How long did you intend to let them run over you?" he countered.

"I don't need you to look out for me, Mr. Willoughby," she barked.

"Well, it sure appears you need someone lookin' after ya," he insisted, a hint of amusement still evident in his eyes.

Angelina drew closer to the large man and lowered her voice, "You've done enough now. You've made up for your hesitancy that summer night. Not that you needed to. Release your guilt in this matter, sir. You are free to move on to a woman whom you truly injured during the war. I'm certain there are plenty who are more deserving of your restitution than I – women whose husbands, sons, or fathers didn't return home because of you. I'm sure they could use your protection much more than I!"

Angelina watched the mirthful twinkle and amused grin drain from Elijah's countenance and a sorrowful frown replace them. For an instant, she felt a twinge of guilt at bruising him with her cutting words.

"I'm sorry. That was horribly cruel of me."

"Yes, it was," he muttered.

"I am sorry. After all, war is war," she apologized but did not give him time to reply before her voice grew more insistent. "All I want to know is what makes me so special? Surely, there are dozens of women more worthy of your constant protection than I? You don't owe me anything. You never did. You especially don't now."

Suddenly, he caught her arm, which waved in front of him. He held it securely at the wrist in a way that restricted her movement but did not cause discomfort.

"What're you doin'?" she hissed as he stepped closer to her, still holding her wrist firmly in his grip. His eyes softened, and his free hand lifted to her face, cupping her cheek softly.

"What're you doin'?" she repeated in a whisper. His hand, which held her wrist, moved to her fingers, lacing his strong hand with hers as he caressed her slender fingers. He lifted her hand to his lips, applying a tender kiss to her wrist, her palm; then lowered it to his chest, holding it securely against him. The rhythmic beating of his heart beneath her palm and the rise and fall of his chest as he breathed assured her that this was no dream. Her insides quivered uncontrollably, her body betraying her with a shiver that she knew he felt.

Angelina's mind swirled trying to comprehend what was happening. She understood very little except one thing. Elijah Willoughby was real, and for the next few blissful moments, he would be hers.

His hand gently caressed her cheek, his fingertips stroking the softness of her blonde locks, his gaze intent upon her. He stepped closer, his eyes lingering upon her mouth as his slowly lowered to hers. When his lips met hers tenderly, Angelina knew that her dreams had not begun to prepare her for the rapture of the experience. She felt his arm release her hand and slip warmly around her waist, tugging her closer to his solid, muscular form. Despite her resolution to deny his protection, she felt incredibly safe in being so near him.

Her hands, having a mind of their own, slipped to his sturdy shoulders, spanning the breadth of them. She marveled at his strength. It was one thing to observe his manly frame as it moved about a room, but to hold it in her arms, to feel the power of him beneath her hands, encircling her in his arms, thrilled her beyond measure. While Jacobsen had taught her to fear such strength in a man, Elijah's gentle touch and warm, lingering kisses taught her that there was nothing to fear. In him, there was a quiet, protective strength, a gentle power that only existed to serve her, to fill her wants, to see to her needs, and to satisfy her desires.

She let her hands slide around his neck, her fingertips playing with his thick, dark hair. He broke from her momentarily, his stormy eyes staring into hers. Such a charge of emotion emanated from them that Angelina caught her breath, surprised by the adoration there. She berated herself for having fussed at him for protecting her, for caring about her. Even though his earlier words to Bonnie had denied it, his eyes conveyed that there was something much stronger than friendship between them.

Completely enraptured by the knowledge that she held the object of her affections, she let her palms slip to his soft bearded cheeks, feeling the warmth of them beneath her hands, and satisfying her curiosity regarding the strength of his jaw, the softness of his beard, the warmth of his skin. When he kissed her again, Angelina felt as if his arms and lips were making promises to her: promises of forever, of a life together, of a heavenly future. He may not have verbalized them with words, but Angelina's heart understood and accepted them like a sweet melody resonating from the smooth strains of a rare violin. In Elijah's arms she felt safe, whole, healed.

But the sweet refrain came to a sudden and screeching halt when Bonnie's voice and footsteps came from the hall toward the parlor.

"Elijah, would you like another cup of - " she broke mid-sentence, observing the couple with wide-eyed wonderment. Quickly, Angelina stepped out of Elijah's arms. She closed her eyes, her cheeks flushing vermilion.

"Oh, excuse me," Bonnie apologized.

"I – I just came down for," Angelina started, but then her voice trailed off, realizing that any attempt at an explanation would be useless.

"I, I best be goin'," Elijah reached to the table and grabbed his hat. "Good night, Angelina," he inclined his head in her direction then stepped around her awkwardly. "Bonnie," he acknowledged the proprietress with a tip of his brow and replaced his hat. Then he was gone.

Mustering her wits, Angelina swiftly stepped to the other side of Bonnie and started toward the kitchen, "I hope there's some food left. I'm starvin'."

Bonnie looked toward the door where Elijah had exited, put her hands to her hips and shifted her gaze back to Angelina who had now opened the door to the kitchen and stepped inside. "If *that* didn't satisfy your hunger, I don't know what will!" Bonnie whispered under her breath with a shake of her head and a set of raised eyebrows.

While curiosity raged through her mind, Bonnie decided the polite thing to do would be to lock up and go to bed without meddling further in her tenant's affairs. She'd already robbed the poor girl of what appeared to be a thoroughly thrilling encounter.

Chapter 21

Elijah climbed atop his horse and started down Bonnie's street on his way home. Just as he started to turn onto Main Street, he met Doug sitting on his gray mare.

"Did you get to see her?" Elijah inquired as Doug turned his horse around.

"I did. She's more beautiful than ever," Doug's soft answer seemed to pierce the still night air.

"I didn't see you around, so I hoped that when we stepped out on the front porch that you were there somewhere."

"I've gotten pretty good at spyin', I'm afraid." Doug brought his horse alongside Elijah's.

"It's time you went home, Doug. Bonnie needs you."

"She looks to be managin' well enough. I heard what she told you – that her business is doin' well. She doesn't need me hobblin' in and makin' a mess o' things."

Elijah shook his head in frustration, "You don't know a thing about women, do you?"

"You're one to be talkin'! You're not makin' any steps toward gettin' a wife for yourself."

"Oh, I've taken steps, all right," Elijah shook his head positively and raised a single knowing eyebrow. "Maybe too many of 'em."

"What's that supposed to mean?"

"Nothin'" Elijah shrugged off Doug's question.

"Oh, no, you don't. No secrets between blood brothers," Doug insisted.

"Yeah, now you remember the whole blood brother thing when it suits your curiosity. You sure didn't remember that promise when you were off hidin' from everybody."

"Don't go changin' the subject. This has to do with you and those steps you've been takin' toward getting hitched. Let's see," Doug rubbed his beard, his whole body swaying with the gait of the old mare. "Wouldn't happen to have anythin' to do with that pretty little school teacher, would it?"

Elijah was glad it was dark so that Doug couldn't see his face turn crimson. "She's promised to another."

"Promised to another?" Doug's quick retort betrayed his surprise.

"Some fella back in Georgia. His name's Paul," Elijah explained.

"Looks to me that her lips were makin' promises to you this evenin'," Doug's words lilted with humored accusation.

Elijah wondered if Doug could see his red-hot face glowing like an ember in the night. The sensations of the encounter were still fresh in his memory. Elijah could still taste Angelina's kiss on his lips and still catch the sweet fragrance of her hair clinging to his clothes. "I don't know what you're talkin' about," he lied.

"Mmmm, mmmm, mmmm," Doug's head swiveled side to side. "We do have a long way to go before we're honest with one 'nother like blood brothers ought 'o be."

"So you were still lookin' through the window?"

"Uhhh hmmm," Doug's baritone affirmation held a melodious quality.

"She got to fussin' at me about interferin' in her affairs and then her nose got all scrunched up, lookin' at me like I was crazy with those blonde curls tossed about her shoulders. The only thing I could think about was kissin' her."

Doug released a belly laugh, "Yep, you're bit."

"You're right about that one. I am bit," Elijah grumbled. "Only problem is she's not available."

"I don't know about you, but if I had a girl as pretty as her promised to me, I wouldn't be back in Georgia, lettin' her traipse around Tennessee and get caught by someone else. Nope, I wouldn't let a filly like that out o' my sight."

"You wouldn't – huh?"

"I sure wouldn't. Somethin' doesn't add up," Doug deduced as if it were a plain scientific fact.

"Then why haven't you come home to Bonnie?"

"That's different," Doug's words spilled angrily from his lips like a guard dog's growl.

"It isn't different. What would you do if Bonnie gave up on ya and found herself another man? Would ya stand by and let him hold her, kiss her, marry her . . ."

"That's enough," Doug's words clipped the air as he pressed his palm to his ears.

Elijah couldn't help chuckling to himself, but he gave his friend a few minutes to simmer down. Then his voice lowered to a calm, rational intonation, "All I'm sayin' is that maybe this Paul fella has his reasons for givin' Angelina some time. So the question is, is it right for me to pursue 'er when she's promised to somebody else?"

Doug didn't answer, but by the light of the moon, Elijah could see the scowl on his friend's face. Elijah knew he'd hit a nerve; he just hoped it was the one that would spur Doug into action. Unfortunately, he was no closer to answers of his own.

~*~

As the cock crowed in the distance, Elijah rolled over in his bed, groaning. Morning came too soon. It seemed he'd barely found sleep before it was time to get up and milk the cows. He'd lain there most of the night thinking about Angelina. One minute he'd be smiling in the darkness, and the next he'd feel guilty for going against Everett's wishes.

Then, he'd remember her angelic face, her long hair spilling around her shoulders. He put his finger to his mouth, still remembering the sensation of her rose petal lips to his own. She'd felt so warm and soft in his arms and when she'd put her hands to his cheeks, it took everything he could muster to contain his emotions.

Elijah raked his hands through his hair and released a sigh as he lay there staring at the rafters. He'd promised to protect her, to help her get over the past. Who was to say kissing her didn't help her do that? After all, he rationalized, she needed to learn that all men weren't like Jacobsen, that what could be between a man and a woman could be something beautiful. But was he really defending her? He certainly wasn't protecting her from himself!

Once again, the cock crowed, and Elijah grumbled, rolled over and pounded his fist into his feather pillow. He scrunched his eyes closed and raked a hand through his tousled hair, then sat up in bed. He rubbed his aching head and put his feet to the floor.

Groggily, he put on his overalls, stepped into his boots and grabbed his coat. With the early morning rays barely visible on the horizon, he went to the stable to begin milking.

As exhausted as he felt, he still whistled as he worked, still caught himself smiling, thinking of Angelina. When he carried the two steaming pails of milk inside the house, he met Doug who was standing on his new leg by the stove.

"Cookin' breakfast for us this mornin'?" Elijah greeted jovially.

"Yep, figured I'd make myself useful for a change."

Elijah came closer and poked his nose over his friend's shoulders. "Eggs and bacon. Smells good!"

"Figured I couldn't mess 'em up too bad," Doug flipped over a fried egg and shifted some bacon in the pan.

"Thanks, I could get used to havin' someone 'round to cook my breakfast!"

"Well, don't get too used to it unless you aim on bringin' that pretty little school teacher home to cook for ya."

"Why? You goin' somewhere?" Elijah asked as he moved toward the table.

"I might," Doug shrugged.

"No more roamin' about, Doug. You've got only two choices now. Stay here or go home to Bonnie."

"Aren't you the bossy one? What right do ya have to tell me where I can go or to set my choices before me?" The expression in Doug's words was still that of witty banter.

"'Cause you can't get away from me. I can outrun your old gray mare on foot!" Elijah laughed.

"Now don't go besmirchin' my horse. She's served me well," Doug smiled, turned around and placed two plates of food on the table.

He leaned his hand on the chair and carefully pulled it out for himself and sat down.

"You're gettin' pretty good on that thing," Elijah pointed to Doug's artificial appendage.

"Thanks," Doug accepted the compliment, reached for a fork and gestured for Elijah to offer a blessing on the food.

After the prayer, Doug watched Elijah dig into his meal.

Elijah ate so ravenously, he didn't notice that Doug never touched his food. Finally, his eyes went from Doug's face to his full plate and back. "What's wrong?"

"Nothin', I've just been thinkin' about your school teacher." He leaned back watching Elijah carefully.

"Oh no, ya don't. Keep your mind on your own woman!" Elijah warned, his voice rising slightly.

"I wasn't thinkin' on her that way, you jealous ninny!" Doug rolled his charcoal eyes and tugged at his beard. "I was just wonderin' who told ya she was promised to another."

"Her father said he wanted me to help her face the past so she could go home to marry the man she loved – meanin' Paul."

"But, did he actually use the word *promised*?" Doug asked thoughtfully.

"No, I guess not."

"Then I don't think you've got anythin' to worry about. Sounds like she's fair game to me. I mean, possession is nine-tenths o' the law. And you most definitely had her in your possession last night," Doug reasoned, a smirk wrinkling the laugh lines around his eyes.

"If that's true, then you better get to possessin' your own woman!"

Doug sighed, "Can you not hold a conversation without needlin' me about Bonnie?"

"All right, all right," Elijah set down his fork and knife, letting them clang noisily against his plate.

"I mean, from where I was standin' it looks like she's quite taken with you. Do you really think a woman could respond to you like that and not care somethin' for ya? Or is there more to this than you're tellin' me? What's the real story between you two?"

Elijah stared at his plate, lifted his fork and swirled it around in his food. "It's a long story," he sighed.

"I've got nothin' but time," Doug leaned back in his chair and folded his arms, waiting for Elijah to explain.

Elijah looked up at him and then hung his head. He thought he'd told this story for the last time when he'd apologized to Angelina, but here Doug wanted him to relive it once more.

"I was in Georgia, summer last. My captain asked me to come along with 'im and scout out a location for our troops. We came upon the Stone farm and commandeered it. It was just the mother and the four children – the oldest of which was Angelina. She was grown, really – beautiful, carefree — or at least she was when Captain Jacobsen wasn't around. Jacobsen was the meanest, lowest. . ." Elijah grimaced distastefully and struggled to find a word that aptly described Jacobsen's reprehensible character.

"Vile one - eh?" Doug chimed in.

"Yeah, vile," Elijah nodded. "He kept eyein' poor Angelina, sayin' crude things. He even grabbed her once, and I had to get 'im off her. Of course, he turned on me and commanded that I remember my rank and such."

"Scum," Doug growled.

"It gets worse," Elijah ran a hand through his hair and then let his head lean against his fist. He felt sick to his stomach every time he thought of it. His finger traced along a crack in the table. "I woke up that night and Jacobsen was gone. I was so bone tired from marchin' and fightin' – never sleepin' in a real bed – that I was lazy and decided he'd probably just taken a trip to the outhouse, especially with all he'd been drinkin' that night. I laid there for a while until this panic seized upon me, and I had this terrible feelin' that Angelina could be in danger. I hopped out of bed, shoved my feet in my boots and ran outside. It was dark 'cause it had been overcast. I stood there strainin' to listen when I heard muffled cries. I went in the direction I thought they were comin' from and it led me to the barn. Just as I stood in the barn doorway, the clouds rolled away from the moon and I saw it." Elijah put his hands over his eyes, rubbing them as if by doing so, he could rub away the memories.

"What happened? Did he . . ." Doug whispered.

"Jacobsen was on top of her. I didn't think." Elijah rose to his feet and paced a step or two. Going through the motions with his arms, he explained what he did next, "I ripped a loose board from the barn and chargin' toward him, I reared back and slammed the two-by-four into his sorry head. He toppled into the hay and lay there still and lifeless."

"Good for you!" Doug shook a triumphant fist in the air.

"And then I saw her," he pointed to the floor in front of him, vividly remembering the scene as if it were happening again. "Her face was beat so bad, I could hardly believe it was the same sweet girl I'd talked with earlier in the day. He'd torn her nightgown to shreds. I closed my eyes. I couldn't stand to see her beaten that way. Not to mention her body was exposed, and no gentleman could stand there and watch."

Doug let out a mournful expulsion of air, "Poor, poor girl." He shook his head piteously. Then his eyes lifted toward Elijah who stood there limp and defeated, as he had felt that night. "Did he? Had she indeed been . . .?" Doug stammered.

Elijah looked up at his friend and knew what he was trying to ask. Had the violation been complete? Elijah shook his head negatively, "I don't think so, not from the looks o' things." He sighed, "But her face was bruised so bad, her lip cut, bruises on her neck. To think what he must have done to cause all that . . . To think of how she must have fought 'im with every ounce of energy she had . . . it just breaks my heart." Elijah pressed the heels of his hands to his eyes.

He turned his back to Doug, not wanting him to see his emotional state. "I couldn't find a blanket to throw over her, and I hadn't taken time to get my shirt. So I just stared at the ground and came toward her offerin' to help. She gathered her shredded gown, clutchin' it to her throat and commanded me to stay back. She tried to stand, but then I could tell she was gonna faint, so I rushed to her, caught her and carried her back inside the house."

"Of course her mother was heartbroken and her brother, Cal. Well, he was madder than a hornet. He went out to the barn and shot Jacobsen right through the head. He probably would 've shot me too if Angelina hadn't protested." Elijah sat back down at the table and paused in his telling of the story.

"What did you do next? Did you stay?" Doug whispered.

"No, Cal put his gun on me and ordered me to leave. I gathered my things, told Angelina I was sorry and pressed my ring into her hand. It was the only thing I could think to do to let her know that I cared what happened to her – that I wasn't the likes of Jacobsen – that there were decent men in the world."

"So that's how she recognized the ring," Doug pointed to the ring on Elijah's hand. "But you're wearing it now."

"She gave it back to me. I felt so bad about not gettin' up and helpin' her sooner that I apologized to her a few days ago. She gave me the ring back and insisted she didn't hold it against me. She didn't want me feelin' obligated to her."

"But you do," Doug observed.

"Of course, I do," Elijah let his hands fall to the table, and he swirled the ring around his finger.

"So is that what you think last night was about? You feelin' obligated and her feelin' grateful?"

Elijah's eyes widened as he met his friend's gaze. Doug had nailed it better than he could've himself. He nodded affirmatively, "Yeah, I think so . . . maybe."

"You really think that a girl who's been through the nightmare that she's been through would be so willin' in her kisses – just because she's grateful?" Doug prodded.

"I don't know," Elijah tossed his head side to side. He didn't feel like he knew anything these days.

"Has a woman ever responded to you like that?"

Elijah raised his eyebrows as he shook his head negatively, "No."

"Maybe she doesn't love this other fella like her Daddy thinks. Maybe she loves you." Doug pointed across the table at Elijah.

"I think we might be stretchin' things a bit here now, Doug," Elijah tugged his collar nervously. "Love's a big word."

"I think ya've got to ask yourself whether you love her, whether you'd marry her if you could. If the answer to those two questions is yes, then you need to find out how she feels about Paul."

"And how Everett would feel about me courtin' her," Elijah added somberly.

As the day progressed and Elijah went through his daily tasks, he pictured Angelina working beside him, imagined her cooking in his kitchen, setting his table, and eating with him. That night as he rested by the fire after Doug had gone to bed, he imagined her snuggled up with him by the hearth, the flame flickering in her meadow green eyes.

What kind of mess had he gotten himself into? He didn't know what to do next. Elijah only knew one thing — he wanted Angelina Stone for his own. The question was could he have her?

Chapter 22

Each afternoon as Angelina stepped from the schoolhouse, she expected Elijah to be there, but he never came. Two weeks passed with Elijah occupying every free moment of her thoughts. She kept seeing his stormy blue eyes and reliving the thrilling sensation of his lips to hers. Just thinking about him sent her heart fluttering.

The Thursday night before Elijah would make his next visit to Bonnie's, Angelina lay in her bed wondering about how she should react in seeing him again. Her mind replayed the conversation she overheard between Elijah and Bonnie two weeks prior. Her heart told her that he cared for her. She'd sensed it in his touch. She put a finger to her lips, remembering his kiss. However, could she trust herself? What did she know of men anyway? Even if he did care for her, he might not be able to deal with her past. It had been two weeks since she'd seen him and with his absence, she questioned the wisdom of her involvement with him.

She rolled over on her side and punched her pillow. What if he couldn't get over what happened – seeing her attacked by Jacobsen – knowing he'd violated her, feeling guilty that it was somehow his fault? Maybe he'd decided the past was too painful and messy.

A tear trickled from her eye and she brushed it away. Could she ever belong to any man after what she'd endured? Maybe Elijah was right to stay away from her. Could she ever completely give herself to him? Was it even possible to get over what Jacobsen had done to her? As much as she thought Elijah could heal her heart, what if even he didn't have the power to do so? It wouldn't be right to lead him to believe that she could love him and then not be able to.

Angelina shifted onto her back and pressed the heels of her hands to her eyes. She wished she could talk to Bonnie, but she didn't want Bonnie to know she'd been eavesdropping. Besides, confiding in Bonnie would mean speaking of that terrible night, and she had only felt confident enough to speak of that with her father. Over the last few days, she'd half hoped that Bonnie would bring up the subject of Elijah, but as much as the woman had teased her about him in the past, all teasing stopped after the night Elijah kissed her. Bonnie hadn't said a word about what she'd interrupted. Angelina found it rather odd and uncharacteristic of the boarding housekeeper not to tease her in some way about what she'd seen.

After nearly an hour of such thoughts, Angelina rolled over and willed herself to sleep.

~*~

Friday evening when Angelina stepped out of the schoolhouse, her eyes widened upon seeing the sight before her. It was her father, sitting atop his wagon, a broad smile spread across his face and there was a familiar sparkle in his eyes.

"Daddy!" she exclaimed and ran to greet him as he hopped down to meet her. "What are you doin' here?"

"Come to visit my little girl," he pulled her to him as she flung her arms about him and kissed his cheek.

"You came all the way up here just to visit me?" she looked up into the face that always gave her comfort.

"That and I did have a delivery to make."

"How long can you stay?"

"I got a room in town," his head gestured toward the street. "I'll be here through tomorrow."

"Oh! It's just so good to see you!" she hugged him once more. "How is everybody? How's Mama, Cal and the children?"

"Good, good, everyone's just spry as spring." He stepped back allowing her to approach the wagon.

He helped her up into the seat, climbed up beside her and jiggled the reins.

"How's school been goin'?" he asked.

"Better. It was pretty rough at first, but it's gettin' better."

"What happened?" Everett's eyes narrowed as he turned the team onto Main Street.

"Some o' the boys were a handful at first: shootin' peas, gettin' up in the middle o' class and walkin' around. You know, frogs and lizards in my lunch pail and hidin' my chalk."

"Oh boy, sounds like a rowdy bunch!"

"To put it mildly."

"How did you get them under control?" he looked toward her, letting the horses travel at an easy gait.

"I got a little more creative with my teachin' methods, and tried to show 'em that I care about 'em." Angelina thought of a conversation she'd had with Harry Todd that afternoon. He'd shown an interest in a story they'd read as a class, and he'd sat down by her at lunch to discuss it. They'd shared an insightful conversation.

"So that helped settle 'em down?" Everett scratched his head.

"Well," she hesitated. "That and one of the men in town took it upon himself to give the two Todd boys a talkin' to. I didn't want 'im to. I asked 'im specifically not to, but he did it anyway."

"You wanted to handle it yourself," Everett observed.

"Yes!" she shook her head adamantly, happy that someone understood her need to do things on her own. "I wanted to see if I could handle it myself." She released a heavy defeated sigh and shrugged her shoulders, "But I guess now I'll never know."

Mr. Rivers was outside the General Store sweeping the sidewalk. Angelina smiled with a nod and a wave. The shop owner returned the gesture.

"I'm sure you could've taken care of it. I'm certain it's your teachin' methods that are keepin' 'em behavin'. Talkin' to's only last so long."

Angelina doubted that. Elijah Willoughby was a formidable man and well respected in town. If he'd threatened the Todd boys, they probably left his presence shaking in their boots and ready to behave from then on.

When they arrived at Bonnie's, Everett helped Angelina down from the wagon, and they entered the house. Bonnie came into the parlor, wiping her hands on her apron, and smiled.

"Mr. Stone! So good to see you again!" she extended her hand in greeting and Everett shook it.

"You too, Mrs. Crestworth. Thanks for taking such good care of my daughter."

"Oh, she's been a big help around here. I'm glad to have her," Bonnie smiled. "Why don't you have a seat and have some peppermint tea."

"I'm just gonna run my books upstairs. I'll be right back," Angelina hurried up the steps, leaving Bonnie standing with her father. When she returned, Bonnie and Everett were sitting in the parlor chatting.

Angelina slipped onto the sofa next to him, and Bonnie rose to her feet. "Well, I better get supper started. You two enjoy your tea."

"Do you need some help?" Angelina stood.

"Oh no, I've got it under control. Stay here and enjoy this time with your father."

Angelina gave Bonnie a grateful nod and sat back down. They talked at length about home, catching up on the family. Then after nearly an hour, Everett's eyes widened. "Oh, I almost forgot somethin'," He reached inside his vest pocket and pulled out a white envelope. "This is for you," he handed it to her.

"For me? From who?"

"Paul sent it."

"Oh, that was nice o' him," she smiled and set the letter on her lap, intent on reading it later when she was alone. She knew her father expected her to marry Paul. But she didn't want Paul. She wanted Elijah. When the conversation lagged, she debated upon whether to tell her father about him. How would he feel about her involvement with a Yankee? Especially one who had invaded their home!

"Were you gonna say somethin'?" Everett prodded.

"No, no, I was just thinkin' about somethin'. It's not important." Just as she waved away the question, the front door opened and Elijah stepped inside, shutting the door behind him.

Angelina's heart leapt at the sight of him. A smile spread across her face as she noticed how handsome he looked in his new black suit and tie. Usually he didn't dress this fancy for dinner, and she wondered what the occasion was. She looked down at her school dress and wished she'd changed into something nicer for dinner or at least taken the time to straighten her hair before he arrived. She patted her hair, making sure she didn't have any stray wisps.

Elijah's head turned toward them, his eyes brightening when he saw her. When his gaze shifted to Everett, his mouth dropped in surprise and stretched into a jubilant smile. He carried a large brown parcel in his hands. He set it on the floor by the door and stepped toward Everett.

"Stone!" Elijah exclaimed. Everett rose to his feet and the two men gave each other a hearty embrace.

"How've you been, boy?" Everett inquired with a jovial slap on the shoulder.

"Good! Doing good! And you?"

"Wonderful. Just as I should be while visiting my Angelina," Everett smiled and gestured to his daughter who had now risen to her feet, surprised that Elijah and her father appeared to be friends.

"You . . . two . . . know each other?" Angelina stammered.

"Sure do, Elijah here's the only Yankee I trust," Everett chuckled and slapped Elijah on the back.

Elijah's mouth straightened into a somber line and he looked at Angelina for a moment. She watched his anxious body stiffen as he fiddled with the ring on his finger.

"So you're here checkin' up on Angelina for me, then?" Everett continued and turned to his daughter, "I hope you don't mind, Sugar. I asked Elijah to keep an eye on ya and make sure ya stay safe. A man worries about his daughter when she's all on her own like this, ya know."

Angelina's face felt like she could scramble an egg on it; it had become hotter than a wood-burning stove at breakfast. She put her hand to her forehead. She could feel the beads of perspiration forming. Here she'd hoped Elijah had been looking after her because deep down he felt something for her, cared about her, but it was all because of her father's request.

She clenched her angry jaw. She didn't need them plotting to protect her. She wasn't a little girl anymore. She was all on her own now; she'd faced the jaws of hell and lived to tell the tale. She didn't need them hovering over her like mother hens making sure she didn't get into trouble. She wouldn't be taken advantage of again. And she certainly didn't need Elijah Willoughby pretending he cared for her, kissing her, just to make her feel protected! The unmitigated gall! To take such liberties with her when he had no intentions toward her! The conversation between he and Bonnie in the kitchen began to make more sense now. He had no true feelings for her, but was only following orders from her father and succumbed in a weak moment.

Everett watched Angelina's cheeks flush and her jaws tighten with the crinkling of her eyebrows. "Somethin' wrong, Sugar?" he asked

She released an angry sigh, "Just explains a lot." Her accusing eyes studied Elijah.

"Explains what?" Everett's puzzled gaze moved from Angelina to Elijah and back.

"Why Mr. Willoughby here has felt the need to constantly interfere in my affairs."

"I have not constantly interfered in your affairs," Elijah defended.

"What about the Todd boys?" Angelina blurted.

"You'd still be pullin' your hair out with that class if I hadn't o' talked to those youngin's, and you know it!" Elijah stepped a little closer to Angelina.

"But ya had no right to do it! I told ya I could handle it," she stepped closer to him and pounded her pointing finger into his chest.

"Ya tried to handle it, and it wasn't workin'," he caught her hand to stop her thumping on his chest.

"Ya didn't give me enough time," she barked, yanking her hand free and shooting him a defiant glare.

"Ya can't even walk through town without gettin' yourself in a pickle!" Elijah retorted.

"I assure you, Mr. Willoughby, that I am perfectly capable of taking care of myself!"

Everett stood watching the quarrelsome pair, his eyes widening in surprise. Their words may have been argumentative, but the sparks passing between them were unmistakable. They reminded him of himself and Lelia when they'd get into an argument. It would not have surprised him in the least if in the very next second Elijah had taken Angelina in his arms and planted a kiss right on her lips. If it had been Lelia barking at him like that, that's what he would've done. She was just too adorable to resist when enraged. Angelina had that same comical spunk when she got angry. Her nose crinkled and her eyebrows furrowed when she looked at Elijah as if he was crazy, just like her mother's did. Everett figured that the only thing keeping Elijah from taking her in his arms was the fact that her father stood in the same room, for the chemistry between the couple was as thick as smoke billowing through a chimney.

Everett watched Elijah run a frustrated hand through his hair. Everett had never expected it, but there was something going on between these two - something intense and evidently not yet verbalized or admitted.

The two stared each other down for a few moments longer, breathing labored breaths until Angelina moved to the coffee table, snatched up Paul's letter and stormed from the room.

"If you'll excuse me, I have Paul's letter to read." She marched out the front door and onto the porch.

The two men watched her slam the door and then looked at each other with raised eyebrows.

"She can be a bit of a spitfire," Everett raised his palms in the air apologetically.

"I'll say," Elijah grumbled.

It was the first time Everett Stone had seen this side of Angelina since before the war. Evidently, Elijah had awakened emotions inside her that she hadn't felt or expressed in some time.

"Looks like you're helpin' her deal with the past," Everett noted.

"How's that?" Elijah released an exasperated chuckle.

"She's been so emotionless since that night. I haven't seen her respond to anyone like this since before the war."

"And you think that's a good thing?" Elijah shook his head in doubt.

"Any emotion is better than no emotion. Looks like she's wakin' up to herself again," Everett said.

"But is hate such a healthy emotion?" Elijah crossed to the window and watched Angelina read the letter.

"She doesn't hate you," Everett released a soft chuckle.

"Sure seems like it," Elijah's eyes remained on Angelina.

"She's still confused about things, that's all," Everett reassured him. "I know my daughter."

"So Paul sent her a letter?" Elijah inquired with casual disinterest.

Everett's eyes sparkled, amused at his friend's demeanor, "Yeah."

"Is he still plannin' on marryin' her?"

Everett stifled a smile as he watched Elijah's gaze remain riveted on Angelina through the window. His friend obviously cared for his daughter. In fact, he was downright jealous. "You'll have to ask Angelina 'bout that. I haven't read the letter."

Elijah stepped away from the window when he saw Angelina turn and come toward the front door.

"Food's ready," Bonnie called just as Angelina stepped inside.

Angelina went upstairs, and called the Forrester sisters to supper on her way to her room. She took a few moments to examine her reflection in the mirror, pinched her cheeks for color, and straightened her hair. When she returned downstairs, everyone crowded around the table, ready to offer a prayer on the meal.

Bonnie asked Elijah to offer the blessing on the food, and upon his conclusion, she passed him a bowl of potatoes. "So, 'Lijah, how do you and Mr. Stone know each other?"

"We met durin' the war," Elijah replied.

"I was a Confederate prisoner and Elijah was my night guard," Everett smiled.

"He stayed awake just to keep me entertained," Elijah gave Everett a reminiscent grin.

Everett chuckled, "More like he let me bore 'im to death with talk of home." Everett paused, his expression somber as he stared at Elijah with admiration and gratitude. "I'd be dead right now if it weren't for Elijah."

Elijah felt himself blushing. "Oh, I'm sure you'd 've made it through. You're too stubborn to die," Elijah winked.

Together the two men related the circumstances and events relating to their meeting and becoming friends. Everyone listened and asked questions while Angelina sat there, never making a comment. Occasionally, Elijah caught her looking across the table at him, and she would drop her attention to her plate.

Near the end of the meal, Dot grew excited, letting her palm slap the table. "Oh! Did ya'll hear about the town social comin' up in a few weeks? I'm lookin' forward to that! Won't it be fun?" Dot grinned as she plopped another mound of potatoes on her plate.

"That's right! I saw a sign up about it in the general store," Edna added.

Elijah's eyes couldn't help glancing across the table to Angelina. She looked radiant, and he noted she'd taken time to straighten her hair. Mentally, he let it down, imagining it wild and free the way it was the day he'd first met her.

He'd planned on asking her to the social, but that was before her father appeared and muddied the water. He'd intended to steer Angelina away from the others tonight and tell her how he felt about her, see how she felt about him, but now he wasn't certain where he stood. Maybe he could still smooth things over with her yet.

"Are you goin' with anyone, Lucille?" Thelma asked her sister.

"Ed Jenkins asked me to go with 'im, but I haven't decided yet," Lucille replied.

"Colin Harper asked me this mornin' when I passed by the General Store," Thelma smiled, evidently pleased with the invitation.

The Forrester sisters continued to chatter on about the dresses they planned to wear. They discussed every aspect of the social with great excitement. Bonnie served them all pieces of apple pie and suggested they move their conversation to the parlor to eat their dessert. The Forrester sisters crowded on the couch while everyone else too seats around the parlor. Elijah sat by the hearth with the fire sputtering behind him.

Suddenly Dot slapped her palm to her head as if she'd had a sudden revelation. "You know what? Elijah, you should take Angelina to the social!" Dot's eyes betrayed her matchmaking intentions as her head bobbed between the pair.

Before Elijah could respond, Angelina did. "Actually, I was thinking of invitin' Paul to come up for the event." She looked to her father, "Would ya take 'im my invitation, Daddy?"

Everett raised a single eyebrow and offered Elijah a dumbfounded glance. He looked back at his daughter, "I – I could do that if you want."

"Who's Paul?" Dot's eyes furrowed with confusion.

"Paul is my friend back home," Angelina replied, folding her hands on her lap, her gaze upon Dot, never looking in Elijah's direction.

"I didn't know you had a beau back home, Angelina! You should've told us!" Dot chirped. "Tell us all about 'im."

"Yes, do tell us all about 'im," Elijah growled, the muscles in his jaw clenching into granite as he leaned back in his chair and folded his arms across his chest.

Angelina's eyes remained on Dot, "Paul and I have enjoyed each other's company for years. His family owns the farm next to ours. He's quite industrious and has always made me laugh."

"So then he's fun to be with?" Edna noted, leaning forward as if she were anxious to hear more.

"Oh yes, we always laugh about the time ..." Elijah tuned out her words. He couldn't stand to listen to her drone on about Paul. Why had she let him kiss her that way if she was so enamored with another man? She continued with her story, looking to the various Forrester sisters, never meeting his gaze. He watched her and decided that her happy laughter and comments looked much too flamboyant for her normal character.

"You seem awfully enamored with this fellow," Elijah observed. "Why is it that we're just now hearin' of him?"

"Yes, I've never heard you speak of him even once," Bonnie added.

Elijah glanced at Bonnie. He knew what she was thinking. She'd seen them kissing and now she was angry about Angelina's fickle attitude. Elijah knew just how protective Bonnie could be of him, and he could see her blood boiling as she stared at Angelina.

"I don't know," Angelina shrugged. "I guess the subject never came up."

Elijah pulled his watch from his pocket, "Well, I hate to leave so soon, but I have a mare that's about to foal. I need to check on her." He rose to his feet and headed for the door.

"Must you leave so soon?" Bonnie protested.

"Yeah, I better go," he glanced at Angelina who picked an imaginary piece of lint from her dress sleeve, never lifting her attention to him. He offered Bonnie a tight-lipped smile, "The meal was delicious as usual, Bonnie. Thanks for havin' me. Perhaps you and I could go to the social together."

Angelina's head darted toward Elijah.

"That would be lovely," Bonnie agreed. With that, Elijah placed his hat on his head and turned to leave.

Everett rose to his feet. "I'm gonna go see if he needs some help," he said, following Elijah.

Chapter 23

"He must really be worried 'bout that foal," Thelma noted.

Without excusing herself, Angelina stood and went upstairs to her room where she quickly took a piece of stationery and penned a note. When she'd completed the letter and sealed the envelope, she tucked it into her pocket and returned downstairs, going straight to the kitchen to wash dishes. After a few moments, Bonnie excused herself from the conversation with the Forrester sisters and followed Angelina into the kitchen.

Bonnie took position next to Angelina, received a plate from her, rinsed it and dried it with a towel. As she put it away, she glanced back over her shoulder at Angelina.

"Angelina, could I ask ya somethin'?" The expression in Bonnie's voice was curious, cautious, yet controlled.

"Yes," Angelina replied, scrubbing another plate in the sudsy water.

"You might think this is none o' my business, but Elijah's a very dear friend o' mine – you could say like my own brother. So as you can imagine, I care very much about his happiness."

Angelina shifted her stance, the muscles in her neck and shoulders stiffening.

Bonnie continued, "I could hem haw around here, but I'll just say what's on my mind."

Angelina braced her hands on the counter in front of her as if preparing herself for something unpleasant.

"If you had a beau back home, why were you kissin' Elijah the other night? Why did you lead 'im on like that?"

"Bonnie, this really is none of your concern." Angelina's voice was authoritative and clipped.

"I'm afraid it is my concern. Elijah hasn't got any parents to look after 'im so somebody needs to watch his back," Bonnie insisted.

Angelina returned to washing the dishes. "He's a big boy; he can take care of himself. Anyway, it's not like you think. He kissed me. He instigated it, not me," Angelina defended.

"That may be true, but you certainly responded to his attentions."

"I don't know what you mean. It was him."

"Not from what I saw! If you're so sweet on this Paul fella, you should've slapped Elijah's face or pushed him away, not grabbed his face in your hands and kissed him all the more!"

"This conversation is makin' me uncomfortable. I don't really see where . . ."

"Watchin' you break my friend's heart is makin' me uncomfortable," Bonnie retorted, thrusting her clenched fists to her hips and staring Angelina straight in the eyes.

Bonnie looked like a mother hen defending her chicks. Angelina looked away and shrugged her shoulders. "I wasn't thinkin' straight. He's handsome. He kissed me, I responded. Any normal girl would. But it doesn't mean anything." Angelina threw up her hands in surrender, her eyes misting with emotion. She lowered her voice to a hurt whisper, "He doesn't want me. Trust me; he's not wounded. I'm sure he's relieved to be rid of me." Angelina bit her lower lip to stifle its traitorous tremor.

"You have no inkling of what kind of man Elijah Willoughby is, do you?" Bonnie looked at Angelina as if she pitied her lack of understanding.

Angelina's voice grew more insistent, "Oh, I know 'im a lot better than you think I do. I know he has no intentions toward me. I know he's only been nice to me because my father told 'im to keep an eye on me. I know that what I feel doesn't matter in the least to 'im. So why should he care who I invite to the social?"

"Are you sayin' that if Elijah did have an interest in you, you'd choose 'im over Paul?" Bonnie's expression lit with sudden understanding.

"Yes, I don't know . . ." Angelina shook her head, obviously flustered, "No, I'm not sayin' that. I – I just know I'm not hurtin' him. He has no real intentions toward me. What happened the other night was just – just nothin'," Angelina stammered, tossing back a stray blonde lock that had fallen into her face.

"Oh," Bonnie's intonation laced with humor, "It was somethin'! I've never seen 'im like that with anyone."

"I'm sure he had no intention of you seein' him like that the other night," Angelina cocked her head to the side and released a nervous chuckle. Then her expression grew somber. "I'm tellin' ya, Bonnie, it meant nothin' to 'im."

"You're wrong. He was hurt tonight when you said you were gonna invite Paul to the social."

"Well, I'm hurt that he pretended to be my friend, pretended to care for me when he has no intentions toward me at all. So in my opinion he gets what he deserves!"

"Listen to yourself! You're admitting that you hurt him and that he hurt you, but how could you hurt each other if you don't care for one another?"

"Bonnie, I really don't want to talk about this anymore," Angelina flung the washrag in the sink, and stormed from the room.

Upon exiting the kitchen, Angelina ran squarely into her father's chest. "Oh, I'm sorry, Daddy. I should watch where I'm goin'," she apologized.

"That's all right, Sugar. Where're you goin' in such a hurry?"

"Nowhere, I – I was just comin' to find you and – and give you this," she reached in her pocket and handed the letter to her father. "Could you give this to Paul when you get home?"

Everett nodded, "All right. But are you certain you want me to give this to 'im?" Everett's eyes narrowed as he studied Angelina's face.

"Of course, why wouldn't I?"

Everett took his daughter by the elbow and led her aside, away from the kitchen door and away from the parlor into a corner of the dining room. He lowered his voice to a whisper, "Be careful playin' with men's hearts. They can break as sure as a woman's can."

Angelina's eyebrows furrowed, "I don't know what you mean."

"Oh, think on it a bit, Angelina. You know what I mean."

Just then, Bonnie exited the kitchen and entered the room.

"Thank you for a delicious meal, Mrs. Crestworth," Everett turned and extended his hand to Bonnie.

"You're welcome, Mr. Stone," Bonnie gave him a cordial smile and took his hand.

"I'm gonna run out to Elijah's place and give 'im a hand with his mare." Everett stuffed Angelina's letter into his pocket and then turned back toward his daughter, taking her by the shoulders and kissing her cheek. "Perhaps you could join me for breakfast tomorrow mornin' before I leave?"

"I'd like that," Angelina agreed.

"I'll pick ya up around eight."

They bid each other goodnight and Angelina watched her father step toward the door. When he reached it, he looked down at the brown package Elijah had brought in with him earlier in the evening. He bent down and lifted it. "Angelina, this has your name on it." He carried it back to her, and then left.

Everyone's eyes were on Angelina and her package, but she ignored them, thanked her father and carried it upstairs, wondering what on earth Elijah had left for her.

~*~

"Sure is a pretty foal, Mr. Willoughby," seventeen-year-old Randall remarked, admiring the newborn that Elijah cleaned with a towel.

"Sure is," Elijah agreed. "I appreciate ya comin' out to help this late at night. Ya be sure to thank your ma and pa for me."

"Yes, sir," the boy nodded.

248

Elijah heard a man clearing his voice and hoped it might be Doug coming back from spying on Bonnie. He looked up toward the stall door to find Everett instead.

"Thanks for comin', Everett. You really didn't need to. Randall and I are just waitin' on the afterbirth now."

Everett leaned against the stall door. "Looks like a healthy one."

"Yeah, she's a beauty," Elijah agreed, as he continued to rub down the foal.

Everett directed his attention to Randall, "If it's all right with your boss, here, I'll stay and help, and you can run along home and get some rest."

Randall shook his shaggy blonde hair from his expectant eyes and looked to his employer for an answer.

"Sure, run along if you'd like," Elijah gestured toward the stable door.

"Thank ya, sir," the boy acknowledged each man with a bob of his head, then scurried away.

Everett entered the stall and sat down next to Elijah, leaning his back against the wall. He pulled Angelina's letter from his pocket and tapped it on the palm of his hand.

"What's that?" Elijah asked.

"Angelina's letter to Paul," Everett replied.

Elijah's mouth twisted into a grimace, his eyes fixing on the foal, but his mind on Angelina.

"She's gotten under your skin, hasn't she?" Everett quirked a single eyebrow, his knowing eyes meeting Elijah's with a hint of mirth in his expression.

"Who?" Elijah shifted uncomfortably and resumed tending to the foal.

"That green-eyed daughter o' mine," Everett tilted his head with an insinuative smile.

"Oh, I wouldn't say that," Elijah lied, trying to brush away the accusation, his pulse racing a little in knowing his interest in Angelina had been so obvious to her father.

"Come on, now, boy. We know each other well enough not to try to fool one another. Angelina's stolen your heart, hasn't she?"

Elijah wished his face hadn't turned red. He would've denied it again, but the heat in his forehead and cheeks was almost unbearable. There was no denying how he felt about the girl.

"Doesn't really matter how I feel about her, she's made up her mind 'bout who she wants," Elijah grumbled.

"Ya talkin' about this?" Everett tapped Angelina's letter on his palm twice.

Elijah didn't say anything, just fixed his stern blue eyes on the letter and frowned.

Everett held the envelope in both hands and acted as if he might tear it in two in the next second, "We could just dispose o' this."

Elijah held up a protesting hand, "What are ya doin'? We can't tear up a letter that doesn't belong to us!"

"Why not?" his hands threatened the envelope once more.

"She'd hate me forever if we did that!" Elijah snatched the letter from Everett's hands and stared at Paul's name in Angelina's handwriting.

"What if I told you it don't matter what that note says, that nothin' would become of it?" Everett eyed his friend.

"I don't understand," Elijah's eyebrows furrowed.

"I don't know what that letter says, but it's not an invitation to the social."

"How do you know? Did she tell ya somethin'?" Elijah countered.

"No, but it can't be an invitation to the social 'cause Paul will be at home eatin' dinner with his wife that night."

"What?" Elijah's heart quickened its pace, and his eyes widened in shock. "Are ya sayin' they're gettin' married right away?"

"No. No," Everett soothed. "Paul's gettin' married Sunday next. I didn't read the letter he wrote Angelina, but I'd imagine it told her as much."

"But, why? Why would she pretend she was gonna invite him to the social?" Elijah asked.

"That must've been for your benefit," Everett's eyes twinkled and his mouth turned up into an amused smirk.

"Why?"

"Because you've gotten under 'er skin, that's why. And she's evidently tryin' to buy herself some time."

"More likely she's tryin' to get back at me for the other . . ." Elijah was going to say she was trying to get back at him for kissing her the other night, but he cut that comment short and started over. "I mean, she's upset 'cause she thinks I only befriended her because you asked me to."

"Yeah, that'd be my guess too," Everett agreed.

"But wouldn't she expect you'd tell me about Paul? She knows we're friends," Elijah reasoned.

"Angelina and I are pretty close. She either thought I didn't know about Paul's marriage yet or assumed I'd play along with 'er."

"Then why didn't you? Why are you tellin' me this?"

Everett placed a hand on Elijah's shoulder, "Because, my daughter is as stubborn as a dad burn mule, and it's time she was happy. And, because it's obvious you two belong together. There's no sense in this silly game playin' and foolish pride."

Elijah swallowed hard and took a deep breath, a bit surprised by Everett's revelation. "So are ya sayin' that ya want me to court your daughter?"

"That's what I'm sayin' – if that's what you want, of course."

Elijah simply nodded, indicating that the thought was agreeable to him.

"Then, court 'er, marry 'er and try not to let 'er dang fool pride drive ya plum crazy." Everett chuckled when a broad smile took over Elijah's face and caused his blue eyes to twinkle. "The only thing I ask is that ya don't let 'er know I told ya about Paul. You've got to let things proceed natural. Just know one thing about Angelina. She cares for ya. No matter what she says or how she protests, have that confidence that in time she'll be yours if you treat 'er right and never give up on 'er. Do ya love 'er that much, Elijah? Enough to fight for 'er?"

Elijah swallowed hard and felt moisture mist his vision. "Yes sir, I do."

Everett patted Elijah's shoulder once more, then took Angelina's letter and shoved it in his pocket. They finished taking care of the mare and foal; then Everett bid Elijah farewell, and returned to the inn.

Chapter 24

Back at Bonnie's, Angelina stared at the unopened package sitting on her bed. Her hands trembled as she ran her hand along her name written on the outside of it. She'd seen Elijah carry it in and set it down by the door, but hadn't thought much of it until her father told her that it had her name on it. She'd already changed into her nightgown for the evening, saving the package for later. What did it mean anyway? Was it a gift? She still felt astonished and guilty with herself for the lie she told. Why had she done such a thing? As she examined her actions and emotions, she realized she'd wanted to push Elijah further away. He'd hurt her feelings and she wanted to hurt his.

They were no good for each other, anyway. The past hung too thick between them. Now knowing her father and Elijah were friends and had conspired to keep her out of trouble made her feel even more foolish. Had they also conspired in Elijah's other attentions as well? Had her father put him up to kissing her - as some means of healing her attitude toward men? Angelina shook her head negatively. Her father would never do such a thing. Would he? No. She shook her head once more and untied the twine around the package.

As the paper fell away, Angelina gasped. It was her mother's quilt! He'd bought it back for her! Angelina couldn't contain the tears that misted her eyes. She raised the quilt to her face and inhaled the remnant scent of home. As she did so, an envelope slipped to the floor beside her bare feet.

She pressed the quilt to her chest and reached down for the envelope. It too bore her name. She set the quilt on the bed and eased down beside it. With quivering fingertips, she opened the seal and began to read.

My Dearest Angel,

I hope you will accept this quilt as a symbol of my desire that all good things be restored to you. Your happiness is my highest aim and your companionship my greatest joy.

Truly yours,

Elijah

Tears glistened in Angelina's joyous eyes as she smiled. Elijah did care for her! How wonderful! No! How horrible! The anguished wave of guilt washed over her like an angry sea. Burying her face in her hands, a flood of tears spilled down her crimson cheeks.

"What have I done?" she sobbed. "What have I done?"

~*~

Two weeks later

"Come on now, Doug, let me just get this one spot around your ears," Elijah scolded as he trimmed the last bit of Doug's shortly cropped hair. Elijah had shaved his friend's face and as he stood back to examine his handiwork, he smiled. "Welcome home!"

"What're you goin' on about?" Doug rolled his eyes, giving Elijah a mock scowl.

"You finally look like yourself!" Elijah grabbed the hand mirror off the kitchen table and held it in front of where Doug sat on a kitchen chair.

Doug's serious eyes examined his reflection and ran his hand along his smooth chin, "Feels strange."

"Well, you know how Bonnie hates beards. You can't go home to her all scruffy."

"That's true," Doug replied. "You really think I'm ready?"

"You've been ready. I never would've thought you could get around as well as you do on that leg."

"Do you think she'll be mad?" Doug turned his head side to side, studying his clean-shaven jaw.

"About what?"

"That it took me so long to come home."

"Of course," Elijah replied and Doug's eyebrows crumpled with worry. "But that's not gonna stop her from bein' beside herself with joy to see ya!"

"Just doesn't feel right showin' up for dinner in front of all those people," Doug muttered, running his fingers through his shortly cropped black hair.

"Well, you may have a point there. Kind of a personal experience for an audience," Elijah agreed.

"Maybe I should wait for another time," Doug sighed and set the mirror back on the table.

"No chickenin' out on me now," Elijah stood beside Doug and rested a hand on his shoulder. "Let's see here," Elijah scratched his beard. "We could go early, and you could talk with her before supper."

"I don't want to ruin her meal," Doug shook his head negatively.

"You're not gonna ruin her supper," Elijah scolded.

"Well, let's put it this way, I'd rather not face a crowd of people right after I come home to my wife," Doug expounded.

"All right, I can understand that. What about after dinner? After everyone's gone upstairs?"

"That'll work, I guess." Doug held up his hand, "Look at that! I'm shakin' worse now than when I went to ask her Daddy for courtin' privileges."

Elijah slapped his friend's shoulder, "It'll be all right. You can get through this. And when you do, Bonnie will be yours, just like she was the last time you were this nervous."

~*~

Elijah greeted Bonnie as he stepped into her kitchen later that afternoon.

"'Lijah! You're early," she smiled over her shoulder as she continued to peel carrots.

"Thought you might need some help with supper," he lowered an armful of logs into the crate by the cook stove. He dusted off his hands, put an arm around her shoulder, and squeezed.

"Thank you," she smiled. "You seem extra chipper this evening."

"It's been a wonderful day, and promises to be a magical evenin'."

"Magical?" Bonnie gave a doubtful giggle. "What's gotten into you?"

"Oh, just lookin' forward to dancin' with ya at the social next Friday night."

"Well, there'll be no dancin' unless you can promise not to step all over my toes!" she teased.

"Argh, you never will let me live that down, will ya?" he rolled his eyes. "I step on your toe one time when I'm fifteen, and I never hear the end of it!"

"It's not my fault you're such a clumsy oaf," she countered, a twinkle glimmering in her eye.

"I am not clumsy. I'll have you know I've become quite the accomplished dancer in recent years," he tugged at the lapels of his suit like a proud peacock.

Bonnie rolled her eyes, "Whatever you say, 'Lijah."

"You want me to prove it? Cause I'll prove it!" He pointed an emphatic index finger at the floor. "Right here, lady, I'll prove it," he stretched out his arms and then grabbed her hand when she set down the paring knife. He put an arm around her waist and the other took her hand and swirled her around, while he hummed a lively tune.

Bonnie broke into giggles as she fell into step with him, and they took a few turns around the kitchen.

Upon opening the kitchen door to find Bonnie in Elijah's arms, giggling like a schoolgirl, Angelina stammered, "Oh, I'm sorry, I didn't mean to intrude. I just thought I'd see if you needed any help."

"You're not intrudin'," Bonnie smiled and patted Elijah on the shoulder. "'Lijah was just provin' to me that he can dance without steppin' on my feet." She stood on her tiptoes to kiss his cheek and hugged him. He returned the embrace, and Bonnie went back to her carrots.

Just as Angelina started to turn around and leave, Bonnie handed a knife to Elijah and then pointed to the cupboard. "Actually, I could use a hand from both of you. If you could peel some more carrots, Elijah, and if you could set the table, Angelina, that would be a big help."

Angelina's stomach churned. She'd been dreading facing him all day. She half expected him not to come to dinner after the way she'd treated him. She turned toward the cupboard to retrieve some plates. They were on the highest shelf in the cupboard, so high that she had to stretch her arms and stand on her toes to reach them.

Elijah continued to hum the tune while he worked. He glanced over his shoulder to observe Angelina struggling to reach the plates. Finally, she managed to grasp them. Just when she felt she might lose her balance and drop them, Elijah's arms reached over her head, his hands covered hers guiding them down until the plates rested on the counter.

"There ya go," he whispered into her ear. His breath on her neck sent a quaking shiver along her spine and down the lengths of her arms. He stood directly behind her, letting his hands linger on hers. "Got 'em?"

"Uh-hmm." She held her breath, daring not to move and hoping that if she remained motionless, he'd stay there longer. Then again, why would he? He must hate her for how she'd treated him!

"Good," he let his hands go to her waist for a brief moment before returning to the carrots. The gesture gave her a glimmer of hope.

Angelina turned around to carry the plates to the dining room, her eyes never leaving Elijah's back. His dark wavy hair lay against his white shirt collar. She couldn't help remembering the feel of it between her fingers. She watched his muscular arms, his shirtsleeves rolled up to his elbows, as they worked peeling the carrots. Angelina grew more uncomfortable, for she did not miss the twinkle in his blue eyes as he laughed and talked with Bonnie. She wished she worked alongside him, that he smiled at her that way, and that he danced around the kitchen with her. But it was her own fault; she'd pretended to choose Paul over him. She couldn't expect him to pursue his affections toward her now!

Irritated with her own stupidity, Angelina set the plates down hard on the table and let the silverware clank into place beside each place setting. When she finished the task, she did not return to the kitchen, but went to the parlor and looked out the front window. She stood there for some time, lost in thought.

Spring was on its way, then summer would follow and the school year would end. She would turn in her letter of resignation and go home to her family. She supposed she'd die a lonely old spinster. How could she ever love anyone as she did Elijah? How could anyone compare to him?

Perhaps she could have been happy with Paul. But even Paul was unavailable. He was marrying Betsy Gables on Sunday. It sure didn't take him long to find someone to replace her! What a fickle man he turned out to be. Then again, she told him to move on with his life, she just hadn't expected him to do so this quickly. The situation with Paul was just one more example of where she'd thrown away a perfectly good suitor – just as she'd done with Elijah. She thought of his precious note and ached for him to speak similar words to her now. She bit her fingernail and shook her head. It would never happen now. Not after what she'd done!

~*~

"Dinner's ready, Angelina," Edna put a hand on the young woman's shoulder.

259

"Oh," Angelina broke from her thoughts and followed Edna into the dining room.

Soon everyone gathered around the table. Elijah and Bonnie carried the food out and placed it on trivets. Just as Bonnie was about to sit down, her necklace came loose and slipped to the floor.

"Uh oh," Elijah bent down to retrieve it. "Here, let me help you with that." He put the necklace around her neck, brushed a few strands of hair out of the way and fastened the clasp.

"Thank you, Elijah," she smiled into his handsome face.

"You're most welcome," he grinned.

Angelina felt a twinge of jealousy. Was Elijah turning his affections to Bonnie now? Was he as fickle as Paul was? As everyone sat around the table discussing their plans for the upcoming social, Angelina said nothing. When Bonnie mentioned Paul accompanying Angelina, she didn't correct her or deny it. She simply nodded and went along, changing the subject to ask Edna if she had an escort. No one had asked Edna or Dot yet, but they still planned to attend.

"I won't let a little thing like not havin' a man spoil my fun! Goodness sakes, if I waited to enjoy life until I had a man, it'd make for a miserable existence!" Edna giggled.

Everyone gave a jovial response, except Angelina. She couldn't keep her eyes off Elijah. He was so handsome this evening! When he wasn't looking in her direction, she studied his face. For all his manly appearance, she believed she loved his smile best. It was no ordinary smile, but one that lit up his eyes and captured his entire face. She envied his hand as it ran along his cheek, her fingertips tingling with the memory of his soft beard and stong jaw.

Her insides melted every time the single dimple in his left cheek appeared as it did right now. It gave him such an endearing, yet mischievous quality. Unfortunately, at this moment his dimpled grin and sparkling blue eyes were directed at Bonnie. Why did she have to be such a proud fool? He could have been hers.

Elijah said something comical and Bonnie put her hand on his, laughing. Angelina rubbed her temples. She had such a headache! Maybe she'd excuse herself early. It was too humiliating sitting here with him – knowing what he'd written in his note and knowing she'd pushed him aside before reading it.

After everyone cleared the table and Bonnie, Edna and Dot washed dishes, Lucille and Thelma settled down to some needlework in the parlor while Elijah read the newspaper. Angelina went to the front door and stepped out onto the porch for some fresh air. March had come in like a lamb. It was an unseasonably warm evening and a gentle breeze brushed her cheek, sending a wisp of her blonde hair whipping against her face.

She groaned to herself, aggravated with the turn of events. She heard the door open and close behind her and footsteps creak across the porch boards. Angelina assumed it was Dot, who often liked to interrupt her moments of seclusion with her continuous flow of chatter. She looked straight ahead, hoping to avoid the inevitable for a few moments longer.

"Nice evenin', isn't it?"

Her heart leapt at the sound of Elijah's deep, alluring voice. "Yes," she turned to glance at him as he came to stand beside her. "It is."

He leaned his back against a porch post as her hands tightened their grip on the rail. She tried to avoid eye contact with him, but he studied her face so closely that finally she turned and met his gaze.

"Thank you for the quilt," she said.

"You're welcome," he nodded and shifted his attention toward the windows of the house. "I'm sorry I interfered with your class," he added.

"No," she shook her head. "Don't apologize. You did me a favor. I should thank you for that as well."

"No, you were right the first time. I was wrong to meddle." His face was sincerely apologetic as he looked at her once more.

She looked into his eyes and then cast hers down toward her nervous hands that twiddled the drawstring of her dress. "I'm sorry about the other night," she whispered, not looking up to him.

She felt the warmth of his palm to her cheek and she closed her eyes, leaning her head toward his touch. "You're not sorry for our kiss are ya?" He whispered, moving a little closer to her.

"Oh no!" her eyes widened and then she bit her lip, realizing she'd protested too vehemently. "I – I just meant, I'm sorry for how I treated you the last time you were here."

Several moments passed before Angelina realized she'd been holding her breath. His body drew closer, and his face lowered ever so near hers. Her heart hammered even harder while she watched him moisten his lips, his eyes lingering upon her mouth. Elijah's gaze seemed to penetrate her soul. Her breathing resumed, shallow, almost painful as she anticipated once again being the recipient of his affections.

His thumb went to the corner of her mouth and grazed the length of her lips. "Just a little bit o' whipped cream there," he whispered. His blue eyes twinkled as his mischievous dimple deepened.

"Come on in, you two, we need ya for the game!" Dot called. Angelina stepped back from Elijah and self-consciously brushed at her lips, attempting to rid herself of whipped cream that hadn't actually been there to begin with. Elijah's hand slipped from her face, leaving a residual tingle that drizzled down the length of her, leaving her weak and breathless. Dot stepped out on the porch and tugged each of them by the arm into the house.

They followed her, but just as they entered the door, Elijah leaned closer to Angelina, placing his warm hand at the small of her back. Her face flushed as his lips drew near her ear and she heard his gruff whisper, "Darn that Dot."

~*~

Doug stood outside the house, lurking in the darkness with his back leaned against a hickory tree. Elijah had left nearly an hour earlier and wished him luck, but Doug just couldn't seem to muster the nerve to knock on the door. He'd watched the boarders return to their rooms, seen their lamps brighten and then dim as they went to sleep.

Bonnie was still up though. He could see her through the window, sitting at the dining room table, evidently making her shopping list. He watched her remove the pins from her dark brown hair, letting it cascade around her shoulders. She shut her chestnut eyes and stretched her arms high above her head and yawned.

How he ached to hold her! He looked down at his feet, clenched the cane in his hand and willed himself to step out of the shadows toward the house. He eased onto the front porch and stood before the door.

Doug took a deep breath and released a long slow expulsion of air. He could feel his lungs quivering from sheer nervousness. He breathed in and out again and then lifted his hand. Maybe he should just turn around and leave, get on his horse and ride out of town. If he left now and didn't come back, Bonnie could move on with her life and find happiness with a real man – a whole man.

The thought sent a fire spark of jealousy through his heart, bolting down the length of his arms and moving his knuckle to the door. He knocked once.

Inside, Bonnie lifted her head from her work and listened. Had she heard something? She couldn't be certain. She waited a moment, but when she heard nothing more, she assumed it was only a stray hickory nut falling on the roof. She directed her eyes back to her shopping list and then there was a stronger knock, three taps.

She pushed back her chair, shoved her dark hair behind her shoulder and went to the door, picking up Elijah's hat on the way. She expected it was him coming back to retrieve it.

When she opened the door wide, her heart, which had been beating in normal time, suddenly stopped, causing her lungs to constrict. Instantly, her stomach drew into a painful knot.

Bonnie released Elijah's hat, letting it slip to the floor. She felt hot and cold simultaneously as the blood drained from her face and a wave of dizziness coated her body with an instantly clammy residue. The next thing she knew everything went black.

Chapter 25

Bonnie's head sank deep into a feather pillow. The room was dark, except the fire in the fireplace in the corner of the room. She realized she was lying down on her bed upstairs. Had it been a heavenly dream? It had felt so real. She replayed the vision – opening the front door to find her cherished husband standing before her, handsome, the deep charcoal eyes she knew and loved staring back at her. What she wouldn't give for the vision to be real.

She heard the bedroom door open and close, and instantly shifted in her bed, sitting up and leaning forward. "Who is it?"

She blinked her eyes as the large figure eased toward her carrying a cup and saucer.

"It's me," his deep voice startled her. He stepped closer until he came to stand beside her bed. "I thought a little tea might help."

"Who? Who are you?"

The man set the tea on the night table and raised the wick on the lamp, illuminating his face.

Bonnie's eyes widened as once again she saw her husband's face before her. Unable to believe what she was seeing, she flung back the covers and stood up, backing away from him.

She rubbed her eyes, "You're a ghost."

"No, I'm quite mortal," he thumped his fist to his chest and a smile twinkled in his eyes. "I'm sorry to scare ya, darlin'."

She eased toward him, looking at him as if he were only a figment of her imagination. She put out her hand and let it rest against his chest. Was he really here? She couldn't believe it. He stood there smiling down at her as she pressed her hands to his cheeks, feeling the strength of his jaw beneath her palms. She rested her thumb in the familiar cleft of his chin.

Then as instantly as he had appeared, she grew angry, drew back her hand, and slapped him square across the cheek.

His mouth dropped in astonishment, his eyes wide as his hand rose to the red mark on his face. "Why did you go and do that? Aren't ya happy to see me?"

"How dare you?" even to herself, her voice sounded like the screeching of fingernails on slate. "How dare you leave me to grieve over you for nigh on to three years? Not a word from ya! Not a single word! What kind of man does that to a woman? And then you expect to just waltz in here, carry me off to our bedroom and have your . . ."

Doug took her by the shoulders, "Listen to me, Bonnie. It's not like that. I wanted to come home so many times. It killed me not to be with ya. I even checked on ya over the years, watched ya, and made sure ya were all right. I just couldn't . . . I knew it wouldn't be the same . . ."

Bonnie raised her hand to slap him again, but he caught it. "You watched me? You mean you've been hovering around, never telling me that ya were alive, that you were well? What kind of horrible beast does something like that?" She wrenched her wrist free and slapped at his arm and shoulder.

He lifted his hands to his face shielding himself from her blows. Tears were streaming down her face as she lashed out at him for all the nights she'd slept alone while this man was hiding from her, letting her believe he was dead! Finally, she pushed him hard enough that he lost balance and teetered sideways, falling onto the bed. Just as he landed, she kicked his leg. Instantly a searing pain started at her big toe and shot up her calf. She sat down on the bed, gathered her toe into her hands and rubbed, trying to soothe away the pain.

"What in the world have ya got stuffed in your boot?"

Doug sat up on the bed and leaned forward, resting his head in his hands, "Wood," he grumbled.

"Wood? Why on earth would ya have wood in your boot?"

Doug leaned his hand on the bedside table and rose to his feet. "I shouldn't 've ever come. I'm sorry I troubled ya," he muttered and started for the door.

But she was quicker than him. She hobbled to her feet and rushed to block his path before he could reach the doorknob.

"Oh no, ya don't! You're not leavin' me now!"

Doug shook his head, an expression of utter bewilderment on his face.

"Don't ya think I deserve an explanation? Why didn't ya come home? Have you found someone else? Is that it? You've met some northern lady of means who nursed ya back to health after a war wound, and ya haven't had the nerve to tell me ya want rid o' me?"

Doug chuckled and shook his head, evidently amused at her outburst.

"Stop laughin' at me!" she cried and slapped his arm again.

"Only if you stop hittin' me! Since when do you hit? I don't remember you ever hittin' me before."

"I don't remember you playin' dead for almost three years before!" she screeched. "So who is she?"

"There's no one else but you, Bonnie."

"I don't believe ya! There has to be someone else! Why else would you stay away?"

"I promise. There's no one else. It's always been you, and there's never gonna be anybody but you."

"Then what in blazes is goin' on, Doug? I just don't understand how ya could do somethin' like this to me?" She felt like her heart was breaking. How could the man she loved and trusted betray her in such a manner? How could he not be truthful? What had he done that he could not come home? What had she done that he could not be with her?

"I didn't want to be a burden on ya, Bonnie," Doug hung his head. "I'm not the man I was. Even now, I don't know that it can ever be the same between us."

"I don't understand you," her head wobbled. She was starting to feel weak again. She'd expended too much energy fighting him after having fainted.

He took her by the shoulders and motioned her back to the bed where she sat down. He took a seat opposite her in a wingback chair and lifted his pant leg to show her his wooden leg, "I lost my leg at Gettysburg and nearly died. I wanted to be with ya, Bonnie – more than anythin' in the world, I wanted to be with ya; but I'm – I'm just not even a whole man anymore. I was afraid you . . ."

She said not a word for several moments, her somber eyes assessing him. "You didn't trust me. Didn't believe I was strong enough to handle it."

"No, you don't understand. It's not like that at all!" he pulled his pant leg up higher. "Up until a few weeks ago, I didn't have this wooden leg. It was just a stump. Put yourself in my position for a second. I'm a man. I'm supposed to take care of ya, protect ya, and provide for ya. I could barely take care of myself – much less be the husband I wanted to be for ya."

Bonnie sat there thinking of the virile man she'd married, his proud way of handling himself in everything he did – from the way he went about his work, to the way he prided himself on his appearance. "Oh, Doug," she rushed to him, kneeling in front of him, encircling her arms about his waist and resting her head against his chest. She closed her eyes and sniffed back tears. "Why didn't ya trust me?" She could feel his warm hands on her shoulders, and then on her head as his gentle hand stroked her hair.

"It took nearly a year before I could get around. A family up North took me in, let me heal at their place. Since then I've just been driftin'. Occasionally, I'd come home and watch ya put the clothes out on the line, see ya sittin' on the front porch or watch ya through the window while ya sat at the dinin' room table makin' your shoppin' lists.

She lifted her head from his chest and stared into his eyes, "Why didn't ya come home and let me take care of ya?"

"That's not your job, darlin'," he put his hand to her cheek, and her heart thrilled, accelerating its cadence with the warmth of his touch. "It's my job to take care of *you*."

She leaned her head against his chest once more, "Then you're ready to take care of me now?"

He put his arms around her, "If you'll have me."

"Of course, I'll have ya, ya silly man, I would've had you three years ago."

"I know you would've, but I didn't want to be a burden on ya. It was Elijah who talked me into comin' home."

"Elijah? You mean that man knew you were here and never told me?" Bonnie's eyes fired with indignation again as her head rose from his chest.

"Easy now," Doug soothed, his large hands caressing her shoulders.

"How long has he known? You mean he let me think ya were dead all these years?"

"No, he found me last month and took me home with 'im. He cleaned me up and made me this leg."

"Why didn't he send you home sooner?" Bonnie's face reddened with fresh anger.

"He tried to, but I wanted to make sure I could get around on this leg. It took some gettin' used to."

"Some friend he turned out to be!" Bonnie grumbled.

"Easy now, Bonnie. I wouldn't be here if it weren't for Elijah. If he hadn't made me this leg, took me in, and made me believe I could go home, I wouldn't 've had the courage to face ya again. It was Elijah who made me believe I could be the man you wanted."

"All right," she sighed, "I suppose I won't slap 'im silly when I see 'im again."

They laughed together and wiped the tears from each other's eyes.

He put his hands to her face and let his fingers rest in her soft locks. "You're even more beautiful than I remembered," he whispered.

Bonnie could feel the heat rise to her cheeks.

"How I've dreamed a thousand times of this day when I could hold your beautiful face in my hands and kiss ya again," his voice was thick with emotion, and Bonnie could see the tears welling in her husband's eyes.

She swallowed back the sorrow she felt for his loss and her own remorse over the lost years they could have shared together. As his eyes filled with adoration, Bonnie's heart quickened, realizing that her husband was truly home again and that she would not spend another night alone.

She put her hands to his neck, letting her fingers slip into his hair. He lowered his lips to hers and with his kiss everything seemed to melt away but the two of them. In that instant all the years, the worry, the grief and the pain were gone. Bonnie could hardly believe he was here, holding her in his arms, consoling her with his kisses.

Despite her earlier anger, she relinquished herself completely to his affections, somehow aware of the necessity of their time apart. Without it, he could never have seen himself as the man she needed, and she would never have come to appreciate the man who had been hers all along.

~*~

The next morning, Angelina came down for breakfast, turned the corner toward the dining room and much to her surprise, found a very attractive man sitting at the table reading a newspaper. Without noticing Angelina, Bonnie entered the room, put a large stack of flapjacks in front of the man, bent down, kissed his cheek, and returned to the kitchen humming a jovial tune.

271

The man folded his newspaper into a neat square, set it on the table beside his plate and reached for the syrup. He looked up at Angelina, his familiar eyes meeting hers, "Good morning," he greeted and drizzled syrup over the stack.

"Good mornin'," Angelina's eyes met his with a quizzical expression. "Do I know you?"

Doug raised his left hand and his thumb tapped the ring around his finger.

Angelina's mouth dropped wide, "It's you! You've shaved your beard."

Doug jutted his wooden leg out to the side of the table for Angelina to see, "And grown a new leg since we last warmed ourselves by the same fire."

"And you are?"

Doug rose to his feet and approached Angelina with an outstretched hand, "Doug Crestworth, Bonnie's husband."

"But, I thought Bonnie," Angelina's eyes shifted toward the kitchen door and whispered, "was a widow."

"So did she, but I wasn't dead, at least not completely anyway," he smiled.

"Then are you Elijah Willoughby's friend?"

"That would be me. Elijah made me this new leg."

"How wonderful," Angelina's eyes widened as Doug took a few adept steps away from the table, turned and went back to his seat."

"So he found ya then?"

"Sure did," Doug pointed toward the chair next to his. "Have a seat and enjoy Bonnie's flapjacks."

Angelina sat down and lifted a few flapjacks onto her plate with a fork. Just as she poured the syrup, the Forrester sisters came bubbling down the stairs.

"Good mornin', Angelina," Edna greeted. When she turned to see Doug, her jaw dropped wide.

"Mr. Crestworth!" Dot exclaimed.

"When did you get here?" Thelma inquired.

"More importantly, where have ya been?" Lucille added.

"Does Bonnie know?" Dot interjected.

"Bonnie knows," Doug smiled at the women. It had been years since he'd been around the Forrester sisters, but it appeared as if they hadn't changed a lick.

"Well, tell us all about it. When did ya get here?" Dot prodded.

"Last night," he replied.

Bonnie entered the room carrying a plate of sausages, "Now, now, ladies. Don't bother my husband with so many questions. You might drive 'im away! It's by the grace o' God he even decided to come back to me at all," she scolded, but there was a glimmer of mirth in her eyes.

Over breakfast, Doug shared his story, and Bonnie sat mesmerized by every word. Angelina didn't believe she'd ever seen a woman so enamored by a man. To think for the past month, Elijah knew that Doug was back! He'd been hiding him at his farm, and trying to talk him into coming home to Bonnie.

Chapter 26

One week later

Angelina survived until the night of the social without admitting to anyone that Paul wouldn't be accompanying her. Then, when all the girls scurried around, helping each other prepare for the event, Edna poked her head into Angelina's room.

"Why aren't ya dressed?" Edna inquired.

Angelina shrugged, "I'm not goin'."

"What about Paul?"

"He couldn't come after all. He couldn't get away from the farm."

"Oh! I'm sorry to hear that!" Edna's countenance fell in sympathy.

"It's all right. I have some readin' I can do tonight," Angelina held up a volume of Shakespearean Sonnets.

"Oh, no you don't! You're comin' with Dot and me! We don't have escorts, but you don't see us sittin' home readin' a book!" Edna stepped closer to where Angelina sat on the bed, removed the book from her hands and set it on the night table. Then she grabbed Angelina's hand and fairly dragged her to a standing position.

"You're goin'! We'll have fun!"

"Oh, I don't know," Angelina grumbled.

"Dot," Edna called over her shoulder toward the door. "Come in here and help me talk some sense into Angelina."

Shortly, Dot appeared at the door. "Talk some sense into her about what?"

"Paul couldn't come so she's plannin' on stayin' home. Tell her she needs to come with us. Won't we have fun?"

"Oh, yes, you have to come! You can't stay home tonight," Dot agreed.

"Here, let's find ya a pretty dress," Dot approached Angelina's armoire and opened the door.

"What were you gonna wear if Paul had come?" Edna queried as she joined Dot in rummaging through Angelina's dresses.

"Oh, I don't know, I hadn't given much thought to it," Angelina stammered.

"I think ya should wear this one," Dot held up an emerald green dress that Angelina's mother made her for Christmas.

"Excellent choice!" Edna agreed.

"It matches your eyes," Dot held the garment up to Angelina.

Angelina started to make more excuses, but the women were so insistent that not going would have been more work than just tagging along.

"Come on downstairs, ladies!" Bonnie called. "Doug's got the carriage ready. Elijah's meeting us there."

At the mention of Elijah's name, Angelina became nervous, started to make excuses, and lagged behind. But Dot took one of her arms. Edna took the other, and they led her down the stairs.

Lucille and Thelma had already left with their escorts. Doug assisted Bonnie, Edna and Dot into the carriage. Angelina held back, still unsure if she wanted to attend the social. She didn't want to face Elijah without an escort. Knowing him, those piercing eyes of his could see straight into her soul and know she'd been lying the whole time.

~*~

Edna, Dot and Angelina sat with their cups of warm cider along the north wall of Mr. Peterson's barn. The band played and couples danced. People stood along the perimeter laughing and talking. Angelina wouldn't have thought it possible, but Dot, excited to be there, chattered on even more than usual.

Lucille danced with Ed Jenkins, whom she'd finally agreed to let escort her, even though she'd rather have gone with Ted Hooper. But Ted was dancing with Millicent Larkin, a petite blonde who batted her flirtatious eyelashes at him. Colin Harper danced with Thelma, and delighted smiles graced each of their faces. Bonnie and Doug danced every dance as a slow dance, completely lost in each other as if they were a couple of newlyweds. Angelina's gaze moved from couple to couple, but mainly she scanned the room for Elijah. She couldn't find him anywhere. She realized that perhaps he'd changed his mind and decided not to attend after all, and she felt deflated at the thought.

If she'd heard her mother warn against the dangers of lying once, she'd heard it a thousand times. "What a tangled web we weave when we first practice to deceive," she'd say. Angelina knew now the full pain associated with deception. The more she thought about what she'd done to Elijah, the more she berated herself for her foolishness. What possessed her to pretend Paul would take her when he was marrying someone else?

She had to admit that it was nothing more than fear – fear of how Elijah Willoughby made her feel – fear of what could follow that feeling – marriage and everything that went with it. She was scared, pure and simple. Frustrated with herself for her cowardice, she rose from her chair, placed her cup on a table and ambled through the throng of people toward the barn door.

The night wasn't too chilly. She wore a shawl and it was enough. Angelina admired the full moon that peeked from behind the clouds as she strolled on past the carriages, toward the barnyard and a fenced corral.

"Where ya goin', girly?" a man's slurred voice called out to her. Her head darted toward the sound to her right. One of the McLean brothers was coming toward her. He raked a hand through his unkempt hair and spit a wad of tobacco on the ground. Juice drizzled down his scruffy beard. He took a swig from a flask, and in the darkness he looked like Jacobsen. Angelina immediately started to flee in the opposite direction, her heart thudding so hard she thought it might beat out of her chest, but she ran into the other McLean brother.

"Oh!" she cried.

"Where you off to so fast, missy?" he put his hands on her shoulders and pushed her back to his brother. Now she was surrounded, a brother on either side!

"Please, just let me go back to the barn," she pleaded, trying to catch her breath.

"Why? You look like ya need a little fresh air, and we're just the fellers to help ya get it," the first brother said, reaching for her.

Angelina struggled against his grip. "No, I – I don't need any help," she stammered, trying to keep the tears from falling. "Let me go," she whispered. They laughed and Angelina took a deep breath before she raised her boot and stomped the toe of the brother at her right and elbowed the one on her left in the gut. Her attempts, while obviously painful to them, were not enough to deter their plans and only served to infuriate them.

They started pulling her backward into the darkness and Angelina closed her eyes against the memories assailing her. God wouldn't let this happen to her again, would he? She screamed, but the music was too loud and no one heard her. As they got to the edge of the property, near the stables, another man appeared seemingly out of nowhere and punched one brother in the stomach and then the other. They doubled over, but the taller one retaliated, punching Angelina's defender across the jaw.

Freed from their grip, she did not bother to wait around to see who had come to her aid, but ran toward the stable and hid inside a stall. She could still hear the yelling and skirmish outside, but then it fell silent and all she heard was the music from the barn. She sat there in the hay, her knees tucked under her chin and her arms tight around her legs. She buried her head in her skirt, feeling the tears wash down her face, a painful lump gripping her throat.

She stayed there, hoping and praying that no one had seen where she'd fled. After what seemed like an eternity of haunting silence, Angelina heard footsteps approach. She saw the light of a lantern sway its luminous oval glow as the person approaching cast eerie shadows along the stable wall. She held her breath, hoping to remain undiscovered.

"Angelina, are ya in here?" She recognized the voice, but she wasn't sure whether she wanted to reply.

"Are ya in here?" Elijah repeated just before his hand pushed against the stall door. He towered over her, holding the lantern. Quickly he hung the lantern on a nail just inside the stall, and knelt before her.

"Are ya all right?" He put his hands on her shoulders and then to her cheeks. "Tell me, girl, are ya all right?"

She wanted to speak, but words wouldn't come. He cradled her face in his warm comforting hands, searching her eyes with his own, "Did they hurt ya?" His voice was stern and demanding, but she discerned a hint of fear in it.

She gestured her head negatively. They hadn't hurt her. He helped her rise to her feet. The moment she did, she leaned into his chest and clung to him, her arms tightening about his waist as if he were a life preserver in a storm tossed sea.

Surprised by her reaction, his arms remained at a distance until a moment later, he let them surround her, pulling her close, consoling her with his embrace and his gentle hand stroking her back and hair.

"I guess it was a good thing my horse threw a shoe on the way over. I had to go back and fit a new one. If I hadn't been late, I don't know if I would've come along when I did."

She clung to him for some time, letting grateful tears trickle from her eyes and spill onto his shirt. When she finally had the courage to look him in the eye, she noticed the gash on his cheekbone that was still bleeding.

"Oh my, you're hurt!" she exclaimed, then pulled a handkerchief from her pocket, and dabbed it to the wound. "I'm so sorry!"

"It's nothin'." He shook his head. "I'm more worried about you."

"This is all my fault. I've done it again, haven't I?" she sighed.

"It's not your fault." He caressed her cheek. "Don't ever think that."

"I guess Daddy was right. I'm just a silly girl needin' protectin'. I'm so sorry I keep causin' ya trouble."

Elijah put his hands to her face just as the band began to play a waltz in the barn, "You're not a silly girl, Angelina. You're a smart, beautiful woman." He took her hand in one of his and put his palm to her side, dancing with her more intimately in the confines of the stable stall than he would have in public.

She shook her head in denial, but he continued with insistence, "You've never been a minute's trouble to me. There's not a man on earth that isn't honored to protect the woman he loves."

Angelina's eyes widened, unsure if she had heard him correctly. She directed her gaze to his shoulder as they danced, unable to meet his mesmerizing blue eyes.

They danced the remainder of the song and when the music ceased, he cradled her face in his hands, his loving eyes staring into hers. "You . . . you . . ." she stammered, unable to verbalize her question.

His handsome face was so close to hers, she could almost taste the sweet peppermint of his breath on her lips. His gaze caressed her face, trailing over her cheeks, speaking to her eyes, lingering upon her lips. His gentle fingertips traced along her cheek. She couldn't pull her gaze from his penetrating eyes.

Angelina's heart raced as his mouth nuzzled against her cheek, then ever so lightly brushed against her lips. "Tell me ya love me too," he whispered.

"I . . ." she stammered, unable to breathe for his nearness and his words thrilled her beyond her ability to concentrate on anything but wanting to be even closer to him. Her hands pressed against his shoulders. For a fleeting second she considered pushing him away. She knew that if this continued she would be hopelessly lost, unable to regain control of her world. But her hands of their own volition slid around his neck, her finger's exploring the soft thickness of his hair.

"I . . ." she halted again, and she felt his lips take hers once more. One of his arms slipped around her waist while the other cradled the back of her head, his fingers vanishing into her blonde locks. She'd worn her hair down this evening, knowing that he liked it this way. She half-hoped he might ask her to dance if she could capture his attention for even a moment. She never dreamed she'd end up like this, alone with him, close to him, tasting the intoxicating flavor of his kisses once more.

He nibbled her bottom lip, the corners of her mouth, her chin. "Tell me ya love me, my Angel," he whispered.

Breathless and unable to contain the beating of her heart, Angelina whispered, "I." His kisses fell to her neck. "Love." His beard tickled the hollow of her throat as he tasted the soft skin below her ear. "You," she clasped his face in her hands and redirected his affections to her mouth.

With the knowledge that his love was truly reciprocated, Elijah's arms enfolded Angelina, and his mouth worshipped hers with an intensity and fire that she had never known. To be held by him, loved by him, was more than her heart could contain, and a single tear escaped the corner of her eye.

"Marry me, my angel. Be my life, my love, my everything," he whispered.

Angelina looked into Elijah's eyes. She did love him, but she was still a little frightened. Would the past come back to haunt them? He, of all people, knew the extent of the damage done.

Noting the shadow of fear in her eyes, he assured, "I won't let anyone hurt you ever again, Angelina."

"I know you won't," she whispered. "But I'm not, not . . ."

"Not what?"

"Not good enough. I'm not," she was too embarrassed to say it, her shameful eyes fell toward the hay-strewn ground as her face turned pink.

"Don't even think it," he held her face in his hands redirecting her gaze to his. "Ya hear me? Don't even think it for a minute!" his words were insistent and demanding. His voice lowered, "Let me love away your pain, Angelina. Marry me. Be mine forever."

Her eyes glistened with moisture, knowing that he was her only hope, her only love. "But . . ."

"I love you," He whispered, his eyes assuring her of the truth of his words. Then he asked her once more, "Will ya marry me, Angelina Stone?"

She clung to him, burying her head against his shoulder. She couldn't fight the feelings she had for him any longer. "Yes," she whispered.

"Yes?" he inquired hopefully.

"Yes," her face lit with a glowing smile.

He hugged her, lifting her off her feet with his jubilance. With his next kiss, Angelina knew he was right. He would love away the pain. Already she felt as if a weight had fallen from her shoulders, leaving her light, free and utterly in love.

Epilogue

Four years later

Angelina looked toward the bedroom where Elijah cradled their son tenderly in his arms. She smiled as she watched his fingertips carress the brown fuzz atop the baby's head. He kissed the sleeping babe's cheek then eased the child into the wooden crib and pulled a quilt over him. Elijah approached his three-year-old daughter's bed, kissed the little girl's forehead, and one of his fingers brushed a blonde curl from her face. Angelina's eyes returned to her sewing as Elijah crept from the room, closing the door behind him.

The floorboards creaked beneath his socked feet as he neared Angelina who sat sewing in a rocker by the fireplace. He stood behind her, put his hands on her shoulders and massaged her aching muscles. She hadn't realized how tense she'd become. His firm strokes on her back felt heavenly.

"Hmmm . . . that feels good," she leaned her head back, looked up into his handsome face and offered him a tired smile.

"Whatcha wrestlin' with?" he bent over and kissed her lips.

"Oh, this darn navy square Edna sewed into the middle of Lucille's quilt!" she sighed and returned to picking at the cloth.

Elijah looked down at the pale green and white baby blanket with a stark navy square sewn into one of the interior rows. He released a soft chuckle, "It's gettin' late. You should get some rest."

"But I've got to get this thing out and replaced before Bonnie, Edna and Dot show up tomorrow mornin' to quilt." Her fingers picked away at the seam. "Ouch!" she exclaimed.

"What happened?" he asked, his brow furrowing in concern as he reached for her hand.

"I poked my finger with this blasted needle!"

He knelt in front of her and took her finger in his hands, examined the puncture wound, rubbed it a little, and held pressure to it. "It's not bad, just painful I 'spect." He kissed the tip of her finger. "I don't think you'll need anythin' on it."

Angelina grimaced and studied her wounded appendage, rubbing it with her thumb.

"Come on," he took the quilt and the needle away from her and set them on the table. "You're too angry with it. You need to stop for awhile."

"But Lucille's baby's due any day now, and we have to get this done. We certainly can't leave that thing in there! We'll never hear the end of it from Lucille if we do."

"Don't you have Thelma's baby quilt started? Why don't you just finish that one tomorrow and give it to Lucille. Then give this one to Thelma later," he suggested.

"But Lucille likes the green, and Thelma likes the blue. I can't switch 'em."

He took her arms, pulled her from the rocker, and hugged her. "Put it aside for the night, and you'll repair it in half the time in the mornin' when you're not so angry with it."

"I still can't figure out where Edna found that navy square anyway," Angelina grumbled as she leaned her head against his chest.

"She probably brought it along with her just for meanness."

"Well, if so, it wasn't Lucille she hurt with her joke, it was me!" Angelina leaned her neck back, trying to work the stiffness from it.

"When did she manage to slip it in there anyway? You were with her, weren't you?" Elijah put his hand to her neck in a gentle massaging motion.

"I guess it happened when I left the room to change the baby. Bonnie and her little girl came with me, and Dot was so busy rattlin' on about her new beau that she wasn't payin' attention to Edna."

"Dot has a beau?" Elijah smiled with one raised eyebrow.

"Chester McNairy. She says he asked her to marry 'im in June."

Elijah sighed, "Poor fella."

"Now, now," Angelina pushed Elijah's shoulder. "Dot's not that bad."

"Not if ya got 'nough cotton for your ears," Elijah's chest rose and fell with his mirth.

Angelina couldn't help but smile. It was true. It would take a special man to endure Dot for a lifetime.

"That'll be my weddin' present to 'em," Elijah laughed. "A box of cotton for poor Chester's sanity, and to keep 'im from lockin' her out of the house for a moment's peace!"

Angelina broke into giggles. Perhaps he was right. She did need a break from digging that blasted navy square out of the baby quilt. She put her palm to his bearded cheek, letting her fingers run along the bristles as she smiled up at him. He could always make her see the lighter side and help her relax when life seemed stressed.

Without another word, he scooped her up in his strong arms, kissed her and carried her into their room. Married four years and two children later, he still made her heart beat faster, still made the nervous, thrilling butterflies flutter inside her. How blessed she was to be his! He'd been true to his word, for he had loved away the scars, helped her heal all the wounds and made her life a heaven on earth, a life fit for the angel he always believed her to be.

About the Author

Marnie L. Pehrson was born and raised in the Chattanooga, Tennessee area. An avid enthusiast of family history, Marnie integrates elements of the places, people and events of her Southern family and heritage into her historical fiction romances. Marnie's life is steeped in Southern history from the little town of Daisy that she grew up in to the 24 acres bordering the famous Chickamauga Battlefield upon which her family resides.

Marnie and her husband Greg are the parents of six children. She is the founder of multi-denominational SheLovesGod.com which hosts the annual SheLovesGod Virtual Women's Conference the 3rd week of October each year. Marnie has served in many capacities within her church in presidencies of the women's and children's organizations, as a Sunday School teacher and pianist. Service as family history consultant inspired her foray into historical fiction.

Marnie is also an internet developer and consultant who helps talented professionals deliver their message to the online world. You may visit her projects through www.PWGroup.com.

You may also read more of her work at www.MarniePehrson.com and www.CleanRomanceClub.com Marnie welcomes reader comments and may be reached at marnie@marniepehrson.com or by calling 706-866-2295.

Other Books by Marnie Pehrson

The Patriot Wore Petticoats
Historical fiction, 224, pages, ISBN: 0-9729750-4-7
Daring "Dicey" Langston, the bold and reckless rider and expert shot, saves her family and an entire village during the American Revolution. Having faced British soldiers, rushing swollen rivers, the "Bloody Scouts," and the barrel of a loaded pistol, nothing had quite prepared this valiant heroine for the heart-pounding exhilaration she'd find in the arms of one brave Patriot. Based on a true story about the author's fourth great-grandmother. Learn more at www.DiceyLangston.com

Beyond the Waterfall
Historical Fiction, 136 pages, paperback ISBN: 0-9729750-7-1
Jillian's feet were precariously planted in two worlds: the Cherokee nation on the brink of extermination, and the world where Jesse Whitmore belonged. On her first meeting with him, the charming and handsome merchant had set her young heart ablaze. Yet, could she trust him? Or was he just like all the other white men she'd encountered? Would he stand beside her while she witnessed her nation ripped apart, or would he join the ranks of the powerful greedy to betray her? Based on family history and local legend.

Hannah's Heart
Historical Fiction, 162 pages, paperback, ISBN: 1-59936-012-8
Hannah Jamison is ready to give her heart away. Unfortunately, the man she's falling for shows no indication of ever reciprocating her feelings. When Mother Nature intervenes in her behalf, all Hannah's dreams seem to be coming true . . . until she discovers that following her heart means losing the ones she loves. Is Hannah willing to pay the price?

Waltzing with the Light
LDS Historical Fiction, 268 pages, Paperback, ISBN: 0-9729750-6-3
Nestled within the valley of the Appalachian mountains, Daisy, Tennessee, seemed like a sleepy little town until depression-era drifter, Jake Elliot, entered it and knocked on the front door of the yellow farm house and met Mikalah, the oldest of the Ford children. Little did he know how his life and his heart would be affected from that moment forward.

Rebecca's Reveries
Historical Fiction, 224 pages, paperback, ISBN: 0-9729750-2-0
Rebecca Marchant had led a sheltered life until she found herself inexplicably drawn to the home of her father's youth. Surrounded by the historical landscape of the Chickamauga Battlefield in Georgia, Rebecca finds herself plagued by haunting dreams and vivid visions of Civil War events. As Rebecca walks a mile in another girl's moccasins through her visions and dreams she learns about compassion, forgiveness, temptation and the power of true love.

You Can't Fly If You're Still Clutching the Dirt:
How to Stop Worrying and Achieve Your God-given Potential
Inspirational Nonfiction, 148 pages, Paperback, ISBN 0-9729750-8-X
Deep down, you know God created you for a reason. He's told you that you're a child of God. You're made in His image, and He has a plan for you. You sense in your heart of hearts that you have wings to fly, but worries, fears, and insecurities drag you down to earth, preventing you from spreading your wings and taking flight.

This book will teach you how to quit worrying and trust God; easily distinguish between what you control and what God controls; find freedom to focus on the two decisions that are yours to make – What you want and Why you want it. Find deliverance from the worry-inducing questions of Who? When? How? and Where?

Lord, Are You Sure?
Inspirational, 152 pages, Paperback, ISBN 0-9729750-0-4
A roadmap for understanding how Heavenly Father works in your life, helping you understand why certain problems keep repeating themselves, how to break the cycle and unlock the mystery of why you encounter challenges and roadblocks on roads you felt inspired to travel.

Packets of Sunlight for Parents
Compiled by: Marnie L. Pehrson
Inspirational, 144 pages, ISBN 0-9676162-4-7
Brighten your day with inspiration for parents of tots to teens! Inspirational quote book.

Packets of Sunlight for American Patriots
Compiled by: Marnie L. Pehrson
Inspirational, 108 pages, ISBN 0-9676162-3-9
Let the founding fathers reignite your love for freedom! Inspirational quote
book.

10 Steps to Fulfilling Your Divine Destiny:
A Christian Woman's Guide to
Learning & Living God's Plan for Her
Inspirational, 124 pages, Paperback, ISBN 0-9676162-1-2
Have you ever said to yourself, "I'd love to do great things with my life, but I'm
just too busy, too untalented, too ordinary, too afraid, too anything but extraor-
dinary"? Inside this book you'll learn how to reach your full God-given
potential.

A Closer Walk with Him
SheLovesGod Study Lessons Volume 1
Inspiraitonal, 212 pages, paperback, ISBN 0-9729750-3-9
A collection of insights and ponderings on the scriptures and how we can
apply them to our everyday lives. Great for the faith-lift you need in the
morning, just before bed, or whenever you need a quick boost of inspiration.
Each lesson is self-contained and independent. Read them in any order the
Spirit moves you or read the 52 lessons in order as a yearly study guide - it's
up to you.

To order call 800-524-2307 or visit
www.MarniePehrson.com

Printed in the United States
72513LV00004B/40-57

9 780972 975094